'I will pa
pounds.'

'I will also pay your passage back to Italy, which is now and must ever remain your home.' Leo saw the glitter in Miranda's magnificent eyes. Ah, that had caught her attention! He took a step closer, trying to intimidate her with his superior height and size. The Countess, however, was tall enough not to be intimidated, and she straightened her back and glared up at him. Leo could not help but be impressed. She had courage; he'd give her that! It was a pity she was totally without scruples, or morals...

There was a moment when she might still have spoken the truth. Cleared up this awful misunderstanding. Like a spluttering candle the moment flickered and died. There was another flame growing inside her. Anger. It burned brighter and brighter until it was too great to be doused. The heat of it flooded through Miranda until every ounce of her usual common sense had melted.

How dared he speak to her in this fashion? How dared he make threats to her when she had come here hoping for the consideration due to Julian's wife? She would make him sorry!

Dear Reader

The Decadent Countess marks my return to writing for Mills & Boon® Historical Romance™ after a ten-year break. The book is a Regency, and I think—and I'm not boasting here—that it was the easiest book I have ever written. Easy, that is, in the sense that it seemed to flow from my fingertips onto the computer screen. The characters were already there, living, breathing people, and I had very little say in how their story would be told. They did all that themselves.

Unadventurous, quiet Miranda, who, to teach the arrogant head of the Fitzgibbon family a lesson, suddenly finds herself impersonating her disreputable stepmother, the aptly named Decadent Countess. And she enjoys the role immensely! And Leo, so staid and set in his duke-like ways, suddenly doing wild and unpredictable things, all because he has fallen head over heels in love with Miranda. They certainly make a wonderful couple...when they finally resolve their problems.

I hope you love *The Decadent Countess*!

Deborah Miles

THE DECADENT COUNTESS

Deborah Miles

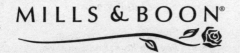

MILLS & BOON®

First published in Great Britain 2003
Harlequin Mills & Boon Limited,
Eton House, 18-24 Paradise Road, Richmond, Surrey TW9 1SR

© Deborah Miles 2003

ISBN 0 263 83499 9

Set in Times Roman 10½ on 12¼ pt.
04-0303-73240

Printed and bound in Spain
by Litografia Rosés S.A., Barcelona

Deborah Miles is an Australian. She lives in Victoria, in a house in an old gold-rush town, with her husband and two children. The family also includes three cats and a dog, who are all very pampered. When she isn't writing, Deborah spends time in the garden, or reading, or embroidering very badly.

Chapter One

Miranda Fitzgibbon tucked her hands into her sable-lined muff, and settled back into the hackney cab with a sigh of relief. Her face, which had been tinted a pale gold by the Italian sun, was presently white with fatigue, while uncharacteristic lines of strain framed a wide mouth more used to smiling. Her hair, a rich uncompromising auburn, shone bright in the gloom.

At four-and-twenty years, she was young to be a widow. Not that her marriage to Julian Fitzgibbon had been an ordinary marriage, but still she had been fond of him. He had been a kind and generous man. Miranda wiped the tears from her lustrous dark eyes, shaking off her sadness and drawing on her impressive store of inner strength. She was not the sort of girl to let regrets weigh down her spirits. She preferred to remember her husband with gratitude and a smile.

He had never wanted her to grieve.

The hackney lurched to avoid another vehicle in the busy London traffic, and the lurch was repeated in Miranda's stomach. Normally, she was a good traveller, but the nine-hour crossing of the channel and seven hours on a crowded coach from Dover had taken their toll on even her robust good health. Still, she was here now, back in England, and safe.

Thanks to Julian, her long years of exile in Italy were at an end.

The hackney cab turned the corner into a quiet street. It was May, and the trees were well covered in their green foliage. The buildings looked solid and dependable, much, thought Miranda, like the English character. Mayfair was an area of London unknown to her. Despite her father once owning a house nearby, Miranda had never lived here. She had resided with her mother in the country and, after her mother died, attended school in Hampshire until she was sixteen, when she had left to go and live in Italy with her father and her stepmama, Adela.

As Miranda recalled, the other girls at the school had pitied and envied her in equal part. Her father, Count Ridgeway, was a handsome but weak man who, having begun to squander his inheritance at an early age, had now completed the task. However, Miranda's stepmama, Adela, had an altogether more exciting reputation.

She was known as the Decadent Countess!

Miranda gave a reminiscent smile. Adela was far away and she, Miranda, was here, in Mayfair and fast approaching an audience with Julian's relatives.

That reminded her... Miranda opened her reticule and searched. The letter crackled in her gloved fingers and she drew it out, despite knowing the contents by heart. It was dated over six months ago, just before Julian died.

His Grace, the Duke of Belford,
Berkeley Square,
London
5th November 1809

Leo,
   The bearer of this letter will be my wife, Miranda, daughter of Count Ridgeway. She needs your understanding and your assistance in establishing herself in English society after a long stay in Italy under somewhat difficult circumstances. You may be familiar with her stepmama, Adela, but be assured, Miranda is a sweet girl whose misfortune it was to be cast into a situation beyond her control.
   I know I can depend upon you, as can she.
   Your grateful and affectionate cousin,
   Julian Fitzgibbon

Miranda smoothed the letter with one gloved finger. She was not expecting to be welcomed with open arms by the Fitzgibbon family—her marriage to Julian had been unconventional, to say the least—but she felt she had a right to their understanding and, as Julian had written, their assistance.

'My family will take care of you,' Julian had told her often enough. 'I'm not pretending they'll be over the moon, but that's only because it's so sudden and they haven't met you yet. Leo's a great gun, he's my

cousin Belford. Go to him if you need help—I always
did. And you'll have The Grange, that's my manor
house. It's old and rickety, but I love it. You can live
there if you don't fancy setting up house with my
mother. I haven't got much of an inheritance apart
from The Grange, but there should be enough blunt
for you to live on. That is, until some rich blade falls
in love with you, Miranda, as he's bound to do!

'Leo will look after you,' he had whispered to her
again as he lay dying. 'Trust him.'

And with those promises echoing in her ears, Miranda had come to London, to Fitzgibbon House in
Berkeley Square, to the head of the Fitzgibbon family.

The vehicle drew to a halt, and she stiffened her
shoulders, unconsciously preparing herself for the
awkward meeting. She had sent ahead of her arrival
and fully expected to be shown into a room full of
disapproving Fitzgibbons, Julian's mother among
them. And of course, his cousin Leo. And yet Miranda, despite never having met the Duke of Belford, had
begun to think of him, and indeed had been encouraged to do so by Julian, as an ally and possible friend.

As she stepped down from the hackney, Miranda
looked up at the imposing house without really seeing
it. Instead she was hearing again Julian's weakened
voice. *Trust Leo.*

Miranda knew that, with very little encouragement,
she would.

'No, no, no! It won't do, Leo. You must find a way
to annul the marriage! Really, this is too much. First

I am shown into your house by that dreadful supercilious Pendle, and now you will not listen to me!'

'Pendle is my butler and has been for more years than I can remember. I cannot see what he has to do with the matter.'

The rather large and imposing lady continued to fan herself vigorously, eyes closed, stiff curls powdered in the old way. The room was overwarm for a mild spring day, a fire burning high in the grate, and Leo Fitzgibbon, the Fifth Duke of Belford, longed to throw open a window.

He controlled the urge.

He seemed always to be controlling natural urges—it was part of being a duke. Instead, he leaned forward, so that the fine cloth of his coat tightened over his broad shoulders and spoke quietly but firmly.

'Ma'am, you make too much of this. Julian was of age, and a sensible, clear-headed man. Just because this lady is not exactly the daughter-in-law you would have chosen does not mean—'

'Oh, you can be so infuriating, Leo!'

Her sharpness surprised him. Leo was not used to being spoken to in such a way, and he raised a dark brow. 'Surely Julian explained his reasons for marrying her in his letter?' he asked, his voice cooler than before.

It was all, he felt, a storm in a tea-cup. Julian had always gone his own road but had never, so far as Leo knew, taken a wrong turning.

'There was some nonsense about her needing his help because her nearest relative had died and left her in perilous circumstances,' Aunt Ellen replied, her voice still on the verge of hysteria. 'My poor boy obviously wrote his letter under duress, or he was too ill by then to...' She swallowed and blinked hard, took a breath. 'Portions of the letter were illegible, but I am sure none of that signifies. It contained no real *details,* Leo, merely an entreaty to be kind to her, to *understand.* And now I know why!'

'Do enlighten me, ma'am,' Leo murmured, bored.

Mrs Fitzgibbon flicked him a furious look, but contained her emotions with a struggle. She was aware that Leo considered her an over-emotional female, but even he would not be so blasé when he heard the facts.

'This...this *Countess Ridgeway,* as she calls herself, is notorious. It would not surprise me if she had never married Ridgeway at all! But then again the man was a weak fool, despite his looks... Well, that is beside the point. When Julian wrote to tell me he had married, I did not at first connect his wife's name with *that* Count Ridgeway. I was disappointed, naturally, but too overcome with grief at the death of my dear boy. If I thought of it at all, I believed he truly had married this girl out of the kindness of his dear heart. You know how he was always so—'

'The point, Aunt!'

'Yesterday I received a letter from Lady Petersham. You know she is currently travelling in Italy? Well, I am sure she couldn't wait to put pen to paper to tell me all the nastier details! Her letter was quite full of blots and scribbles. Dreadful creature.'

Leo gritted his teeth.

'Evidently Count Ridgeway had hardly buried his

first wife—a sweet little creature!—when he married
a second, and whisked her off to Italy of all places.
He died a year ago and left her a widow. Lady Petersham writes that *she* is the woman my poor, poor
boy has married.'

Leo wondered where all this was leading. It had
been last year when his aunt informed him of Julian's
marriage and, in quick succession, his death. There
had been matters to deal with, and Leo had dealt with
them. He had grieved for his cousin then, and still
did, but he had thought the subject finished.

Then, yesterday evening, while Leo was at his club,
a note had come from his aunt expressing, in somewhat garbled terms, her dismay upon learning the
identity of Julian's wife, and that the new Mrs Fitzgibbon had written to inform the old Mrs Fitzgibbon
she would be presenting herself at Berkeley Square
on the following day.

Leo had been about to call upon his aunt this morning when she had arrived on his doorstep.

He was not pleased.

At thirty-five, Leo considered himself a man of experience, and rightly so, for he had come into his
inheritance eighteen years previously. He was a handsome man, but there was a coldness about him which
made some people ask whether he had a heart at all.
His cousin Julian, who had the fortunate ability of
being able to see straight to the core of a matter,
would have recognised that coldness as Leo's response to the heavy responsibilities which he had
been thrust into too young, and a life he often found
shallow and disappointing.

Unmarried, with a yearly income of twenty thousand pounds, his life was ordered very much as he wanted it. And yet lately Leo had felt the lack of something more. A niggling, irritating little wrinkle in his starched and ironed existence. Had he been a romantic man, he might have thought he lacked... well, romance, but Leo considered himself too phlegmatic to be romantic.

'Surely Julian could be trusted to find a wife who would shame neither his name nor his position?'

'You don't understand, Leo,' Mrs Fitzgibbon replied in shrill tones. 'She's quite, quite *unsuitable!* I don't know how Julian could have been taken in by her, really I don't. Clearly this Countess inveigled her way into the poor boy's affections, hoping to obtain for herself a respectable name. She entirely lacks one of her own!'

He shrugged indifferently, further infuriating his aunt.

'Oh, Leo,' she cried, 'it is just too much! If you do not care for my feelings, then think of my poor, poor boy. You must *do* something.'

Leo bit back an impatient snort. He looked at his aunt again, her flushed cheeks and heaving bosom. She was certainly not the most intelligent woman of his acquaintance, but he had never seen her this agitated.

Grudgingly, he supposed that even level-headed young men had their weaknesses, and possibly this Countess Ridgeway had been Julian's. And, if that was the case, as head of the Fitzgibbon family, it behoved Leo to act. He was not intimidated by the idea of confronting the cuckoo in the Fitzgibbon nest and sending her on her way as quickly as possible.

'Leo!'

Ellen Fitzgibbon's sharp, irritated cry caused Leo to raise his dark brows over his dark blue eyes, a faint smile of enquiry curling his firm lips.

'Leo,' Mrs Fitzgibbon went on, her voice taking on a wheedling note in case she had offended him—it would never do to offend Leo when she needed his help. 'As head of this family—'

Leo sighed. 'Yes, Aunt Ellen, I am well aware of my illustrious position. When are we expecting this…this harpy?'

Mrs Fitzgibbon slumped in her chair with relief, her corsets creaking.

'Any moment now. She wrote to advise me she would be arriving on the morning coach.' An expressive shudder. 'Do you know what they call her? Lady Petersham mentioned it in her letter, and as soon as I read it I had to call for my smelling salts.'

'Do enlighten me, aunt. What do they call her?'

'The Decadent Countess!' Mrs Fitzgibbon gasped out the words, her corsets once again creaking dangerously.

Leo's blue eyes narrowed.

All signs of amusement and boredom dropped away from him. He had had no idea it was this bad! Why had his aunt not told him this at the very beginning? Countess Ridgeway, the 'Decadent Countess', was notorious for her loose living. Leo only vaguely remembered Count Ridgeway, they had hardly mixed in the same circles, so that when his aunt had mentioned that gentleman before he had not immediately connected the two. He recalled him now: Count Ridgeway, a tall, laughing man who always lost at cards—one of his main reasons for fleeing across the channel—had been a harmless fool and of good family whatever his later actions.

His second wife was neither of those things.

Leo had not had the misfortune to meet her—her circles were not his—but he had heard enough about her to make her current position as his cousin-by-marriage unpalatable in the extreme.

'What was Julian thinking of to saddle you with such a daughter-in-law?' he asked, a hint of crossness creeping into his voice.

Mrs Fitzgibbon smiled triumphantly. She knew the signs. Leo was angry. Leo understood *at last* her own feelings.

'Very well,' Leo went on quietly, looking even more cross. 'I'll buy her off and send her back to Italy.'

His agreement came none too soon, for the next moment Pendle, the butler, was tapping discreetly on the door. It opened to his pinched and disapproving face, and he informed them, in the voice of a man who has eaten sour fruit, that there was a person at the door calling herself Mrs Julian Fitzgibbon and asking to see the Duke of Belford.

Ah, now I understand everything!

Those were the first words to enter Leo's mind upon seeing Julian's wife.

He meant, of course, that he understood why his

cousin had married a woman with the dubious title of
the Decadent Countess. This understanding was followed by a sting of envy, something to which he had
previously believed himself a stranger.

How had the amiable Julian captured this fiery
beauty, with her russet hair and dark flashing eyes?
And then he reminded himself it was quite probable
that *she* had captured *him*.

Even so, there was something about her... That
organ in Leo's chest, which so many of his peers
thought dead, quivered violently and began to beat to
a wildly unfamiliar rhythm.

Miranda was also surprised, so surprised that she
instantly forgot the frosty reception given her by the
manservant who had opened the door.

Before this moment she had imagined Julian's eyes
to be the deepest blue imaginable. Now, she knew
she had been mistaken. The Duke of Belford's eyes
were far darker and deeper and altogether more fascinating than Julian's had ever been. Indeed, she was
having great difficulty in directing her gaze away
from them.

Julian's cousin was as tall as Julian, but broader
across the shoulders, and he had glossy dark hair cut
close to his skull. He also radiated strength. No wonder Julian had trusted him and urged Miranda to follow suit. How could one fail to trust so imposing and
handsome a gentleman?

Belatedly realising she was being addressed by the
other person in the room, Miranda turned to Julian's
mother, murmuring a polite, 'Excuse me, ma'am?'

Short and plump, Mrs Fitzgibbon was the antithesis

of her son, the only feature they shared being the same pale fair hair. And yet there was something comforting about Mrs Fitzgibbon, a motherly air which further alleviated Miranda's fears.

Everything, she decided with relief, would be fine after all!

Miranda smiled her wide, brilliant smile. Julian's mother's response was to purse her lips and wrinkle her brow, her eyes like grey icicles. It was only then, at long last, that Miranda became aware of the definite chill in the air.

'The Duke of Belford is the head of our family,' Mrs Fitzgibbon said, giving the impression of having uttered a non sequitur. 'You must address yourself to him. Indeed, I am still far too overcome with grief to speak with you at all, Countess.'

'I am not—' Miranda began, confused. She wanted to say she was not Countess Ridgeway, she was not Adela. However, before she could do so, she was interrupted by the deep and confident tones of the head of the Fitzgibbon family. She turned to face the Duke, bewildered, the anxiety she had a moment ago relinquished returning in full force.

'I fear, Countess, you have travelled far for very little purpose. My cousin, Julian, though rich with charm and sweetness of character, was not rich in any other form. But you must have realised that already. There is The Grange, of course, but it is unbelievably drafty, falling down in fact. No sensible woman would marry for The Grange!'

'Falling down?' she managed. *It's old and rickety,*

but I love it, Julian had said. Surely he would not have bequeathed her a derelict building?

'Well, not quite *falling* down, Countess, and there is the legend—'

Mrs Fitzgibbon stopped abruptly and Miranda caught the edge of the sharp glance Belford sent to his aunt. She knew then that the Fitzgibbon family were rallying against her, drawing up their battle lines in some mistaken belief that she was the Countess Ridgeway.

That she was the enemy.

Leo hid his annoyance with difficulty. With luck the Countess would not have heard of the legend his aunt was alluding to. That The Grange was the Fitzgibbon talisman, that if ever the old house left the hands of the Fitzgibbon family the Fitzgibbons would be finished. He didn't believe it himself, but he certainly did not wish to supply the Countess with fresh ammunition.

'Perhaps you married Julian for love alone?' Leo asked now with deceptive gentleness. 'In which case no one would be better pleased than I. Did you marry him for love alone?'

A flash of memory obscured the elegant drawing room and Miranda's growing fears that she was being outmanoeuvred. Julian with his lean, almost gangly figure and wan good looks, sheltering on the terrace from the hot Italian sun. 'I'm awfully concerned about you, Miranda,' his dark blue eyes growing even darker with emotion, until they were the colour of the Mediterranean on a sunny day. 'You know I'm dying, don't you? Of course you do! Everyone does. I've made no secret of it. I'm here because my family insisted—they believed the climate would do me good—and I didn't want to disappoint them. But I fear no amount of Italian sun or Italian wine will cure me now.'

In the year Miranda knew him, Julian had always been very matter of fact when it came to his illness. He hadn't allowed anyone to feel sorry for him. Or sad. He had lived his life, he said, and had no complaint. There had been only one more thing he wished to do before he passed on, and that was to marry Miranda and, as Julian had half-jokingly avowed, rescue her from her wicked stepmama.

'I am a respectable gentleman and I come from a good family,' he had declared. 'The Fitzgibbons go back for centuries, you know, and every one of them was determined to have his way. And they usually did. So you see, Miranda, it's no use refusing me. I mean to help you, and help you I will!'

Miranda blinked and Julian was gone. She was back in the house in Berkeley Square, back in the nightmare. The Duke of Belford was watching her. 'Countess?' he murmured, waiting for the answer to his question. And then suddenly, startlingly, he smiled. It was a revelation. If he had reached out and brushed his fingers over her face, Miranda could not have been more affected.

'Countess?' he repeated. Now a frown creased that broad, strong forehead and drew down the well-shaped brows. Suspicion narrowed his remarkable eyes.

Miranda stared back at him and wondered if she

had by some mischance wandered into the wrong house. That the Duke and Julian's mother had mistaken her identity was obvious. Equally obvious was the fact she must set them right. She opened her mouth to do so, at the same time reaching into her reticule for Julian's letter, but she was again interrupted by Belford.

'So, it was not love after all? A pity. Well, let us be frank, Countess. I believe you are a woman who likes to be…frank.'

He made the word sound almost obscene. Adela, the real countess, would have laughed and made some ribald reply. Miranda was so startled the words of explanation dried up in her throat. Meanwhile, Belford continued matter-of-factly, as if he were saying something quite unremarkable.

Miranda could not know that, beneath his civilised exterior, Belford was just as bewildered as she.

And the lack of his usual equilibrium was making him angry.

'I will pay you ten thousand pounds, the amount to be placed in a bank in Italy for you to draw on as required. I will also pay your passage back to Italy, which is now and must ever remain your home. It goes without saying that The Grange will revert to the Fitzgibbon family.' Again he smiled, that devastating stretch of the lips, but now it had lost its magic for Miranda.

He was a devil, and she was beginning to hate him.

Leo saw the glitter in those magnificent eyes. Ah, that had caught her attention! She wasn't happy to be

rumbled so soon into her nasty game. Well, she'd be
even less happy when he was finished with her!

Leo took a step closer, trying to intimidate her with
his superior height and size. The Countess, however,
was tall enough not to be intimidated, and she
straightened her back and glared up at him. Leo could
not help but be impressed. She had courage, he'd give
her that! It was a pity she was totally without scruples,
or morals…

Startled at the direction his thoughts were taking,
Leo mentally ordered himself back to the point. His
voice grew quiet but deadly. 'You may believe that
in marrying Julian you have found the goose that lays
golden eggs. Be quite certain, madam, that this is the
only golden egg you will ever receive. If you come
back for more I will not be so generous. I consider it
bad form to hoodwink innocent men into marriage.'

His eyes dropped downwards. 'What is that?'

Miranda blinked. His ultimatum—for that was
clearly what it was—had frozen her to the spot. Now
she followed the direction of his gaze and realised
she had taken Julian's letter from her reticule, meaning perhaps to show it to him, to explain his mistake.

There was a moment when she might still have
spoken the truth. Cleared up this awful misunderstanding. Like a spluttering candle the moment flickered and died. There was another flame growing inside her. Anger. It burned brighter and brighter, until
it was too great to be doused. The heat of it flooded
through Miranda until every ounce of her usual common sense had melted.

How dare he…they…*he* speak to her in this fashion! How dare he…they…*he* make threats to her when she had come here hoping for the consideration due to Julian's wife!

She would make them…*him* sorry!

Miranda crushed the letter in her fist. 'This?' she repeated in a loud and brittle voice. 'Why, this, sir, is a list of my expenses!'

Her eyes lifted to his and flashed fury.

Leo, momentarily taken aback by those glittering eyes, drew a quick breath. By God, she was a beauty! A pity she was such a hardened harridan. Once again, he saw how easily a susceptible man could be drawn into her clutches. That flawless skin, the wide mouth and proud chin, that slim, straight body…

A jarring thought occurred to him.

Leo frowned. Surely this woman was too young to be the Decadent Countess? When she had entered the room, he had vaguely noticed that she was somewhat drawn and tired from the long journey. Now she seemed to have thrown off her weariness and fairly burned with vitality. And youth. Leo's eyes narrowed.

Could it be that Italians had aids to beauty yet unheard of in England?

Once one anomaly had entered his mind, Leo found others. When she had arrived she had seemed unsure of herself, lacking the assurance of a woman of the world. Almost an innocent. Not at all as Leo had expected her to be after his aunt's damning description. Was that part of her duplicity or…what?

Leo's frown deepened, and he stepped yet closer. He was not quite sure what he meant to do or say, only that it was imperative he question her further.

'What do you mean by expenses, Countess?'

Miranda bared her teeth at him in a patently false smile.

'My charges are a little high, I am told, but well worth the paying.'

'Charges!' Mrs Fitzgibbon gasped, reeling back, her hand clutched to her bosom. 'My poor, poor boy—'

All of Leo's burgeoning doubts vanished. Only a harpy could speak so boldly. However sweet and innocent the Decadent Countess might have looked upon her arrival, he now knew that Julian's wife was even blacker than she had been painted. He would rid his family of her if it was the last thing he did! However, when he spoke, his moderate tones betrayed nothing of the intensity of his true feelings. And only someone who knew him very well would have noticed the splash of colour high on his cheek bones or the deepening of the blue of his eyes, both indicating his extreme anger.

'I am sure, Aunt Ellen, the Countess is a sensible woman. She will accept my offer.'

Miranda laughed. Her own anger made her reckless. She wanted to grab this man by his immaculate coat and shake him. Hard. She did the next best thing, and shook him with her words, which she spoke in a brilliant portrayal of Adela's offhand manner. So they thought her vulgar and unworthy to bear the Fitzgibbon name? Then let her show them how vulgar she could be!

'I suppose I will consider it. That is all I can say for now. I have come to London to enjoy myself, and that is what I intend to do. Tell me, your Grace, where are the best shops and the best houses? I hope I can obtain tickets for Almack's. And what is a gaming hell? Oh, I mean to sample everything!'

Mrs Fitzgibbon blanched and gasped. 'But…a woman unaccompanied! You cannot mean to—'

'Oh, I am sure there can be no harm in Mrs Julian Fitzgibbon going about on her own. The name is so respectable, is it not?' The look she gave them was arch in the extreme. 'In Italy, I do very much as I please, but of course you have heard that.'

There was a meaningful silence.

'Where do you stay while you are in London?' Leo enquired softly. 'The docks?'

Miranda did not know the docks were notorious for seedy taverns, but she guessed it from the savage gleam in his eyes. *Devil!* Her heart beat harder and her fingers turned white as they gripped the strings of her reticule. If only it was his throat she held between her hands, she thought with uncharacteristic venom, if only she could squeeze and squeeze until his bullying look turned to contrition.

'I thought I would stay here,' she announced, idly glancing about her at the elegant room, pretending to find fault with the tasteful decor. 'But, no, it will not do. I am used to more colourful surroundings. Italy is so *vivid.* Who would have thought a duke's house would be so dull? No, I will put up at a modish hotel. Can you suggest one?'

He stared back at her as if he'd like to throttle her. It was Julian's mother who spoke, her words breathless and stumbling. 'I—I believe Armstrong's Hotel is very good, C-Countess.'

'Thank you, ma'am!' Miranda curtsied prettily. 'I will go to Armstrong's then, and send *you* the bill, your Grace.'

Leo bowed low, insultingly low.

Miranda turned and swept from the room.

Mrs Fitzgibbon turned and stared at her nephew. Her mouth was ajar, her eyes as large as duck eggs. 'You said you'd deal with it,' she managed in a shaking voice. 'Leo, you have made it worse!'

Leo turned his back on his aunt and went to stand at the window. He was very shaken. Some deep turbulence was at work inside his usually unflappable interior and his head felt quite light. This was so uncharacteristic of him, he wondered if he were coming down with a cold. That would also explain his unusually clumsy handling of what should have been a simple matter.

The truth was Leo had grown too used to getting his own way, to ordering things very much as he wanted them. His life had been in his control, and now quite suddenly the reins had been snatched from his hands.

At that moment a slim figure appeared on the street below him.

The Countess straightened her hat and then stared down at her hand. Leo watched her hesitate and then slip her crumpled list of expenses back into her reticule, before marching to her waiting hackney. The vehicle pulled away from Fitzgibbon House and joined the sedate traffic. It left the Duke of Belford, normally so imperturbable, a deeply troubled man.

Chapter Two

Armstrong's Hotel was large and comfortable and definitely modish.

Unfortunately Julian, as Miranda had been reminded by his odious cousin, had not been wealthy, and Armstrong's was clearly for those who were. But Miranda didn't presently care about such minor details. Still riding high on the crest of the anger that had carried her from Berkeley Square, she ordered a room, was granted it, and ascended the staircase with her boxes and trunks carried behind her.

She had had the foresight, before she left Italy, of obtaining a letter from her father's bank. Her father's credit had never been good, but the bank was too polite to say that. The main purpose of the letter was to confirm Miranda's identity, and, equally importantly, her relationship-by-marriage to the Duke of Belford.

Armstrong's couldn't do enough for her.

When the door had closed and silence filled the

room, Miranda sank down on a comfortable brocade-covered chair and considered her options.

They were few enough.

Belford—*Trust Leo, Miranda!*—had failed her and, by association, Julian. She would never now be welcomed into the Fitzgibbon family; indeed, she would be lucky if they ever spoke to her again. Not that she cared! Oh, no! As far as she was concerned, they could think her Adela, the Decadent Countess, *forever*.

If it were not so infuriating, the mistake would be laughable. Despite her excellent state of preservation, Adela was at least forty. Still attractive, though increasingly reliant upon cosmetics, she was not at all like Miranda. Adela was petite with dark hair and a small, pixie face... Miranda reminded herself that the Fitzgibbons had obviously never met Adela.

But people met strangers every day and did not accuse them of being who they were not!

The Decadent Countess!

Miranda had overheard the sobriquet at school in Hampshire and had never forgotten it. She could not say that the scandalous nickname exactly suited Adela, but she could see how it came about. Adela had a wicked smile and an equally wicked gleam in her eye. Even before Adela had married Papa, she had been a trifle rackety; now that she was widowed, she declared herself beyond caring when it came to social strictures and niceties. She therefore gave herself permission to do exactly as she pleased.

When Miranda arrived in Italy she had tried to dislike Adela. Adela was so very different from her own gentle and diffident mama. Adela was lazy and care-less and lacking what Miranda had always believed to be quite a few of the more important morals. But she was also great fun, had a ready and infectious laugh, and a genuinely kind and generous heart. Adela was the sort of woman who could never resist a sad story or a charity, and subsequently her house was always full of those deserving—and not so deserving—of her generosity.

Miranda had tried many times to persuade Adela to rein in her kind heart, as well as her purse strings, but restraint was not her strong suit. And so, even before her husband died, Adela had presided over a villa filled with the odd, the pitiable, the genuinely desperate, and sometimes, the unsavory.

When her father died over a year before, Miranda had not deserted her rackety stepmama—indeed, where would she go? Besides, despite her shortcom-ings, or maybe because of them, Miranda had grown very fond of Adela.

Even Julian had been fond of her, disapprove of her as he might. Certainly he had been appalled by Miranda's domestic situation. Upon arriving in Italy, Miranda had lived a hand-to-mouth existence with her father and stepmama. She had felt safe enough while her papa was alive; he had looked after her in his own careless way. Unfortunately, her papa had caught a fever and died, and then it had been just Miranda and Adela in the increasingly dilapidated Villa Ridge-way with Adela's increasingly disreputable guests.

That was when Julian had begun to grow seriously worried.

'Don't misunderstand me.' Julian had smiled his amiable smile. 'I think your stepmama is great fun. One could never be bored at her soirees. But, Miranda, you have to admit, it isn't quite the thing. Not for a girl like you. Only think what might have happened last week if I had not come along when I did?'

Miranda had thought, and shuddered. She had been followed on to the terrace and kissed wetly by one of Adela's many so-called admirers, although this 'gentleman' appeared more smitten with Miranda than her stepmama. Until that moment Miranda really had thought herself safe.

She preferred a quiet and unassuming existence, or at least that was what she had always told herself. 'Dear Miranda takes after her mother,' the Count had often said, sometimes with disappointment, sometimes—if Adela had been particularly exhausting—with relief. Miranda was a subdued and practical girl, who liked to paint—not very well—and take long walks. Hers was a calm beauty, all the more so when set against Adela's vivaciousness.

Until her stepmama's admirer kissed her, Miranda had truly believed herself happily immune from the disreputable element at the villa.

After the kiss, she knew she was not immune after all, and her safe world rocked alarmingly upon its axis. She realised that Julian, whose concerns she had previously dismissed with a laugh, was right. Miranda began to gaze into her looking-glass with new eyes. A girl such as she, tall and slender, with hair the colour of autumn leaves, was sure to attract attention in Adela's drawing room. No matter how quiet she might try to be, she could not help but be noticed. And although Adela had sent the offending 'gentleman' off, there would be others.

Julian was right, things could only get worse.

At that stage Miranda had known Julian for half a year, and although she enjoyed his company she certainly did not—could never—love him with the mad passion Adela appeared to exhibit whenever a new admirer entered her sphere. But, as Julian said, he was very fond of her and it would please him to be of use to her. In fact, Julian begged Miranda to let him help her, to let him give her his name and the protection it afforded. She could travel back to England and reside among the respectable Fitzgibbons and be safe.

Reluctant but at the same time thankful, Miranda had accepted Julian Fitzgibbon's proposal.

They had married within weeks, but by then Julian was already too feeble to stand without assistance. His illness, which until then had seemed content to move sedately, set off at a gallop. Instead of being Julian's wife, she had become his nurse. A month after their vows, he was dead.

Miranda sighed, allowing the past to slip from her. Her current situation presented her with quite enough problems without dwelling on those left behind!

Had the Fitzgibbons not read Julian's letter? He had promised Miranda he would write to his mother and explain everything, that she would have nothing to worry about, that Leo would take care of her. Take care of her!

Anger burned through Miranda again as she remembered the scene at Berkeley Square. How dare that man speak to her in so insulting a manner! Offering her money in that careless, arrogant voice. As if he had always had, or been given, everything he wanted. Well, he would learn disappointment! Miranda would make him wish he had never laid eyes on her.

Oh, yes, he would learn!

Miranda simmered for a few more moments, pacing about the room and staring unseeingly from the windows at the busy street below. The contrast to her home in Italy caused her a sharp pang. She felt more alone at this moment than she had ever felt in Adela's chaotic surroundings. But the emotion was brief and had more to do with her encounter with Leo than any real wish to return to the uncertainties of the Villa Ridgeway. *This* was her home now, and she would not be frightened away by an overgrown bully, even if he was a Duke!

It was strange, but when she had first stepped into the drawing room at Fitzgibbon House and been confronted by Belford, Miranda had found herself attracted to him. She had not thought him arrogant or bullying then. She had thought…well, there had been an odd sense of recognition. Not because he was Julian's cousin, but…well, because he was Leo.

Miranda shook her head. She must have been very tired from her journey to have woven herself such a fantasy. She sank back into her chair and stared at nothing. Her thoughts turned to The Grange. She quickly dismissed Belford's attempts to frighten her into giving it up. Julian had been very fond of his manor house, and now that it was hers she would pay his memory the courtesy of viewing the house before making a decision. Julian had spoken of The Grange often, especially in the last days of his illness. Of course, nearly everything had been prefaced with 'Leo and I', which at the time Miranda had found poignant, but now...well!

They could not stop her from moving down to Somerset and living there. In fact, Miranda thought that the two Fitzgibbons she had met so far would be very glad to see her go. Perhaps the odious Leo would decide Somerset was almost as good as Italy in regard to its distance from London and, when he discovered that she meant no mischief, leave her alone?

Until she left, however, she would make him very sorry for his behaviour, oh, yes! Miranda had no intention of following up her threats, but how was Belford to know that? As far as he was concerned she was the wicked Adela, capable of any mischief.

Another thought entered Miranda's head: the empty vow she had made to the Duke that she would send her hotel bill to him. Of course she had not meant to do so—she would rather die than take credit from his Dukeship!—but her fury had overcome good sense, and Miranda had found herself directing the cab driver to Armstrong's and soon after ordering herself a room when she had always intended to find modest lodgings at a modest inn.

She had little enough money and now a goodly portion of it would have to go on the bill. Miranda took a deep breath. It could not now be helped, but first thing in the morning she would call upon Julian's bank and discover exactly what her present financial situation was. As well as paying Armstrong's, she would require some funds once she reached The Grange, even for the frugal life she envisaged.

Miranda experienced a faint flutter of unease at the idea of living alone in a strange house. Villa Ridgeway had always been full of people, people of all sorts, stations and ages. Adela, the hostess, had never had much of a practical head on her shoulders. It was left to Miranda from her first days in residence to juggle accounts and order the servants. She was a clear-headed, clear-thinking girl, certainly not prone to extremes in behaviour. Which made her current conduct so puzzling, not least to herself.

Still, and Miranda quashed her doubts, it would never do to let cowardice cripple her plans. If she was so afraid, she may as well turn tail and hurry back to Italy now.

There was an alarming thought!

Fond of Adela as she was, Miranda had no desire to return to the past. No, Julian had left her The Grange, and she owed it to him to take full advantage of his generosity. At least she would be safe there. None of Adela's wet-lipped admirers would be lurking on the terraces or in the corridors, waiting to pounce. And there would be no arrogant dukes to enrage her…

Miranda sighed—she told herself it was a sigh of relief. Her mind made up, she rose briskly and set about making use of the warm water, soap and towels which had been left her. She would brush her hair and change into a crisp muslin gown—despite their reduced circumstances, and their often depleted larder, Adela had always made certain they were well dressed.

They would be serving luncheon downstairs shortly, and Miranda was suddenly very hungry.

The evening had been exceedingly dull. Leo made his excuses as soon as was politely acceptable and, collecting his hat and cane, strolled out into the night. A brisk wind swirled the edges of his coat, but he didn't feel the cold. He was pondering the puzzling fact that he had been quite looking forward to tonight's dinner at the Torringtons, and now suddenly it was…well, *dull.*

Cautiously, as though he were probing a tender spot, Leo asked himself whether his dissatisfaction might have something to do with a woman with hair the colour of autumn leaves, liquid dark eyes and a wide, full-lipped mouth. Such a face had been hovering in his thoughts since the moment the Countess entered the drawing room at Berkeley Square. He had held it at bay, telling himself—somewhat foolishly, he saw now—that if he did not think of her she would cease to annoy him. He had made a mess of their first meeting; anger—or something very like it—had taken possession of his usually imperturbable tongue. That was why he had felt so agitated ever since.

Aunt Ellen, he recalled, had displayed an insulting ingratitude, telling him he had only made things worse. Leo had been sorely tempted to give her an uncharacteristic, icy set-down, but instead informed her that he was not finished with the Countess yet.

He would visit her the following day at her *modish hotel,* and persuade her to accept his offer.

It was the way in which he said 'persuade' that pacified his aunt. She eyed him sharply, then set aside her handkerchief and smelling salts. By the time she left him, she was in much better spirits, and talking of everything soon returning to comfortable normality.

Normal? thought Leo now, as he strolled along the deserted street. What was normal? And comfortable, what was that? He had thought his life both until today. Now he was wondering whether the last thirty-five years had been just a dream, and he had at last awoken to reality.

'Belford! Wait on, man!'

Leo turned with a frown. He would as soon be left in solitude, but he could hardly tell Jack Lethbridge to go away. They had been friends since childhood. Jack's family lived on the opposite side of the village from Ormiston, the Fitzgibbon country residence. Jack even indulged in the hope that one day Leo would marry Sophie, Jack's sister. Leo had no intention of marrying Sophie, and as Jack had not mentioned his sister lately—she had remained in the country after one disastrous season—Leo hoped his friend had forgotten his fond dream of uniting the Fitzgibbon and Lethbridge families.

Not that Sophie wasn't a very sweet girl. Leo would even admit to her being pretty, in a washed-out sort of way, but girls like Sophie bored him, though he would never hurt his friend's feelings by telling him that he had seen too many girls like Sophie over the years, and they held no surprises.

'I thought you were deep in a game with Lord Ingham, Jack. What, have you lost already?'

Jack laughed good-naturedly. 'You know I have no head for cards, Leo. Can never remember what's trumps. No, I left them to it, went in search of you, and then someone said you'd just left. I thought you might have something more entertaining in mind.'

Leo strolled on and his friend fell into step beside him.

'I'm sorry to disappoint you.' Leo spoke in his usual mild tones. 'I was going home. I have a particular problem occupying my mind and I am afraid I am not very good company tonight.'

Jack gave him a blank stare. After a moment he cleared his throat. 'I know I'm not the brightest spark, Leo, but I hope you know that if you're in any difficulty you can talk to me about it?'

Leo smiled. 'I know I can, Jack. However, this is family business. To do with my cousin Julian, actually.'

'Julian? A good chap. Sad to hear he was ill, and then that he'd lost his fight. I sent a letter.'

'Yes, you did, thank you, Jack. This "difficulty" doesn't concern Julian so much as…his wife.'

Jack scratched his head. He was a good-looking gentleman in a round-faced, innocent sort of way. His eyes were brown and trusting, and his mouth often hung partly ajar. The kinder of his friends said this was because he was pondering some great mystery. Those less kind said he was thinking about his dinner.

'Didn't know Julian was married,' he announced now, very surprised.

'No, it is not widely known. Yet.'

'He never showed the least partiality to anyone in my presence, Leo. Not a runaway marriage, was it?'

Leo shook his head. 'No, Jack. My cousin didn't run off with anyone, although in hindsight I wish he had.' His eyes narrowed. 'He fell into the talons of a woman in Italy, a *lady* my Aunt Fitzgibbon would be loathe to allow in the rear door, let alone the front. In short, Jack, he has married the Countess Ridgeway, otherwise known as—'

'The Decadent Countess!'

Leo turned to his friend in surprise. 'You've heard of her?'

Jack was goggling at him. 'Hasn't everyone? She's infamous, Belford! Don't tell me Julian fell for *her*? Well, this is beyond anything! And she's now a Fitzgibbon? If you want my advice, Leo, you'll make damned sure she remains in Italy. Pay her if you have to, you can bear it. Pay men to watch the ports, too, and if she so much as sets foot on a boat have her arrested!'

Despite himself, Leo laughed. When he had sobered enough, he said, 'Thank you for your advice, Jack. You know I always value it. Sadly it comes too late. The Countess is already in London and I have had the pleasure of meeting her.' He looked thoughtful. 'I wonder, is "pleasure" the right word? Yes, I do believe it is. Have you seen her, Jack? She is very beautiful.'

Jack's round eyes opened even rounder. 'No, I

haven't seen her, I only know of her. But look here, Leo. You're not falling into her clutches, too, are you?'

Leo raised an eyebrow. 'Of course not. I hope I can appreciate a thing of beauty without being taken in by it. Some of the most vicious and dangerous creatures in the world are beautiful, but that doesn't mean I would like to cuddle up to them.'

Jack contemplated this for a while, then shook his head. 'Maybe not, but you're the right age, old boy. If you were going to make a fool of yourself over a woman, it'd be now. Have you forgotten the Fitzgibbon curse? The first Fitzgibbon married a scarlet woman and they've been the downfall of the male Fitzgibbons ever since. Remember your grandfather and that actress, what was her name?'

'Thank you, Jack,' Leo replied drily, 'I'll keep your warning in mind. But if you want my opinion the Fitzgibbons have a damned sight too many curses and legends! Now, my apologies, but I'll bid you a goodnight.'

Surprised, Jack looked up, and saw that they had reached Belford's house. 'Will you be travelling down to Ormiston this month?' he asked casually.

Leo shook his head. 'Not that I'm aware. Why?'

'Oh, I thought I might mention it to Sophie. If you were, that is.'

Leo sighed inwardly. 'Goodnight, Jack.'

What was it about some men and their sisters? he asked himself, as he climbed the steps to his front door. He was quite fond of Clementina, his own sister, but he did not try and run her life for her, and he certainly had not attempted to find a husband for her. Tina had been quite capable of doing that herself, and had made an excellent choice. She was at this moment at home in the country, having recently been brought to bed of a second healthy baby boy.

Pendle opened the door to him.

'I'll take brandy in the library, Pendle.'

'Yes, your Grace.' Pendle pursed his lips as if his evening meal had disagreed with him, but his master didn't notice. Pendle had been a part of his life for so long now that Leo took his bossiness, his frosty demeanour, and his loyalty, for granted. Indeed, he appeared to regard Pendle with a tolerant affection quite bewildering to other members of his family.

'No messages?'

Pendle allowed himself a thoughtful moue. 'No, your Grace, no messages.'

Of course not, Leo told himself impatiently, why should there be? The Countess had only to await his next move, after all, she held the best cards.

When Pendle had brought the brandy and closed the door, Leo sank down in his favourite chair, lifting his feet on to a padded footrest. The room was quiet, and smelt of tobacco, leather and books. A man's room, a refuge from the rest of the great house, which he sometimes found very large and very empty, although he would never have admitted that to anyone.

The Fifth Duke of Belford was the most urbane of men, the most tranquil of men. Ask anyone in the *ton*. He never got angry or excited or even mildly upset over *anything*. It was rumoured by those jealous of his good fortune that he was a very cold fish indeed.

In fact, hardly human. For if one could not feel, then one could not show emotion, and Leo rarely showed any.

They had not, of course, known him when he was young. Then, Leo had been a passionate boy, full of wild promise. The death of his father and the laying of great responsibilities upon his youthful shoulders had dampened down those earlier high spirits. Leo had tried hard to become what he believed a duke should be, and until now imagined his ambition to have been achieved.

But tonight all certainties had come undone, like buttons popping off a coat one had thought securely fastened. He felt a queer restlessness, and the usual peaceful silence of the library had become an irritant rather than a balm. He found himself wondering what it would be like if he had a wife waiting for him. Children, too, to greet him with their laughter and noise. Usually such imaginings were rare for the Duke of Belford, but tonight, deep inside, where the private man dwelt, Leo experienced an aching aloneness.

With his yearly income of twenty thousand pounds, an estate in Somerset, a hunting box in the Shires, and a house in London, Leo had been the object of many a flinty-eyed matchmaker. He knew of at least a dozen titled young women who would willingly accept the position of his duchess. Lately he had been considering the Honourable Miss Julia Yarwood as a possible contender. A Duke had to produce an heir— it was his duty, and Leo had never been one to shirk his duty.

Yesterday the Honourable Julia had seemed quite an attractive prospect, but now…

Leo closed his eyes. 'Damn the woman!' he burst out, and he wasn't thinking of the Honourable Julia. For some reason he didn't yet understand, this was all that woman's fault. She was turning his mind topsy-turvy. She had taken what had been a perfectly comfortable way of life and shaken it ragged! Tomorrow morning he would track her down and compel her to take up his offer. He would have her out of London if it was the last thing he did!

His sanity demanded it.

It was not quite ten when Leo called upon Miranda at Armstrong's.

Ten might have been too early for some ladies, and indeed that was what Leo had hoped. He told himself he wanted to fluster the baggage, catch her unawares.

He was disappointed.

Miranda had been up for several hours. She had not slept well, which was no fault of Armstrong's excellent bed but rather her own disturbed thoughts. She was washed, dressed, breakfasted and had been on the point of setting out to visit Julian's bank when a maid brought her the news that the Duke of Belford was awaiting her in one of the private downstairs parlours.

After ascertaining which parlour, Miranda thanked the girl calmly, her manner in no way betraying the strange conduct of her heart, which seemed to be trying to leap out of her chest. As soon as the maid had gone, she ran to check her appearance in the looking-glass. The green walking dress she was wearing was both flattering and fashionable, with its long, close-fitting sleeves and a muslin ruff at the throat. Kid-skin gloves, stout walking shoes and a warm cloak completed the outfit.

Miranda smoothed a truant lock of auburn hair back into the knot on her crown. If Belford found fault in her then it would not be because of her appearance.

She met her own eyes in the glass, and a slow, guilty flush spread upwards from the muslin ruff. What did it matter what he thought of her? In fact, the worse he thought of her the better! Julian's cousin had sullied her good name with his inferences and bullying behaviour. He had allowed his bias to blind him to the truth, when any other man would have seen at a glance that she was not Adela.

He was deserving of the severest punishment and she would see that he received it.

Miranda lifted her chin, straightened her already straight shoulders, and, with her reticule and her umbrella clasped firmly in her gloved hands, left her room to face her persecutor.

Indignation carried her downstairs to the private parlour in question, but once she had opened the door, Miranda hesitated. The Duke of Belford was standing with his back half-turned to her, one hand resting on the mantelpiece, his dark head bowed. He did not look like a bully now. He looked pensive, almost... troubled. And *very* handsome.

Miranda decided he could not have heard her enter, for he continued his silent examination of the small circle of flames in the fireplace. While knowing she should clear her throat to draw his attention, Miranda continued to remain silent, taking the opportunity to run her eyes over him. There was, she told herself firmly, nothing wrong in thoroughly scrutinising her opponent.

He was dressed for riding in a dark blue coat and brown breeches, with top boots so shiny Miranda was sure she would see her face in them, if she cared to look. His neckcloth was clean and neat but not ostentatious, and certainly not foolish, as had been the one worn by a man in the dining room last evening. In fact, everything about him was quiet and understated. He seemed the perfect gentleman.

Miranda struggled to dredge up her earlier anger, but for some reason all she could find was a ridiculous but no less painful longing that she and Julian's cousin had met in other, more congenial, circumstances.

'Do I pass muster, Countess?'

At the sound of his voice, Miranda's chin jerked up and she met the reflection of those deep blue eyes in the gilt-framed mirror above the mantel. He was smiling but there was no warmth in it, rather he looked smug and supercilious. A man who was used to women's adulation, she told herself, and longed to set him down. She lifted her chin another notch as the anger she had been seeking in vain a moment ago surged through her.

'You're passable, your Grace, but I have seen better.'

A reciprocal spark of anger flared briefly in his

eyes. He veiled them with dark lashes. 'Indeed,' he replied smoothly, with a hint of cruelty. 'But then, you draw from a vast experience.'

Untrue though they were, his words stung. 'Oh, vast!' Miranda retorted, and smiled back with clenched teeth. 'What do you want? I am just on my way out.'

'So I see. Then I will delay you only a moment.' He hesitated, coolly examining the impatient beauty before him. She was even more lovely this morning, despite the smudges of weariness beneath her magnificent eyes. Had he put them there? Reluctantly he dismissed the thought. She might disturb *his* sleep, but he very much doubted he disturbed *hers*. At least he was himself this morning. There would be no repeat of yesterday's unforgivable clumsiness.

'Will you not sit down, ma'am?' Leo spoke now with a frigid politeness. 'There are matters we must discuss and we may as well be comfortable while we do so.'

Miranda's stomach fluttered but she did not show it. Instead she replied with equal iciness, mixed with a fair dose of stubbornness, 'Thank you, but I am very comfortable. I prefer to stand.'

'As you wish. I understand you are calling yourself Mrs Fitzgibbon while you are staying here?'

'It is my name.'

'For the moment.' That smug smile again.

Miranda laughed in a manner completely alien to her. She felt reckless, slightly mad, capable of anything. Her family and friends would not have recognised her. Indeed, she felt like a stranger to herself, and yet at the same time it was a heady, liberating feeling.

'I did not realise you were able to effect divorces, sir!' She spoke with a degree of sarcasm she would never have believed she possessed.

'I am capable of many things, Countess. You do not know me yet.'

Was that a threat? His tone had sounded very soft and very menacing.

'Julian spoke of you often, so I feel as if I do,' she replied airily, as if she had not a care in the world.

At the mention of his cousin, Leo stilled, his gaze narrowing. 'Oh? Julian spoke of me?'

'Often. You were his hero. He—' She choked back what she had been about to say. The realisation came to her that it was in her power to hurt him by withholding Julian's regard for him. And yet, even as she determined to do just that, Miranda knew she couldn't. Whatever Leo's true character, Julian had believed him a generous and trustworthy man. She owed it to Julian to tell the truth.

Miranda looked into Belford's eyes and said simply, 'Julian thought a great deal of you.'

Leo appeared startled, and for a brief moment almost defenceless. And then his brows snapped down into a frown and Miranda knew she must have imagined it.

But Leo was caught off guard. He had not expected such generosity. A moment ago, with her eyes wildly glittering, she had seemed more inclined to murder him than offer him compliments.

Why then this sudden change of heart?

Leo felt like a tiny boat on a stormy sea—off balance and dangerously adrift. It had not occurred to him that the wicked Countess would suddenly develop a heart. Mentally, he shook his head. If he allowed himself to be sidetracked he would never gain the upper hand. The only way to bring this matter to the desired conclusion was to stick to the point.

'Have you reconsidered my offer, Countess?'

Ah, that was better! Her eyes were glittering again, and she was clenching her fingers about the handle of her umbrella as if she would like to break it over his skull.

'Your offer?' she cried, tossing her head, pretending at a carelessness he now knew she didn't feel: 'No, I haven't. Nor do I intend to. England will be my home from now on, and, whether you approve or not, here I will stay!'

A curl of auburn hair fell incongruously over one eye and she made an impatient sound and tucked it behind her ear. Her cheek appeared soft, smooth and defenceless. Her slim fingers were trembling.

Leo frowned.

Again he had the distinct feeling that there was something wrong, something jarring in the scene before him. The Countess wasn't being honest with him. He sensed it, and his instincts were rarely wrong. Determined to get to the bottom of the matter, one way or another, he closed the distance between them.

Miranda stood her ground, refusing to be intimidated by his broader shoulders and bigger body. They faced each other, he still frowning and she attempting to act out the part of her stepmama while inside she was feeling increasingly wobbly.

'Italy is your home, Countess,' Leo said softly. 'You would be far more comfortable there. And with fifteen thousand pounds, you could live very comfortably. If you were careful.'

Miranda searched his expression with narrowed eyes. He had upped the price, and probably expected her to capitulate. He did not realise the money meant nothing whatsoever to her. She would not have accepted his bribe had it been a million pounds!

'I am never careful,' careful Miranda answered artlessly.

She saw confusion gleam briefly through his cool mask, and then anger took its place. He stepped forward again, and now he was uncomfortably close.

'I will pay you twenty thousand pounds, but that is my final offer. If you still refuse to leave London, it will be necessary for me to take measures you will find extremely unpleasant. Be warned, madam, I am not a man to trifle with!'

No, she was sure he wasn't. Miranda licked her lips. The movement seemed to rivet his attention. His eyes slid to her mouth and fixed there. Suddenly Miranda was having difficulty breathing.

Leo was having difficulty remembering why he had come here in the first place. He was close enough now to smell the scent of her soap—lilac—and see the faint trembling of her hands as she clasped and unclasped them around her reticule and umbrella, both objects large and practical rather than the froth and frivolity he'd normally associate with a Decadent

Countess. But he was far beyond taking in such small discrepancies.

Instead, Leo was thinking that she was only a few inches shorter than he. Perfect, an unfamiliar voice inside his head affirmed, when it came to kissing. A slight adjustment, a comfortable tilt of the head, and their lips would be joined. He wondered what she would taste like. Something sweet, yes, warm and sweet.

God, he wanted to kiss her! More than he had ever wanted anything in his entire life. And for the first time in that life, Leo bent his head and gave full vent to his urges. A moment of pure paradise. Her lips were as soft and sweet as he had imagined, but, oh, so much warmer. His arm curved into the indentation of her waist, and her body leaned to his. Trustingly. Meant to be there.

Leo deepened the kiss.

With a cry, Miranda pushed him away.

She had to exert no little pressure to make him stop. Leo blinked, dazed, and stepped back. He took in her flushed and furious face. Reason returned full force, like the slam of a door in his face.

'Your Grace,' Miranda managed, her voice a breathless squeak. 'Whatever you may think of me, I *never* kiss strange men in hotel parlours.'

He laughed. Despite everything, he laughed. When *do* you kiss them? he wanted to ask, but knew that would be unforgivable. As unforgivable as that which he had just done. And then all humour left him.

Miranda's shock and indignation was excessive for a woman of such dubious reputation, but Leo did not think of that. He was too mortified by his actions. How could he, the most reasonable of men, have so completely lost his reason? How could he have been knocked off his calm and steady axis, and by the very woman he had come to send packing?

Leo bowed, his movements a stiff caricature of his usual self-possession. 'Madam, I beg your pardon.' His eyes were full of the truth of his words, startling Miranda with their clear honesty. 'Whatever ill feeling there may be between us, there was no excuse for my presumption.' He cleared his throat. 'Will you accept my apology?'

Miranda hesitated, gazing into his eyes. Somewhere deep inside her was the naughty, hoydenish acknowledgment that she had enjoyed his brief kiss very much, and that it had felt inexplicably *right,* but it was buried beneath an avalanche of confusion. And now he looked so very…sorry. She had meant to tear strips off him, or burst into tears. Instead Miranda found herself saying, 'I will accept your apology, sir. It will be as if it never happened.'

Their eyes met and slid away uncomfortably.

Leo cleared his throat. 'And you will accept my offer of twenty thousand pounds?'

He waited while she seemed to take an inordinate length of time to consider his question. There was a churning sensation in his stomach, but he told himself it was because he so wanted her to say 'yes'.

'No, Duke, I will not accept your offer.'

There was no readable expression on his face—he had himself well under control again. Instead he turned aside to stare into the flames.

'And may I ask why not?' Even his voice was blank.

Miranda matched him as well as she was able, though her heart was still beating uncomfortably hard and her breath was shaky. 'No, sir, you may not. But never fear, you will not have to endure the contamination of my company much longer. I am removing to The Grange as soon as I am able. I am sure you will agree that will be a relief to us both.'

He turned to stare at her as if he couldn't believe his ears. The words burst out of him before he could stop them. 'The Grange? You cannot mean to live there?'

Miranda was equally taken aback by the shocked disbelief in his face and voice, but she hid it with a brittle laugh. 'Of course I mean to live there. It is my home now, sir.'

'The Grange has been—'

'In the Fitzgibbon family for centuries, yes, Julian told me. But I am also a Fitzgibbon…now.'

Leo smiled grimly at her droll reminder. The momentary loss of the cool mask which he had worn for most of his life would not be repeated. 'As a matter of interest, do you know where The Grange is situated, Countess?'

Miranda watched nervously as he collected his hat and whip from a small side table. 'In Somerset, sir, near the village of St Mary Mere. Is that far enough away for you?'

He did not immediately answer, instead striding to the door. Once there he hesitated, before turning back to face her. She braced herself for she knew not what.

'You will regret your refusal to deal with me, Countess,' he told her quietly. Again that quick, searching look. He bowed again. 'Good day.'

The door closed behind him.

Astonished, incapable of any reply, Miranda stared after him. She was awash with a dozen emotions. She had no doubt he had meant exactly what he said. He wanted to be rid of her, and he would not rest until he was. Did he loathe her so much? Miranda, who had wanted him to loathe her, now took exception to that. How dare he speak so to her? And yet, on another level, Miranda tingled with an attraction so potent, she hardly knew how to explain or manage it. He had kissed her! And she had not been repulsed, not at all. She had not wanted him to kiss her, not expected it, but when he did...oh! What bliss.

Realising the ridiculous direction her thoughts were taking, Miranda put a stop to them. Whether she had enjoyed it or not was beside the point. No gentleman should make unwelcome advances towards a lady.

And what if he did not think her a lady?

Miranda groaned. Of course! He thought she was Adela, an experienced woman of the world. He thought she would welcome such advances, or at least know how to deal with them. And she had allowed him, even encouraged him, to think it!

So did that mean she had only herself to blame? Miranda did not think so. If this was anyone's fault, it was *his*. He was the one who had jumped to conclusions in the first place, and it was he who had insulted her and infuriated her to the point where she had had no choice but to punish him.

Miranda touched her lips and remembered the warm wave of pleasure which washed over her when he kissed her. And something else…a sense of belonging. Leo Fitzgibbon, the Duke of Belford, was evidently even more dangerous than she had thought.

Just as well she was retiring to The Grange. There she could live in quiet solitude. Indeed, she thought wryly, with so few funds she had little choice. And she did not resent it, no, indeed! Although Miranda had enjoyed Adela's soirees, she had never sought excitement in her life. Since childhood, she had led an uncertain existence. It was certainty she craved, and a sense of security. The Grange would give her that.

The memory of Leo Fitzgibbon's eyes intruded on her comfortable picture. It could not be that she would miss that hateful man? she thought, appalled. He had done nothing but insult her since the moment she met him. No, she disliked him intensely, and if she never saw him again—which she certainty would not!—it would be too soon.

Chapter Three

Leo itched to gallop his chestnut stallion. Send it careering recklessly along the quiet paths of the Park, frightening ladies and gentlemen as they strolled beneath the leafy trees.

Of course he did no such thing.

To do so would be completely, entirely out of character. And yet Leo was beginning to wonder just what was *in* character for him.

He was still reeling from his complete loss of control in the parlour of Armstrong's Hotel. If he had thought his handling of the situation yesterday was bad, this was far worse. And, try as he might, he could not understand why he would want to kiss a woman who was like a thorn in the side of the Fitzgibbon family. A woman who was, to be blunt, blackmailing him into paying her far more money than he cared to.

What was wrong with him?

All these years, Leo had prided himself on his restraint. He was a man to be relied on in a crisis, known for his good manners and cool control. He had even heard himself described as the perfect gentle-man. Well, this morning had put an end to that!

Leo twitched uncomfortably in his saddle. It was now more imperative than ever that the Countess agree to his terms and return to Italy. His life would not be the same again if she did not. Obviously he could not trust himself in her presence, *ergo* her presence must be removed.

And now she was threatening to take up residence at The Grange! Could it be she was not aware of the upset her plans would cause him and his family? Did she not know that The Grange was on the opposite side of the village to Ormiston, the Fitzgibbon family estate? And yet she had indeed seemed unaware of this fact. One moment she was one thing, and then she was another. Just when he had decided she was the very antithesis of the wicked schemer she had appeared five minutes before, she would do or say something to throw him once more into confusion.

Leo cursed softly.

There was an empty stretch of path ahead. His rest-lessness could no longer be contained. Leo spurred the chestnut into a gallop. By the time he pulled up again he was feeling a little calmer, and was able to make polite bows to a number of his acquaintances. They did not, he told himself with relief, seem to notice any alteration in him. He was himself again.

The season was in full swing, and a number of mothers and marriageable daughters were to be seen in their carriages, taking the air. The knowledge that he was once more a prime target caused a flicker of irritation to crease his brow. Had he ever really en-

tertained the thought of marrying a Miss just out of
the schoolroom? They all seemed so insipid. More so,
he admitted uneasily, since he had met the Decadent
Countess.

Leo found himself wondering idly what it would
be like to be married to Julian's widow. Certainly he
would never be bored. Probably he would be distracted within a day and mad within a week.

He groaned aloud at his own stupidity, causing a
gentleman in a yellow waistcoat to turn and stare. Leo
exited the gates of the Park and set his horse in the
direction of Berkeley Square. There were matters
awaiting his attention, and he would need to send a
note to his aunt informing her of his latest encounter
with her daughter-in-law.

Leo had an uneasy feeling the old Mrs Fitzgibbon
would be even more ungrateful than she had been
yesterday.

The bank had been most accommodating. Miranda
had learned Julian had left her a modest inheritance,
enough to allow her to live frugally. Mr Ealing had
been keen for her to sell The Grange and buy a somewhat smaller dwelling. A cottage in St Mary Mere
village, perhaps? Miranda had listened politely, but
refused to make any decision until she had seen the
house for herself.

Julian had loved The Grange, and therefore she felt
it an obligation that she visit the house first, before
Mr Ealing and fate had a chance to remove it from
her grasp.

A brief shower had swept the streets clean while

she was inside the bank, and now the air was fresh and clean. Miranda crossed the road, carefully avoiding a phaeton pulled by gleaming black horses and driven by a gentleman with a neckcloth so high he could barely turn his head and a coat so tight he could barely move his arms.

If the Duke of Belford looked like that, she decided, it would be an easy matter to despise him. Instead his sober but well-cut clothing proclaimed him a man of sense. In other circumstances she might have thought him a very elegant gentleman indeed, but no one, having been kissed by him so thoroughly in the parlour of Armstrong's Hotel, could believe him any sort of gentleman at all!

Miranda felt her face growing hot. A tingle of excitement stirred in her blood, making her wonder if she was coming down with an illness. She could not remember ever before behaving in such an ill-considered and nonsensical manner. In Italy, her stepmama looked to her for plain, practical and level-headed advice, and described her as 'composed'. No, this was all his fault. He was turning her into a Bedlamite, and the sooner she escaped to the quiet of the country, and The Grange, the better.

Surely, he would not follow her there?

Or would he?

Miranda had the sinking feeling that Leo Fitzgibbon was capable of anything when it came to getting what he wanted. What was it Julian had been fond of saying to her? *Down the centuries every one of the Fitzgibbons has been determined to have his way, and usually did!*

She reached Armstrong's just as more rain drops began to fall. Inside, branches of candles had been lit to combat the dull day and fires burned merrily in the many fireplaces. Miranda thought it all looked very nice indeed, but the knowledge gave her no joy. The bill loomed large over her. She would have enough money to pay it, but it would leave her uncomfortably short until the bank was able to send on some of Julian's legacy.

She should never have allowed herself to be goaded into putting up here. It was convenient to blame Leo Fitzgibbon, but Miranda was honest enough to apportion herself part of that blame.

Miranda had begun to climb the stairs to her bed-chamber when one of the maids called out to her, begging her pardon, and handed her a letter. Puzzled, Miranda continued on to her room, where she tore open the unfamiliar seal.

A quick scan of the single sheet of paper disclosed that the letter was signed by a Mr Frederick Harmon. Miranda had never heard the name before, and sat down to read.

Mr Frederick Harmon stated that he was a distant cousin of the Countess Ridgeway, and had been asked by that lady to make himself known to Miranda as soon as she arrived in London. He wondered if Miranda would allow him the pleasure of dining with her this evening at Armstrong's? A note to his rooms would confirm or deny him this treat.

Miranda put a hand to her brow, where a faint, niggling pain warned of the beginnings of the head-ache. It had been kind of Adela to write ahead of her arrival, and ask Mr Harmon to visit her—a typical Adela gesture—but her stepmama's friends were unfortunately not always the most respectable of people. Miranda hesitated, wondering whether she should accept his invitation, or refuse and take her meal in her room.

The latter sounded so comfortable that she was on the verge of refusing, when a thought popped into her head. Leo Fitzgibbon would hate to think of her dining alone with a strange gentleman. It would confirm all of his worst doubts about her.

That settled the matter. Miranda crossed briskly to the desk by the window and, her headache forgotten, wrote a brief note of acceptance.

Leo looked across the colourful sea of guests, noting those he might seek out and those he might avoid. He had already accepted this invitation to the Ingham ball, or else he might have cried off. He had planned to begin his courtship of the Honourable Julia Yarwood tonight, but that seemed eons ago—yesterday, before he met *her*.

Now Leo knew he would neither court nor wed Miss Yarwood. He would probably die a sour old man, the last of his line.

That was *her* fault.

His aunt's reply to his note, and her blunt criticisms, hadn't lessened his unfamiliar feeling of depression. His eye caught that of an acquaintance. Leo fixed a smile to his mouth and bowed. In his black evening wear, he made a handsome picture. Not a vain man, he was nevertheless well aware of the number of ladies watching him from behind fluttering fans.

If they but knew the state of his mind, he thought grimly, they would run from him in terror.

For half an hour he strolled through the rooms, doing his duty as the Duke of Belford. He danced once with the Honourable Julia, and wondered what on earth he ever found in her dull, monotonous voice and lifeless smile to attract him. He knew now that, married to her, he would die of boredom within a year. At least he could comfort himself with the thought that he had never once given her to hope theirs was more than a polite friendship.

As soon as possible, Leo escaped to the card room, where he found Lethbridge. Losing. Jack grinned at him, and made his excuses to his opponents.

'You've sent her packing, Belford?' he demanded, pouring them both a glass of claret.

'I will, Jack. Soon.'

Jack frowned, then shook his head. 'It's as I said, old chap. She's got her hooks into you. You'll never be free of her now.'

Leo laughed lightly. 'Not at all. She's running scared.'

'Is she?' Jack was thoughtful. 'Didn't look scared when I saw her an hour ago. Harmon didn't look scared, neither. Looked to be enjoying themselves too much to be scared.'

Leo narrowed his remarkable eyes, fixing his friend with a stare that made Jack feel, he later admitted, rather queasy.

'What are you talking about?'

Jack edged back. 'Steady on, Leo! I just said—'

'I know what you said,' Leo retorted, teeth clenched. 'Harmon? You don't mean the blackguard Harmon?'

'Well, yes. Went to school with him, you know.' Jack gave his friend a startled glance. 'Well, so did you!'

Leo gritted his teeth. 'For God's sake, Jack, concentrate. Where did you see them?'

'Armstrong's,' Jack replied mildly.

'What were you doing at Armstrong's?' Leo demanded, the edge of impatience in his voice giving way to astonishment.

Jack cleared his throat. 'I…eh…I thought I'd take a look at Armstrong's. You know, sometimes one has friends visiting from the country. Want to put up somewhere. Thought I'd take a look just in case.'

Leo stared at him in disbelief. 'You mean you went to Armstrong's Hotel to spy on the Countess?'

Jack widened his eyes, but his flushed face gave him away. 'Not exactly spy. Just a bit of a peek. I asked one of the maids to point her out. Wanted to see what she was like.'

'And did you?' Leo mocked.

'Yes.' Jack looked suddenly grave. 'I can see why you're not yourself, Belford. Like I said, it's the Fitzgibbon curse.'

Leo smoothed his cuff. 'I am very much myself, thank you, and I don't believe in curses. Tell me the rest.'

Jack obliged. 'She was dining with a gentleman in the dining room. Not a private room, mind. Just the two of them at one of the tables. Perfectly respectable. Laughing and talking, like old friends. It was Harmon, Belford, I couldn't mistake him after what he did to Sophie last season… *You* know. I would have called him out then, but Sophie begged me not to. Said it'd make it all worse for her.'

'And so it would have,' Leo replied.

'Well, I can tell you, Belford, when I saw him tonight it made me come over a bit strange. Sitting there with your Countess, bold as brass. You know I'm a mild sort of chap, but I wanted to walk in there and plant him a facer.'

'She's not *my* Countess,' was all Leo said to this admission. But there was something strange happening in the region of his midriff, a sort of churning, lurching feeling, like a rowing boat pitching on a rough sea. The thought of the Countess and Harmon together, dining, laughing, was building like a dark and turbulent storm inside him. He found that his hands had clenched into fists, and quickly slipped them into his pockets and out of sight.

Jack was eyeing him nervously. 'You're not going to make a cake of yourself, are you, old chap?'

Leo laughed, and it didn't sound like his laugh at all.

'Wish I hadn't told you now,' Jack muttered. 'I won't let you go alone, though. I'll come with you, to lend support.'

'There's no need for you to come. I merely want to see this pretty portrait you've painted me in the flesh. Simply to confirm it. I have no intention of coming to blows with a creature like Harmon.'

Jack still looked dubious, but Leo said a brief good-bye and went to take his leave of his hosts. Jack poured himself another glass of claret and shook his head.

'Worst case I ever saw.'

Mr Frederick Harmon had arrived promptly at Armstrong's.

A man of Belford's age, he was smaller and less good-looking than the Duke, with a long narrow face and carefully arranged brown hair beginning to thin on top. There was, however, a casual air about him, a lack of stiffness, which Belford did not possess and which was rather attractive.

In other circumstances, Miranda might have been drawn to his smile and the friendly gleam in his eyes. But she had met the Duke of Belford, and, although she did not yet know it, he had spoiled her for all other men.

Mr Harmon's greeting was warm, but reserved enough not to cause Miranda alarm. He was, he confirmed, a cousin of Adela's.

With a hint of self-depreciation, he explained to Miranda how he had invested his small inheritance unwisely and fallen upon hard times. Adela had generously helped him out, allowing him to regain his feet. He was now, he jokingly assured her, well and truly 'back in the black'.

'I am always most eager to do anything I can to repay Adela's kindness and when she wrote of her concern for you, well...' He smiled. 'You will understand how readily I agreed to her request to seek you out.'

Miranda smiled back, and sipped chicken soup from her spoon. The dining room was quite full, but here in the alcove by the window, she and her companion were surprisingly private. Miranda imagined this to be mere chance, and could not know that Mr Harmon had made certain of that 'chance' by greasing the palm of one of the hotel's less scrupulous employees.

Freddie Harmon was a man who rarely left anything to chance.

'You *were* very prompt in seeking me out, sir,' she ventured.

Her companion twinkled at her guiltily. 'I must confess to you, I have a contact in the shipping office. He sent word you had arrived and I made haste to present you with my note. I hope you don't find me too presumptuous, Mrs Fitzgibbon, but I wanted to offer you the benefit of my experience as soon as possible. Adela seemed to think you might need advice from someone who has lived in the metropolis for most of his life.'

His air of earnestness, kindness and honesty made Miranda more than willing to forgive him, if forgiveness was needed. 'Of course, Mr Harmon. I meant no criticism, believe me. I can truly say that never have I been more in need of a friend!'

He hesitated, as if he might ask more, and then let the comment pass. Time enough later to storm her barricade, he thought, but for now he would tread lightly. He leaned forward solicitously, and refilled

Miranda's wine glass. 'I was sorry to hear of your loss,' he said. 'If I may say so, you are very young to be a widow.'

Miranda accepted his sympathy with a sober nod of her head. 'Are you married, Mr Harmon?' she asked him with more politeness than curiosity.

'I was.' He allowed his voice to drop. 'Alas, I am also now alone.'

His demeanour, while perfectly proper for a bereaved husband, suddenly struck Miranda as false. And yet there was no reason why it should. Puzzled by her own reaction, Miranda smiled gently but firmly. 'Tonight, sir, we must put aside our grief.'

Mr Harmon agreed to this readily enough, and soon afterwards Miranda decided she must have been mistaken. He was a lively companion, and he would have been a charming one, too, if Miranda's thoughts had not been centred elsewhere. But whenever she looked into Frederick Harmon's earnest brown eyes she saw instead a pair of cool blue ones.

Perhaps it was guilt at her own lack of attention which caused Miranda to be far more friendly, and far less cautious, than she might otherwise have been, for when the meal was finished, she allowed Mr Harmon to order coffee in a private parlour.

It could not hurt, she told herself. She was a widow, with no need of a chaperon, and this was a very respectable hotel. Besides, Mr Harmon was Adela's cousin, and, despite Adela's reputation, Miranda knew she would not purposely harm Miranda's by throwing her into the company of a bad man.

Soon, Miranda found herself telling Mr Harmon

about The Grange, and her plans to remove there as soon as possible.

'It has been in the Fitzgibbon family for centuries,' Miranda announced, her voice so loud and strangely boastful, she bit her lip in consternation. Mr Harmon had pressed a number of glasses of wine upon her, and it was only now she wondered if she might, in her efforts to please him, have imbibed too much.

Mr Harmon was nodding sagely. 'I imagine the family will be glad their manor house is safe in your hands.'

Miranda laughed, her apprehension forgotten. 'Glad! They'd do anything to get it back.'

Harmon stared back at her aghast, whilst secretly delighted. He had been almost certain that that was the case, and now she had confirmed it. He recalled the exact words of Adela's letter to him.

My dear stepdaughter will be an innocent among those Fitzgibbon wolves. I know she thinks they will welcome her, but I believe differently. Belford in particular has the reputation of a hard, callous man. I'm afraid they will soon strip her of the little Julian left her. The Grange is like a good luck charm to them and they will try anything to get it back. Please, Freddie, in remembrance of what I have done for you in the past, look after her!

Freddie Harmon blessed the day that letter came into his hands, and had been watching for Miranda's arrival ever since. How could silly, soft-hearted Adela know that, if it were not for Belford and his idiot friend Jack Lethbridge, her cousin would at this moment be comfortably leg-shackled to the rich and gullible Sophie Lethbridge?

He had been within a beat of closing his fist on her, when Belford struck. Frederick Harmon didn't just dislike Belford, he hated him, and he would do anything to pay him back.

'Perhaps you would allow me to speak to the Duke of Belford in your stead?' he asked now, his voice carefully diffident, his expression reflective. He leaned forward and took her hand, patting it like a kindly uncle.

Miranda didn't notice. She was thinking it would do Leo Fitzgibbon a great deal of good to have another man to bully rather than a defenceless female. But before she could tell him so, they were interrupted by the bully himself.

His voice was soft and deep, and she found that already she knew it well.

'Are you trying to increase my offer, Countess?'

Miranda looked up in astonishment to where Leo stood inside the parlour door. His eyes seemed fairly to blaze out at her from the shadows beyond the candles. He was very angry, and very, very jealous, but Miranda could not know that. Seeing his anger, she gasped and shrank back into her chair.

In contrast, Mr Harmon rose smoothly to his feet, his smile a smug caricature of concern. 'Belford,' he said, and bowed so slightly it was a clear insult.

Leo glanced at him dismissively. 'If you planned to impress me with the company you keep, Countess, you should have chosen someone other than Harmon here. I bloodied his nose when we were boys and have no doubt I can, and will, do it again.'

Harmon flushed angrily, but forced himself to remain steady. 'Mrs Fitzgibbon has asked me to tell you she has no intention of giving up The Grange. She—'

'The Countess can tell me her intentions herself,' Leo sneered.

Harmon frowned. 'Why do you call her—?'

Miranda sprang unsteadily to her feet. She felt suddenly breathless and rather dizzy. At the same time she was able to read perfectly well in Belford's face what he thought of her. The contempt was in his eyes and the curl of his lips. She should have been pleased, but instead she wanted nothing more than to convince him that none of the insulting things he was imagining were true.

It was of the utmost importance he understand.

'Mr Harmon is a distant relative of my...of mine,' she said firmly, forcing the tremble out of her voice. 'He was kind enough to...that is, we dined together. In the public dining room. And then he suggested coffee and I... There is no reason for you...there is nothing—'

'He was holding your hand.' Belford cut through her garbled explanation, his voice like ice.

Miranda blinked. 'Was he?' She looked at Harmon and frowned, then back to Leo. She sighed. 'Oh dear, so he was. I suppose it was the wine. I drank several glasses. I seem to have lost my perspective.' Defeated, she sank back into her chair.

'Do you normally drink so much?' Leo demanded. 'I don't recall my Aunt Ellen describing you as a sot.'

'No, I do not,' she snapped. 'If I were a—a sot, do you think I would have had any compunction about telling you so? Even in Italy, where one normally drinks wine in preference to water, I never drank much. Perhaps if I had I would not now be in this predicament. Besides, Mr Harmon kept refilling my glass and—'

Leo closed the distance, hands clenched at his sides. 'Are you telling me that this man forced strong drink upon you?'

'No, I didn't mean that!' Miranda cried. 'Will you stop trying to start a fight?'

Harmon, who had been listening with interest, smoothed his cuffs. 'I don't mind if he starts one, Mrs Fitzgibbon, for I will certainly finish it.'

'No!' Miranda said, and then put a hand to her eyes. It was a nightmare and she had had enough. 'Please, both of you, go away. I have the headache and I have a long journey to undertake tomorrow. I am removing to The Grange.'

Leo frowned, a shadow moving in his blue eyes. 'Alone?' he asked her sharply.

Miranda lifted her head, her eyes blazing back at him. 'Of course alone!'

Leo almost smiled. Instead, he bowed. 'Then I will leave you to your preparations, Countess. Be assured, however, this matter between us is far from finished. Do not think this is the last you will see of me. Goodnight.' His glance skimmed Harmon, rather as one would glance at a small and not very interesting beetle.

Once more the door closed behind him.

Harmon, full of questions, turned to Miranda. She was staring towards the window so that only her profile was visible to him. She looked pale and young, and desperately in need of a shoulder to cry on. A perfect opening for him. He decided on the outraged tone.

'His behaviour was quite incredible! Who does the man think he is? Such ill manners! And yet I had always thought Belford the epitome of the English gentleman. Or, at least, he puts it about that he is.'

'Does he?' Miranda murmured wearily. 'I hardly know him.'

'And what did he mean by calling you "Countess"? Does he not know that *Adela* is the Countess Ridgeway?'

Miranda lifted a dismissive hand, her face still averted, her shoulders slumped. 'A mistake on his part.'

'A mistake? I would not have thought Belford lacking in wits. Are you—?'

'Please.' Miranda stopped, swallowed, then went on. 'I know you mean well, sir, but I would prefer it if you went now. I—I am very tired and I must pack for tomorrow. Thank you for your company this evening, Mr Harmon. I am grateful for your time and trouble. If we do not meet again then…goodbye. I don't expect to be travelling up to London very often.'

He stared at her in astonishment. Could she mean to dismiss him so easily? And yet it seemed that she did, and, playing the part of the gentleman, he had no option but to accept her dismissal.

'My dear lady,' he murmured gently, 'I will leave you now, but you must not think I am deserting you. If you need me, you have only to write and I will hasten to your side.'

His words were melodramatic, but Miranda did not notice that. Rather she found his concern for her gratifying and her lips wobbled pitifully as she tried to smile.

With a sigh, Harmon bowed and left her. Outside Armstrong's Hotel, he stood staring into the darkness, puzzling over what he had just witnessed. There was something between Belford and Miranda, any fool could see that, but what exactly was it? Maybe he could use the 'it' to his advantage? Belford wanted The Grange, and soon Frederick Harmon, as Miranda's close and dear friend, would be in a position to bargain with him.

For a price.

With a smile, Harmon strolled off into the night.

Leo shifted out of the shadows, turning to watch Harmon walk away. If it was true that Freddie Harmon was the Countess's cousin, his presence was explained. If not... Leo could not help but wonder if the two of them were in league. Harmon had an unsavoury reputation and was not above trying to elope with young, impressionable girls, while the Countess was, well, the gossip on that subject was not pleasant listening.

Perhaps Jack was right, perhaps the Fitzgibbon curse or legend, or whatever it was, was working on him. He'd be another such as his grandfather, chasing after totally unsuitable women to the consternation and embarrassment of his nearest and dearest relatives.

Leo glanced up at the square, solid façade of Armstrong's Hotel, softened by the glow of many candles. It looked rather fortresslike in the darkness. He found himself thinking: She will be safe there. And then wondered why he should be concerned for such a woman's safety. It defied explanation. Besides, she would be leaving in the morning for Somerset and The Grange.

Leo allowed himself a smile. She thought she had escaped him, but Ormiston was mere miles from Julian's old home. So simple to pay her a visit.

The decision lifted him from the wave of gloom which had washed over him at the thought of her leaving. It was about time he made one of his infrequent trips to Ormiston. London had grown inexplicably stale. Yes, he would begin making arrangements in the morning.

Leo set off towards Berkeley Square with a decided spring in his step.

Inside the hotel, Miranda had reached her bedchamber and now sat curled in the chair before her fire. An odd combination of regret and depression assailed her. Leo Fitzgibbon had seen her this evening exactly as he expected to see her. And he had drawn the worst possible conclusions. Now, she could never make him as truly and deeply contrite as she wished. He would never grovel for forgiveness at her feet, for even when he discovered she was not the Decadent

Countess, he would still think just as badly of her. Miranda could hear him now, his cool voice cruelly dismissive. 'Like stepmama, like stepdaughter.' No, he would never now beg her pardon or look at her with surprised and delighted wonder in his magnificent eyes...

Miranda shook herself angrily. What was she thinking! Leo Fitzgibbon was an arrogant bully and he meant nothing to her. She would travel to Somerset and make her home at The Grange and, despite his empty threats, never see the Duke of Belford again.

It was what she wanted, after all.

Wasn't it?

Chapter Four

Miranda lay under the counterpane, face turned towards the windows. Or, the bedcurtains being closed, where the windows should have been. It was an old bed, dark and ornate, with heavy, faded draperies and a lumpy mattress. Miranda would have preferred not to be hemmed in, but she knew from experience that outside her warm cocoon the room would be icy. She had been at The Grange for a week now, and felt that she already knew the best, and the worst, it could offer her.

Tugging the embroidered bedcurtains to one side, she peered out. Sunlight was shining through old mullion windows, making rainbows on the uneven wooden floor of the bedchamber. The Grange, Miranda had learned, was extremely old, parts of it dating back to the days of Henry the Eighth.

Old or new, the house was far too large for Miranda, as well as being dilapidated, leaky and impossible to keep warm. And Miranda loved it. She had loved it from the moment she saw it.

Arriving exhausted from her journey from London, the final three-mile leg having been made by very rickety cart from the village, her first sight of The Grange had lifted her weary heart. The golden bricks had glowed in the afternoon sunshine and the tall chimney stacks had risen solid against a pale blue sky. Miranda had been filled with joy.

She had known at once this was her home and that she would never sell it, whatever Mr Ealing advised.

Neither the ancient manservant who had answered her repeated pulls on the bell, nor the damp sheets and unaired rooms had dulled her bright enthusiasm. That first night she had ordered a fire lit in the great hall, and sat in a carved wooden chair eating stale bread and cheese, surrounded by shadows and the shades of Julian's ancestors.

Remembering it now, Miranda sighed and snuggled further under the covers.

Although her love for the house had remained constant, her enthusiasm had dimmed over past days. The waning of the latter had begun after a long ramble along The Grange's dusty corridors had given her a better grasp of the manor's state of health. Rain dripped through holes in the roof, floorboards were rotten, and dust and damp collected everywhere.

If The Grange had been a person it would have died from neglect years ago.

When she allowed herself to consider the amount of money which would be needed to repair and restore the building to its former glory she felt quite dizzy. It was certainly more than she had or was ever likely to have. Indeed, sometimes she wondered if she had merely exchanged the penury of Villa Ridgeway for a similar, possibly worse, situation.

Of course, you could accept Leo Fitzgibbon's offer, wheedled a voice in her head.

Miranda gave it a stern talking-to. If she accepted the Duke of Belford's bribe, she would be bound to return to Italy, taking the money with her. She would never see The Grange, or England, again.

And never see Leo Fitzgibbon again.

This time Miranda ignored the voice. She had no intention of accepting the Duke's offer. It would be against her principles to do any such thing. What an arrogant and rude man! How amiable, generous Julian could have had such a cousin was beyond her. And that he should actually have admired and liked him! Well, Miranda could only think that Julian had been a very poor judge of character.

A light tap on the door heralded the arrival of Nancy, a raw-boned woman of indeterminate years. She was carrying a jug of lukewarm water in her arms. Miranda knew that it was lukewarm, it had been lukewarm on her first morning, and had remained so no matter how many times she had pointed out this unfortunate fact to Nancy. Nancy blamed the myriad staircases and corridors she had to traverse from the kitchens. It was true that The Grange resembled a series of mazes, all upon different levels, so that one was forever climbing up or down to get somewhere.

Miranda was still finding her way around.

'The house is old and so are my legs,' Nancy was fond of saying. It was her stock answer to any of the tactful suggestions for improvement Miranda might make.

This morning Nancy had a skinny young girl trailing behind her. She was wearing a cap which would have been too big on Nancy and was therefore enormous on the girl. She peered shyly out at Miranda.

'This here is Esme from the village,' Nancy announced. 'She's to help in the kitchen.'

Miranda raised her eyebrows. 'How many servants have I now, Nancy?'

Nancy shrugged. 'They come and go, mistress. This is an awful big house and my legs aren't what they used to be.' She turned to mutter to Esme. 'Make your curtsy, girl.'

Esme wobbled a quick curtsy, her expression anxious.

Despite her doubts, and the knowledge that she and Nancy would have to have a serious talk before long, Miranda's heart went out to Esme, and she smiled kindly.

'Welcome to The Grange, Esme. I hope you are very happy here.'

'You've a visitor, mistress.' Nancy did not hold with sentimentality.

Surprised, Miranda sat up. 'A visitor? What time is it, Nancy?'

'Going on for nine, mistress. Some folk have no notion of what's proper.'

Miranda ignored this. 'Who is it?'

'Miss Sophie Lethbridge, mistress, from Oak House.'

As this meant nothing to Miranda, and Nancy did

not appear to be willing to elaborate, she decided she had best hold her questions until she met Miss Sophie Lethbridge face to face.

Miss Lethbridge would be her first visitor to The Grange. Despite the early hour and her other concerns, Miranda experienced a sense of excitement and anticipation. From the moment she had stepped back on to English soil, she had been determined to build a proper life for herself, the sort of settled existence which she had never before been lucky enough to own.

Nancy's dry tones intruded. 'You'll want your tea and toast then, mistress?'

'Not this morning, thank you, Nancy. That will be all.'

Nancy bobbed a grudging curtsy, dipping her chin to hide her smirk, and with Esme on her heels, left the room.

As soon as the door closed behind her, Miranda jumped quickly out of bed, pulling on her warmest cloak, and tipped the water from the jug into the basin. She had been wrong. The water was not tepid this morning—it was cold.

Quickly, shivering, she dressed, slipping on a pair of thick and ugly woollen stockings beneath her skirts. They were hardly high fashion but no one would know, and The Grange was very cold.

When she was dressed, Miranda sank down in front of her dressing table. Her auburn hair hung in tangles about her shoulders and her eyes were shadowed. Despite the old mirror's golden glow, Miranda could see that this morning she was not looking her best. Worry and a good night's sleep did not seem to be mutually compatible.

With a sigh she picked up her brush. It would never do to keep her first visitor waiting.

Nancy's father, Bennett, was standing in the hall as Miranda descended the stairs. He was looking particularly villainous this morning.

'Miss Sophie Lethbridge in the parlour, mistress,' he informed her with his thick Somerset burr.

'Thank you, Bennett.'

'Nancy even lit the fire in there, mistress. Looks right cheery.'

'Well, that will be a change, won't it?'

The old man appeared to find great amusement in this, for he chuckled to himself as he tottered away.

Miranda wondered if that meant Bennett had accepted her at last, or whether he was simply amused by her attempts to play the part of mistress of The Grange. Since she had arrived the servants, led on by Nancy and her father, had treated her as an interloper. She supposed she should be grateful they had not asked for their wages, something she had been dreading and yet expecting daily. They must not have been paid for some time.

Miranda was not even entirely sure just how many servants were employed at The Grange.

Of course, there was Nancy, and Bennett, her old father, and there was Nancy's son and daughter, and a scruffy-looking old woman who pretended to dust but, in Miranda's opinion, was either too blind to do a proper job or simply didn't want to. And now, as well, there was young Esme from the village!

They were all related and the sort of servants who had been attached to the one house for a very long time—they had probably come with the Fitzgibbons. That was why, no matter how unfair it was, they considered *her* the intruder in *their* home. Miranda was not used to having her orders questioned or smirked at, and she was not used to evasion and downright lies.

They did lie to her, she was certain of it. There was the question of an almost complete ham going missing from the larder, and the reason for so many empty spaces on the walls in rooms where pictures had once hung. According to Nancy, Julian had sold them before he left for Italy. Miranda had no reason to disbelieve her, except that she did.

How could Julian have borne such a ramshackle arrangement?

But she knew the answer to that. Julian had been so amiable, the only time he had ever stirred himself was to save her. He would not have cared a jot what his servants did as long as they served him his dinner and didn't trouble him with tedious matters.

Like dusting.

Miranda took a deep, sustaining breath. There would be time for all of that later. Right now she must greet Miss Sophie Lethbridge.

Nancy had indeed lit a fire in the parlour. It was small and a little smoky, but it did brighten the drab room considerably.

A slight, fair creature rose from a sagging, needle-point-inflicted chair, her blue riding costume and jaunty hat making her seem very much out of place. But her gloved hand was outstretched, and her smile was friendly.

'Mrs Fitzgibbon?' Her voice was high and sweet. 'How do you do? I am Sophie Lethbridge.'

Miranda smiled in return. 'How do you do, Miss Lethbridge?'

'I am sorry for calling so early. I was out riding and I had a sudden thought that I should call upon you... My thoughts are always sudden! If I am inter-fering with your other plans, I shall leave immedi-ately.'

'Oh no, I have no other plans. You are my first caller since I arrived at The Grange, Miss Lethbridge, and you are very welcome.'

This seemed to satisfy Sophie, and when Miranda sat down she also resumed her seat. She appeared to be a fidgety little creature, although Miranda sensed it was due to an excess of energy rather than ner-vousness. She was young, probably still some years under twenty.

'I live at Oak House,' she spoke very quickly, 'on the other side of St Mary Mere. With my father, Sir Hugh. I imagine you have been very busy settling in? It is a very long time since I have been in this room. When Julian's mama was first married, she and Ju-lian's father lived here, but then it was very different. I am afraid the house has been rather...neglected.'

Miranda laughed. '"Neglected" is positively generous! It is in a disgraceful state and I don't know how I shall ever bring it about.'

Sophie laughed back. 'Julian did not notice, and if he did he did not care! He loved The Grange just as it is.'

'You knew my husband well?' Miranda asked curiously.

Sophie's green eyes sparkled with easy tears. 'Dear Julian. I knew him all my life. My brother, Jack, too, although he is more Leo's friend than he ever was Julian's. They were at school together, you see.'

Miranda blinked. The room seem to swim a little at the edges of her vision. 'Your brother and Julian were at school together?'

Sophie gave another gurgle of laughter. 'Oh, no, I meant that *Leo* and Jack were at school together. They are great friends, you know.'

In Miranda's mind there was only one Leo. It couldn't be him. She shifted uneasily in her chair. A little hard knot of dread was twisting in her stomach. 'I don't quite understand you, Miss Lethbridge. You cannot…is it possible…are you speaking of the Duke of Belford?'

Sophie's green eyes widened in her pale, pointed little face. 'Why, yes! Am I gabbling? Jack always says I gabble and confuse everybody. I don't mean to, it's just that the thoughts come into my head so very quickly and I can't seem to get them out without mixing them all up. Does that make sense?'

'I—I think so.' Miranda wondered if she was going mad, but knew with a cold, dreadful certainty that she was not. It could not be, oh, let it not be…

'Did you know that Jack, my silliest of brothers, has it in his head that I should marry Leo? He cannot see that we would never suit, never in a hundred years, Mrs Fitzgibbon! Leo would be bored with me within a day, and probably strangle me the next. You must know that he has been used to the most beautiful and clever women, and is yet to show the least partiality to any of them. Some people say he has no heart and that is why he cannot love, but I don't believe that. Leo can be so kind, and I think that a man with no heart would be quite incapable of kindness. Don't you?'

Miranda stared. 'I-it seems to follow, I agree.'

Sophie barely took a breath before launching into speech again.

'I have received a letter from Jack this very morning, which is why I am out riding so early. I am quite cross with him. He has written to tell me that Leo is travelling down to Ormiston, and that I must make myself *agreeable* to him, if you please! As if I would ever be *dis*agreeable, for I have known Leo as long as I have known Jack, and I am never disagreeable to him, although there have been times when I wished very much to be disagreeable and—'

She broke off, eyeing Miranda uneasily.

'Are you quite well, Mrs Fitzgibbon? You are gone very pale.'

Miranda had not gone pale. The colour had been bleached completely from her face. She had to clear her throat several times before her voice would emerge.

'How can Leo…do you mean that the Duke of Belford is coming here, Miss Lethbridge? But...the Duke of Belford lives in London!'

Sophie nodded gently, as one would humour an invalid. 'Well, that is true, but Ormiston is the Fitzgibbon family seat. Are you thinking he should reside at The Grange? I believe the family did live here in the early days, but The Grange was never large enough or grand enough for the Dukes of Belford, so they built Ormiston and The Grange was left to Julian's branch of the family.'

She continued to rattle on.

Miranda no longer heard her. Leo Fitzgibbon was here, in the same county. He was not safely in London. He was lurking dangerously close... She sat up with a jolt. Just how dangerously close was he?

'Where is Ormiston?'

Sophie stopped her chatter in mid-word, not at all disconcerted. She must be used to being interrupted. 'Ormiston is some five miles beyond the village. Belford and my father are neighbours, although of course Ormiston is a very large estate indeed. Why, Mrs Fitzgibbon, didn't you know? Did Julian not tell you? How utterly amazing! Perhaps he did not want to frighten you. Not that Leo is frightening, exactly, just a little intimidating. He came into the title very young, you know.'

Miranda was far too shocked to reply. How could she have known that on the other side of the village where she had thought to make her home was a nest of Fitzgibbons? Just waiting to strike out at her.

Oh, good Lord, what must Leo Fitzgibbon have thought of her when she told him she was going to live at The Grange and he need never see her again? He must have laughed himself sick, or decided she was a complete fool. She remembered now his stunned expression in the private parlour at Armstrong's, and his words, 'As a matter of interest, do you know where The Grange is situated, Countess?' And then, that last time, after the appalling scene with Mr Harmon, 'Do not think this is the last you will see of me.'

Miranda almost groaned aloud.

And worse, still worse, what would he tell his friends and neighbours about her? He was now convinced she was the Decadent Countess—she herself had convinced him! Her life here would become insupportable!

'Mrs Fitzgibbon, are you quite well?' Sophie's bright, inquisitive eyes met hers. 'Have I given you the headache? Jack says I give everyone the headache!'

With an enormous effort, Miranda rallied. It would never do for Miss Lethbridge to guess the awful truth, and if Leo should mention the small matter of the Decadent Countess, Miranda wanted Sophie to be able to find no parallels between his views on her character and her own observations.

'No, no, I am quite well. I am sorry if I have been distracted. It is just that I believed Belford a London creature, more at home there than in the country. Do you know why it is he visits Ormiston?'

'Oh, you are wrong, for he very much enjoys the country. He is a great rider, you know. As to why he comes, I had thought he was making this visit to see you. To assure himself you were properly settled in at The Grange. He always prides himself on doing everything that a man in his position should.'

Miranda nodded, pretending to listen with close attention, but really her thoughts were elsewhere. It was just as she feared. He had come to see *her*. Or rather, he had come to see the Decadent Countess.

What was she to do now?

Sophie had been rattling on again, but now she ended with, 'You are probably wishing me a dozen miles away, Mrs Fitzgibbon. Jack says I am rather like a whirlwind, creating chaos wherever I go.'

Despite all that had befallen her over the past half-hour, Miranda was rather proud that she was able to laugh at this. 'You must tell him from me, Miss Lethbridge, that I was very glad of your visit.'

Oh, yes, what if Leo had come upon her without Sophie's warning! It didn't bear thinking of!

Sophie leaned forward impulsively. 'Please, do call me Sophie. You are so much younger than I had imagined. Do you think we could be friends? I am on the shelf, you see, and you are a widow. We might keep each other company.'

Now Miranda laughed without restraint. She considered the other girl, with her bright curls and bright eyes. 'On the shelf? You are very pretty. I do not for a moment believe you are on the shelf. Are the gentlemen of Somerset blind or foolish? Both, perhaps.'

Sophie blushed becomingly. 'Oh, no! I have had my season in London, you see, and it was a dismal failure. My father says that one idiotic waste of money is enough, and as I didn't make a hit or snare a rich husband I shall stay home now. Not that I am not very happy to do so!'

Sophie, thought Miranda, did not seem terribly happy. There was a brittle edge to her vivacity. Was her father the kind of man who would prevent his only daughter from finding happiness, preferring to keep her as his housekeeper?

'Then we must be friends by all means,' she said kindly. 'And you must call me Miranda. Will you visit again soon, Sophie?'

Sophie said that she would, and they parted.

Friends in adversity, Miranda decided with grim amusement, as she stood in the hall with a beam of sunlight shining through the dust motes. It was as well she had some friends. She would need them when Leo Fitzgibbon, whom some said had no heart, unleashed his wrath upon her.

But what Miranda felt most in need of right now was a brisk walk.

Fetching her cloak, she set out for the copse which fringed the edges of a steep rise to the north of The Grange. The exercise lifted her spirits and the shadow of depression which had begun to fall over her. And, unexpectedly, when she reached the top of the rise, she found that because of the clear day and the rather flat cast of the rest of the countryside, she could see for miles in all directions.

For a moment she paid particular attention to her own house, gazing over the tall chimneys and golden bricks of The Grange. There was evidence of what had once been a moat surrounding the house, but it was almost completely filled in now, swallowed up

in the wilderness of garden. Bennett, when she had
approached him about it, had replied that it was dangerous and 'smelled like rotten fish', so it was decided
to fill it, 'long before I were thought of'. Which, considering Bennett's age, must have been a long time
indeed!

Miranda could not help but wonder what The
Grange had looked like when it was new, and what
sort of people had lived in it. Fitzgibbons, of course,
but were they kind and amiable like Julian, or darkly
handsome and dangerous, like Leo?

The village of St Mary Mere appeared as a jumble
of cottages and smoking chimneys. Several largish
houses were visible in the distance beyond, but although Miranda strained her eyes she could not make
out which was the Fitzgibbon home five miles past
the village. The estate was large, Sophie Lethbridge
had said.

Had Leo Fitzgibbon arrived yet?

Just as the question occurred to her, a movement
caught her eye. Glancing towards the road that led
from the village, Miranda saw a horseman approaching The Grange. Even at this distance, there was
something familiar in the set of his shoulders.

Miranda's heart stuttered and began to pound.

Not yet, she could not face him yet!

A wave of heat washed over her, and she pressed
her hands to her mouth as if she might cry out.

As she continued to watch, the rider reached The
Grange, dismounted and strode to the door of her
house. He was only gone a moment when he reappeared and, standing darkly silhouetted against the

golden façade, peered upward towards the hill and the copse where Miranda was standing.

She held her breath, as if that might cause her to become invisible. While she stood there, trembling, waiting, she was assailed by conflicting desires. On one hand she wanted Leo Fitzgibbon—for she knew it was him—to climb once more upon the back of his chestnut horse and ride away. On the other, she longed for him to ride towards her, galloping up the hill like a knight impatient to reach his lady.

It was preposterous.

It was ridiculous.

Not surprisingly, he didn't do the latter. He remounted, hesitated a moment, then turned back down the driveway until he reached the road to the village. He gave his horse its head.

Miranda stood and watched him go, watched him until he was nothing but a moving dot in the distance.

'Good,' she murmured to herself. 'I'm glad he's gone.'

After another moment, she turned and began to trudge slowly back to The Grange.

Chapter Five

Miranda woke to the soft patter of rain against her windows and Nancy's pronouncement, made over the unappetising smell of burnt toast, that she had received a letter.

On further investigation, Miranda found that it was indeed a letter, and the paper was of a superior quality. For a moment Miranda thought, her heart jumping about in excitement, that it might be from his Grace the Duke of Belford—he had not reappeared at her door since she saw him from her hidden vantage point. However, the letter's seal was not that of the Fitzgibbon family, and her heart returned to normality.

Nancy had plunked down the jug of tepid water and moved to draw the bedcurtains.

'I have some business to attend to this morning, Nancy,' Miranda said in a brisk voice. 'Be sure to light the fire in the library, won't you? Mr Thorne is coming.'

Nancy smirked. 'Aye.'

Thorne was Julian's estate manager. Not that there was much of an estate left, only a very few acres and two tenants. However, those tenants had been quick to present themselves to Miranda. Their complaints were valid, and honestly represented the state of their houses and Thorne's total lack of interest in his job.

Ever since then, Miranda had been trying to obtain an interview with Thorne, but he was well versed in avoidance. Several times Miranda had sought to run him to ground, only to have him slip away at the last moment. To make matters worse, his craftiness at eluding these meetings had become a joke among the servants.

Then, yesterday, he had sent a note with a promise, sworn upon his mother's grave, that he would present himself at the house at nine o'clock sharp.

Nancy had finished her duties, but seemed inclined to linger. She was probably hoping Miranda would open her letter so that she could discover who had sent it and what it contained—all good gossip for the kitchen. However, Miranda had no intention of opening it in front of her, and in the end Nancy bobbed a bit of a curtsy and left the room.

Alone with the sound of the rain, Miranda fought the depression which was threatening to settle over her shoulders like a weighty cloak. Problems appeared to beset her at every turn, and although in Italy she had been used to ordering her stepmama's and her own affairs, here it was, well, different. Lack of funds, Thorne, and servants who smirked at her orders—all these things constantly threatened her authority and the dreams she was attempting to make real.

She had even thought of accepting Adela's cousin's kind offer of assistance. If nothing else, Mr Harmon could give her advice and at the moment Miranda felt herself sorely in need of that. And yet, in her periods of deepest anxiety, it was not Mr Harmon who sprang into her mind.

Dark hair and remarkable eyes monopolised her thoughts whether she willed them to or not. Several times she found herself, for no apparent reason, standing lost in dreams rather than setting about her tasks. Knowing he was so close, only five miles on the opposite side of the village, had acted powerfully upon her emotions. In her wilder moments she imagined his presence like a beacon, beckoning her forth.

No one needed to tell her how foolish she was being, and how ridiculous it was to dream of a man who thought her her wicked stepmama and wanted nothing so much as to be rid of her...when he wasn't kissing her.

If only there were some medicine she could take to erase her mind of all memory of the wretched man!

To distract herself, Miranda broke the seal of the letter. She spread the sheet of crackling paper and ran her eyes over the message. It was brief and to the point, and had the effect she desired.

Dear Mrs Fitzgibbon,
    I regret there has been an unexpected delay in releasing the monies of your late husband's es-

tate to you. Please be assured we will complete
this business as speedily as possible.
Yours etc.
Mr Ealing

Miranda read it once, twice, and then set it aside.
Slowly she lifted her head to gaze beyond the window. She had been in desperate need of Julian's
money. Not only because there were urgent repairs to
be made to The Grange, but because her new household required the bare necessities of survival.

How could there have been a delay? Was it possible that Belford had something to do with this?
Could he have interfered in her affairs? Was he so
devious? Was he even now laughing at the mischief
he had made?

An involuntary shiver ran through Miranda. If Mr
Ealing's delay was Belford's doing, he would find her
no weakling opponent! Whatever madness had assailed her in London was past; she was herself again.
Calm, practical and determined. She had not come all
the way to Somerset to turn tail and flee just because
a few minor obstacles were thrown in her pathway.

No, indeed!

The Duke of Belford would do well to reconsider
if he imagined he could bully Miranda into doing anything she did not wish to do. She would live on tea
and toast, if necessary.

Burnt toast!

Thorne was not waiting in the parlour. Why had
she expected him to be? Her spirits, a moment ago
buoyed up with indignant anger, plummeted again.

She tried to lift them with the observation that the table in the hall had been dusted and flowers arranged—more or less—in a vase. Nancy had not, however, lit a fire in the library and it was cold and dank and filled with the smell of mouldy books.

Bennett tottered towards her from the shadows leading down to the kitchen.

'That Thorne won't come to see you, mistress,' he said gummily. 'He knows that if he do come you'll tear strips off him. He's too slippery for 'at.'

'He deserves strips torn off him, Bennett.'

'You'll never get the best of that Thorne, mistress.'

'Indeed! Well, we shall see.'

Miranda took a moment to eye the old man critically. As usual, he looked like a compost heap on bowed legs.

'Bennett, you have a large stain on your coat.'

Bennett grinned and smacked his lips. 'That'll be Nancy's mutton pie. Best in Somerset, mistress.'

'I didn't mention the stain to compliment Nancy on her cooking, Bennett.'

'Oh, aye?'

Miranda would have said more but her eye caught the vase of flowers again and she realised there was something else different about the hall. The picture over the table had gone.

It was not a particularly pleasing picture, being dark and concerned with cattle in a small pen, but it had been there yesterday evening when Miranda went up the stairs to bed. She turned to question Bennett, but he was already shuffling back the way he had come. Indeed he was moving faster than she had ever seen him move, which was suspicious in itself.

Slowly, Miranda returned to the library and stood in the doorway. No fire, though she had specifically instructed Nancy to light one. What else? She began a list in her head of all the tasks in urgent need of attention.

The linen cupboard was in an atrocious state, there was dust and dirt everywhere, the larder was near enough to empty, there was another picture missing, and Julian could certainly not be blamed for its absence this time.

Miranda shivered. The silence of the house suddenly struck her as unpleasant. Where were the servants? Where was Nancy?

It was time for some plain speaking.

It was time the servants of The Grange learned that, young though she might be and a stranger, Miranda was their mistress and they must obey her.

She set out in search of them.

The most likely hiding place was the kitchen. Miranda made her way quickly down the cold flag corridor towards that area of the house. She had visited the kitchen before, but had not as yet thoroughly examined it…apart from the larder.

Perhaps she had erred in that. Perhaps she should have asserted her authority from the first, no matter how unpopular it made her. But she had thought—she had hoped that by showing kindness, by giving the Bennetts time to adjust to her presence, she would win their trust and thus gain their loyalty.

Hah!

As she descended the final three steps to the kitchen door, Miranda heard a burst of loud laughter barely muffled by the thick wooden panels. If she had not known better, she might have thought there was a party in progress.

A party, she thought angrily, at her expense!

Miranda moved to open the door.

'And what does her ladyship say but "Bennett, you have a large stain on your coat"!' It was rather a good imitation of her voice, considering that the imitator was an elderly man with a strong west country accent.

'Aye, that were a lovely mutton pie!' Nancy's son declared above the laughter. 'Is there any left, Ma?'

'I sent the rest of it to Cousin Annie in the village, and that nice piece of ham. I'll see her ladyship gets some more in—the last lot went so quick she only got a tiny slice!'

More laughter. A chill struck Miranda, followed by a hot blast of anger. She wondered at her own stupidity in not realising before that her servants were playing her for a fool. In Italy, she had been vigilant for just such goings-on, but somehow, here, in Julian's home, she had thought it would be different. That they would welcome her, eventually, as she longed to be welcomed.

She swung open the door.

The laughter stopped abruptly and the persons taking their leisure by the roaring fire turned to stare at her. Remembering the tiny, smoky fire she was normally privy to, Miranda glared back. They were all there, Nancy and her old father and son and daughter, as well as the scrawny woman who didn't dust, and the skinny young girl called Esme, who was peeling vegetables over a pail.

She appeared to be the only one who was actually doing any work.

Miranda let her eyes linger on the greasy surface of the kitchen table, the sumptuous, half-eaten meal, the soot coating almost every uncluttered surface. Bennett shuffled to his feet, smirking at her in an ingratiating manner that she found particularly repulsive.

Miranda took a deep calming breath.

'I do not employ servants who do not work,' she said, forcing herself not to shout. 'Nor do I employ servants who steal or give away what belongs to me. From this moment on matters will change. If you wish to leave The Grange, then go now. Those who want to stay, come to the library and we will discuss the new terms of your employment.'

'We're owed wages!' Nancy burst out. 'You can't send us away. You owe us money!'

Was that why the servants, under Nancy's tutelage, had so thoroughly abused her generosity? Because they believed themselves immune from retribution, because they were 'owed wages'?

Miranda took a step towards Nancy, and, such was her anger, the woman actually cringed back. Miranda allowed her gaze to rest on the groaning table. 'If I ever owed you wages, you have more than made up the deficit!'

She turned away, but not before Nancy cried out again. 'We've been here longer 'an you! You can't toss us out, we belong here! There've been Bennetts at The Grange since King Henry's time. 'Tis you who should go!'

Miranda kept walking until she reached the library. She was trembling with emotion, she was angry, disgusted and upset over what she had just overheard and witnessed. This latest incident was almost too much for her.

She waited a very long time before the timid knock sounded on the door. It cracked open and Esme peered in, her cap so big the brim of it rested on her eyebrows. A pair of frightened eyes met hers.

'Ma'am?' she whispered.

'Come in, Esme.' Miranda forced a reassuring smile. Esme came in, inching nervously towards the desk. 'Is there anyone else out there, Esme?'

Esme shook her head warily. 'No, ma'am, they all be gone.'

'I see.' Miranda sighed inwardly. She knew she was better off without Nancy and her family. Even if Nancy had gone and the others had stayed, she would have had difficulty in trusting them—they seemed to be completely in Nancy's power, either too afraid or too indebted to her to say no to her. But she was going to find it difficult to replace them.

'Never mind, Esme,' she said bracingly, trying to buck up her own spirits as much as the young girl's. 'I'm sure we shall do very well without them.'

Esme nodded uncertainly. 'I can cook a little, ma'am, but 'tis an awful big house.'

'Yes, Esme, it is. But don't worry, we'll get more servants, and things will improve.'

More servants, from where? Money to pay them,

from where? Miranda did not know the answers, but Esme would not know that. She opened her mouth to suggest they start by lighting a fire to warm the chilly library, when a sound outside caught her attention.

The crisp clip of hooves on the gravel drive. Miranda came out of her chair and moved to the narrow library windows that overlooked the front of The Grange. A horseman had pulled his chestnut stallion to a halt and was now dismounting.

Miranda gripped the window sill hard.

For a crazy moment she thought she would send him away, but almost at the same time she knew that would not do. More than likely he would not go, but, apart from that, to send him away, to hide here, was cowardly and Miranda had never been a coward. No, she must face him and vanquish him once and for all.

'Esme,' she said, her voice surprisingly mild for someone whose heart was leapfrogging into her throat and whose blood was running hot and cold, 'there is a gentleman come to see me. You must bring him in here. Can you do that? We will discuss your duties later.'

The girl nodded, bewildered, and went out. Miranda returned to the chair behind the desk and sank down.

Why, oh, why had he come now! Of all times, *now,* when everything was in such an uproar!

A scratch on the door announced Esme's return. 'The Duke of Belford to see you, ma'am,' she whispered.

At once Leo Fitzgibbon strode into the library, closing the door on Esme with a snap. He removed his hat and tossed it, and his whip, on to a table. A small cloud of dust rose and hung in the chilly air.

Miranda could not think of a thing to say, and if she had tried to stand she was certain she would have fallen over. She felt frazzled and dowdy—for some reason an image of her ugly woollen stockings came to mind. No, she was not at all up to this encounter.

In contrast Leo was immaculate, his riding boots mirror-clean, the fit of his coat perfection. The dark blue of his eyes bright with some emotion Miranda could not immediately place and was too overcome to try.

Leo raked her with a glance. 'Oh, very good, Countess. I suppose I am to believe from your pose behind that desk that you have the reins of your household firmly in hand? Well, I regret to inform you that I have just met your servants at your gate!'

Miranda lifted her chin and glared back. 'Not *all* my servants,' she retorted huskily.

'Oh, yes,' he mocked, 'there is that child outside the door remaining to run the household with you. What on earth do you think you're doing?'

Pride came to Miranda's rescue. She would not allow him to browbeat her when she was down. And if her dark eyes were a little brighter than usual, Belford would put it down to temper rather than tears.

'They refused to work, and they were cheating me. What was I to do? Give them an increase? I expect that is what you will do! It pleases you very much, does it not, that I have had such a welcome to my new home?'

Miranda's tirade seemed to have quenched Leo's

fire. 'What did you expect, Countess?' he retorted more mildly. 'Bouquets and red carpets?'

'I expected...I expected...'

'As for stealing,' he went on thoughtfully, as if she were not spluttering for an answer, 'I must agree with you there. By the look of the cart they had with them, they were making off with half of your household.'

White-faced, Miranda rose on shaking legs, but Leo's next words halted her.

'Be still, I have dealt with them. They will return what they have taken or I will know why. Unlike you, Countess, I am a force to be reckoned with.'

Slowly, shakily, Miranda dropped back into her chair.

'I must thank you—' she began, wondering how it could be that he had turned the tables on her so swiftly.

'Please, think nothing of it. I would do the same for anyone. Even *you*, Countess.'

That strange light was back in his eyes, as if he mocked himself. Miranda tried and failed to think of something to say. Moments ago, she had been in full spate, and now he had deflated her like a pricked balloon. She felt a shocking urge to throw herself into his arms and indulge in a good cry.

He was watching her curiously, as if trying to read her mind.

'I would offer you refreshment,' she rallied, 'but I doubt Esme can spare the time from her other duties.'

Leo gave a reluctant crack of laughter. 'I shouldn't think so. It will take her from dawn to dusk to deal

with this barrack of a place. What are you going to
do about it?'

'I will employ other servants—'

'From where?' with an arch of his left eyebrow.

'The village.'

'I doubt it. Half the village is related, and by the
time Nancy Bennett has finished with your character
no one will dare work for you. Besides which, you've
dried up the free food supply for a good many of
them. They won't love you for that.'

Miranda stared back at him and found herself once
more fighting the tears. 'I am growing used to being
not loved,' she said huskily.

Leo froze, as if, she thought afterwards, she had
struck him.

'I would imagine a woman like you would receive
a surfeit of love rather than too little.' His voice was
strange, his gaze compelling.

Miranda swallowed.

He leaned towards her over the desk, so that she
was obliged to tilt her head. An auburn curl brushed
her cheek. Slowly, as if he were compelled, Leo
reached out and tucked the bright strands behind her
ear.

'Love may elude you, Countess, but I would not
see you starved for food and comfort as well. I will
send some of my people from Ormiston to replace
your servants.'

Mesmerised by the expression in his eyes, Miranda
struggled to break this strange spell. 'I don't think
I—'

'I had no right to interfere in Julian's household's

affairs before, but I should have done something about Nancy Bennett when he died. I suppose I did not wish to interfere in your domain. Now, as head of the Fitzgibbon family, I wish to make amends.'

'I can't—'

'I have come to make you another offer, Countess.'

His change of tack startled her, waking her from whatever dream she had been in. Her cheeks flushed becomingly. 'You are wasting your time—'

'Let me finish first.' Leo stepped back, straightening his cuffs with brisk movements. 'I want to buy The Grange. My offer is extremely generous, considering the state of the place, but this house has been in the Fitzgibbon family for generations—it was built by the first of our name—so you must blame my lack of good business sense on sentimentality.'

'Forgive me, but I doubt you possess an ounce of sentiment! You are wasting your time. I do not need your permission to remain here. This was Julian's house, and he left it to me because he wished me to live in it, and live in it I shall!'

Leo's eyes darkened, but he went on as if she hadn't spoken. Miranda could not know the unexpected bolt of jealousy that had shot through him at the mention of his cousin.

'You will have plenty of money to return to Italy and to live well. You may even procure for yourself another husband, only this time, Countess, make quite sure he has plenty of blunt.'

It was unforgivable.

Miranda shot up out of her chair. 'How dare you! I do not want another husband! The Grange belongs to me. You cannot force me to sell no matter how much money you throw at me!'

'No,' he agreed mildly, 'but I can make things very uncomfortable for you, Countess.'

Miranda laughed wildly. 'They are already uncomfortable! How much more uncomfortable could you possibly make them?'

The truth of what she had said startled them both into a brief silence.

Miranda went on, desperately trying to regain control, though her hands were clenched and her eyes shooting fire.

'We may live at opposite ends of the same village, Duke, but we need not see each other. Indeed, I did not know you lived here at all until someone told me. The news was, you can imagine, most unpleasant. I had hoped to have left you, and your offers, behind me in London. You are an intelligent man. Can't you grasp the fact that I never want to see you again?'

Leo collected his whip and hat, his stiff movements at odds with his coolly polite tone. 'I do not need to see you to know that you are here, Countess.'

'Then pretend I am not, I certainly shall! I shall be pretending you are at the other end of the world!'

'The Grange belongs to the Fitzgibbons,' he said flatly. 'It always has.'

'As I keep reminding you, I *am* a Fitzgibbon.'

'You are a brief and undesirable holder of the family name, Countess. Agree to my offer now before it is too late!'

Somehow Miranda restrained the terrible, roaring wave of anger he had generated in her so effortlessly.

'Get out,' she whispered, her voice trembling. 'Get out before I have you thrown out!'

He laughed. God rot him, he laughed.

'No, thank you, I won't put Esme to the trouble. Consider well what I have said, madam.'

The door shut.

Miranda sank her head between her arms, not knowing whether to scream or howl. He had found her at her lowest ebb and promptly set about abusing and insulting her. He had threatened her, intimidated her, he had—

Suddenly Miranda lifted her face and stared, open-mouthed, at the closed door. He had threatened, yes, threatened her servants into returning what they had stolen! And now he was sending replacements from his own household, so that she would not suffer the inconvenience of their loss.

It made no sense. Why had he done that? When it would have suited his purposes so much better to have been cruel and left her alone but for Esme in a cold, empty, broken-down house.

Now, as head of the Fitzgibbon family, I wish to make amends. Was that what it was? A sense of duty?

Leo is kind, Sophie Lethbridge had said. Could that be true, too? Why, then, if he was so kind, had he used his influence to prevent Mr Ealing from sending her Julian's money? If indeed he had. Why hadn't she thought to ask him when she had the chance?

Miranda dropped her head back on to the desk again and this time she did groan aloud. Her life was a mess and even she, who had always prided herself on her ability to untangle disorder, felt it to be beyond her.

Leo kicked his horse into a gallop. There was a bitter taste in his mouth, and he looked neither left nor right. He knew the driveway to The Grange well enough. He had spent much of his time here as a child. Although the house had always been Julian's, he knew its history and its beginnings, and the legends that had been wound about it. The Grange was part of the Fitzgibbon family history.

Now that woman was there, the scheming beauty who had captured his foolish cousin's heart.

Leo Fitzgibbon was not a man used to losing control. He prided himself on his strength of character, his reserve, his tranquillity. Until he met the Decadent Countess he had never imagined he was capable of such rash behaviour, such reckless urges. Now he was afraid to be in a room with her in case he throttled her.

Or kissed her.

Some of the words he had just uttered to her were unforgivable. *You may even procure for yourself another husband…* How could he have said such a thing? He hardly understood it himself, except that when she had begun speaking of Julian in that soft, longing tone something inside him had broken.

He was jealous.

Leo Fitzgibbon, the Fifth Duke of Belford, that gentleman famed for his cool head and cooler emotions, was jealous. It beggared belief! And yet it was so, and it was jealousy that had betrayed him into speaking words which should never have been spoken, even to such a woman as she.

And yet, he frowned thoughtfully, when he had first entered the room she had not seemed dangerous and deceitful. Her beautiful eyes had been sad, and he had wanted nothing more than to take her in his arms and protect her.

And kiss her, of course, that went without saying.

Leo knew he had been wrong when he said she was an undesirable person to bear the family name. She was a very desirable person, very desirable indeed. And, by reputation at least, bore an uncanny resemblance to the first Fitzgibbon wife.

Could there be something to this talk of the Fitzgibbon curse after all?

Leo knew that if he had any sense he would pack up now and return to London. Unfortunately, he appeared to be singularly lacking in that faculty.

Because he had no intention of going anywhere.

Chapter Six

The Ormiston servants arrived the following morning, a veritable army of them. Miranda's instinctive protests were overridden by the army's commander, an upright man with silver-grey hair and the expression of someone who had eaten a very sour plum. He was also vaguely familiar, and when he informed Miranda that his name was Pendle, that he had been in the service of the Fitzgibbon family all his life, and that he had come to take charge of her domestic affairs, she remembered where she had seen him last.

At the Fitzgibbon home in Berkeley Square.

Despite her determination not to be intimidated, Miranda found that she was. But the idea that someone could come in and take over her house was infuriating to say the least, and soon restored her courage.

'When the Duke told me he would replace my servants I expected one or two, not...not...' Words failed her.

Pendle didn't move and yet still gave the impression of peering superciliously into every dank and dusty corner.

'One of two would not be nearly enough, madam.'

It was true. Miranda's face coloured but she held her ground, chin raised. 'I must be frank with you, Pendle. I cannot afford this many servants. I cannot pay their wages.'

Pendle stiffened like a pedigree hound offered second-rate offal. 'You mistake the matter, madam. These are *his Grace*'s servants. To offer them recompense would be the direst insult, to them and to him.'

'Direst insult?' she repeated hotly.

Pendle allowed himself a faint, humourless smile. 'As head of the Fitzgibbon family, his Grace has a duty to care for his relatives. Gratitude is all that is required from you, madam.'

Miranda opened her mouth, but what could she say? She was in the most awkward of situations.

Pendle gave her a slight bow. 'Excuse me, madam, there is a great deal to be done if we are to set this house to rights.'

Outflanked, Miranda retreated into the parlour. She dearly wanted to send the lot of them back to Ormiston. She wanted to storm up to *his Grace*'s door and tell him exactly what she thought of his, and Pendle's, high-handed behaviour.

But she did neither.

From the moment she had arrived in that rickety village cart, and fallen in love with The Grange, Miranda had dreamed of living here. But her dreams had never included a chronic shortage of funds, dishonest servants and lack of the same. For a person of practical disposition she had been very naïve.

If she sent the peremptory Pendle away now, she might as well sell up and return to Italy. He was right, she did need help in getting the place into some sort of order, to make a proper beginning. And she did need help until Mr Ealing was able to send her the monies Julian had left her. To make a scene and demand Pendle leave might gratify her momentarily but it would be very short-sighted.

Miranda sighed. In any other man but the Duke of Belford, this sort of high-handed action might be classed as a kindness, and at first Miranda had believed he *was* being kind. Pendle's arrival had violently changed her opinion.

Miranda had heard that the Duke had a highly developed awareness of his position and the duties attached to it. It was *this* that had sent him—albeit unwillingly—to her rescue. Even though he detested her, and she detested him equally, in some perverse manner he was probably enjoying her gratitude.

'Mistress Fitzgibbon?' Esme's shy, whispery voice broke into her reverie.

Miranda looked up and forced a smile. The girl was hovering in the doorway. 'Yes, Esme?'

'Will you…will you still be needing me here at The Grange. Now that Mr Pendulum's here?'

Miranda bit back a smile. Pendle would not enjoy being renamed, but it helped to reduce his ogrelike presence to something more mundane.

'Certainly I will still need you, Esme! All of these people are very efficient, and no doubt The Grange will soon be spick and span, but they are the Duke's people, not mine. Eventually they will go, and we will be left again to fend for ourselves.'

At least she hoped so!

'My brother works in the stables at Ormiston, mistress,' Esme confided, pushing back her over-large cap.

'And does you brother like working there?' Miranda asked curiously.

'Oh, yes!' Esme squeaked. 'He says it's better even than going to London!'

'Well, there's no accounting for tastes,' Miranda replied. 'Thank you for staying, Esme. I am grateful, and I won't forget.'

Esme blushed and bobbed one of her wobbly curtsies before closing the parlour door behind her. Miranda picked up the list of urgent tasks she had begun yesterday, but it was useless. She could not settle to it. Beyond the door the movements of Leo's invading army constantly disturbed and distracted.

She would have to thank him.

The acknowledgment caused her to wiggle uncomfortably in her chair. Remembering their conversation yesterday, or as much of it as she could bear to, she could not find a proper thank-you in it anywhere. Not that he had behaved at all well himself! In fact he had been overbearing and rude and—

Miranda stopped herself. *His* behaviour did not excuse *hers*. A true lady would have been icily polite and unfailingly civil. Though Belford did not, she reminded herself, think of her as a 'lady', true or otherwise. He believed her to be the wicked and flirtatious Adela, and she had allowed him to believe it in order to punish him for his error at their first meeting.

Quite suddenly she wondered what he would do if she were to be wicked and flirtatious with *him*. The idea held appeal in a shocking sort of way. Would he resist or would he be quite willing to forget his scruples and enjoy a little flirtation with the Decadent Countess? She rather thought, and Miranda allowed herself a knowing smile, remembering that kiss at Armstrong's, that it might be the latter.

But reality soon reasserted itself. Miranda glared at the defenceless list. As if Leo Fitzgibbon would ever be drawn into a desperate flirtation with someone like Adela. He was far too cold and far too proper. Yes, and far too aware of his own consequence.

No, she would leave such fairytales to Mrs Radcliffe.

Leo gave his mount its head, exhilarating in the stallion's power and grace as they raced across the countryside. He had not had many moments of freedom of late. He had been busy with estate matters, and it was now several days since he had sent the incomparable Pendle to create order at The Grange.

Leo felt an unfamiliar twinge of guilt. He need not have sent Pendle, there were others who would have done nearly as well. Pendle demanded perfection, and not many people were tolerant of perfection. But Leo was well aware that Pendle would have The Grange running perfectly, faultlessly, in no time. The Countess would have nothing more to worry about—that frightened, desperate look he had momentarily glimpsed upon her face when he came upon her that day would be erased.

That, he told himself, was his main reason for sending the faithful Pendle.

And Pendle had, when the matter was explained to him, risen magnificently to the occasion.

Apart from Leo's good intentions, there *was* the question of the effect the arrival of such a paragon would have upon the Countess. Leo had spent many quiet moments since, reflecting upon the scene. Pendle's appearance at her door, the Countess's fury…it must have been prodigious. Leo would not have been surprised if Pendle and his band had been returned to Ormiston forthwith.

But that, of course, would be underestimating Pendle.

Pendle had not returned, and Leo had even received a polite note thanking him for his kindness. It was signed Miranda Fitzgibbon, by which name, Pendle informed him, the Countess preferred to be known. The note had been so stilted and so unlike the woman Leo had had dealings with so far that he had tossed it aside in disgust.

He didn't want her thanks. He hadn't acted in the expectation of receiving them. To be honest, he did not himself fully understand why he had done what he did. Except that she had moved him in some profound and surprising way.

In the past, Leo had never felt the least compulsion to help Julian out of his financial difficulties, despite the fact that he'd known for years The Grange was falling to pieces and the servants were dishonest. Julian hadn't cared about those things, so why should Leo? Besides, Julian would have been mortified if his cousin had interfered.

What had swayed him this time? He had claimed he felt a family responsibility, and maybe that was partly so. But what about the rest?

Had he been moved by the woebegone look in her lustrous dark eyes? The faint tremble of those soft pink lips? Although not a cruel man, Leo would not have said he was particularly compassionate. Within his own sphere he was fastidious in fulfilling those duties he felt due to his tenants, family and friends— some people thought this kindness—but to the world in general he was largely indifferent.

Why, then, this sudden urge to play the good Samaritan? He could pretend it was due to a dislike of what others would think if he left his cousin's wife in such dire circumstances, but Leo well knew that at the time such considerations had not occurred to him.

To add further to his worries, Aunt Ellen had had the news of his impulsively generous act from her cronies, probably the Misses McKay, a pair of voracious gossips who lived in genteel poverty in the village. Julian's mother had written him a letter which had the distinct aroma of smelling salts about it, and was crossed and re-crossed so many times as to be almost unreadable.

Leo had replied with a letter of his own, hinting that he was playing a deep game with the Countess and Aunt Ellen should not listen to idle gossip. He supposed, in a way, he was telling the truth. He *was* playing a deep game. If the Countess was grateful enough to him for his assistance in her time of need, she might well agree to his proposal and quit the country.

His mount quickened its stride, and Leo saw the wall directly in front of him. It was constructed of piled stones and appeared dangerously uneven. He still had time to pull up and normally that's what he would have done.

But today he did not feel like pulling up. He was tired of pulling himself up. Leo bent low in his saddle and allowed the horse its head. They jumped...and landed safely.

Leo's heart was pounding. How long since he had taken a jump like that and damn to the consequences? How long since he had put himself at risk for risk's sake? Too often he thought only of his position as the Fifth Duke of Belford.

How long since he had felt truly, tinglingly alive?

When he had been a boy, Leo had dreamed of performing mad and daring deeds. Sailing his boat directly into a storm, jumping from the highest tree in the grounds at Ormiston with only a handkerchief to see him safely to earth, wagering the entire estate on the turn of one card. Staggeringly crazy things. Things that made his heart thud and his blood pound, things that made him laugh aloud.

What had happened to that boy?

Not that the man he was now contemplated for one moment attempting such senseless and dangerous acts, but that wasn't the point, was it?

Leo pulled his mount to a halt and took a deep, gulping breath. Had he really become so joyless? He thought of his life and what it had been and would be, stretching out before and behind him like a straight and steady road, and suddenly wondered how he would bear it. And yet the position he held demanded he behave in a certain way, and that could not be changed. His life could not be altered because he had suddenly decided he no longer enjoyed it.

He was the Duke of Belford. It was fact, and he must learn to endure.

Voices in the distance alerted him. Leo looked up and realised he had ridden much further than he had realised, for there, in the hollow below him, were the tall chimneys of The Grange.

She would be there, flashing him angry looks from her marvellous eyes. Offering him, in a way he did not as yet understand, a glimpse of something he was beginning to crave.

For a moment the temptation to go on was so strong Leo had actually urged his horse forward. It was doubt and confusion, rather than good sense, which drew him up. He could not go down there, he could not so soon engender another scene between himself and the Countess. He could not meet her again now, not when he did not feel at all himself.

Whatever that was.

No, he must wait. He must...he must consider. Every particle of sense inside him was crying out for him to turn back, to remember who he was, to do the proper thing.

Leo turned his mount for home. He rode with exaggerated caution. He did not jump any more fences. He told himself that he had done the right thing, the proper thing. He was the Duke of Belford, and she…she was a nobody with an appalling reputation.

Then why did his restraint give him no joy?

Two days later Leo was back in Miranda's house. He had found it impossible to stay away longer, but he told himself that was because he needed to ascertain if she had thought over his offer and come to a decision.

It could have nothing to do with his need to set eyes on her again, no, indeed!

The visit did not proceed as he had envisaged.

When Pendle let him in, it was to find that the vicar had also decided to pay Miranda a visit, and she was presently engaged in pouring tea and handing out sandwiches. The cool glance she gave him upon greeting was enough to inform Leo that he had little option but to put aside their differences. He prepared to join them in a polite tête-à-tête.

The vicar was an affable fellow, though sometimes a little too obsequious for Leo's taste.

'Your Grace is in good health? And your sister? And, of course, your dear aunt, sir, how is she?'

Leo's murmured replies to the vicar's polite questions were distracted. He was watching Miranda and wondering, in some amazement, how the simple act of pouring tea could suddenly have become so enticing.

The sun, shining through the long windows, had become entangled in her hair, like gleaming threads of golden and copper. She held her chin firm, but there was a softness to her jaw, that vulnerability he had sensed before, so at odds with her hardened reputation. A flush of pink highlighted aristocratic cheekbones, and her lips were tender and full. And, dear God, so kissable.

The vision before him shimmered, drew him in like the sirens on the rocks in Homer's tale. Of a sudden Leo imagined her seated in the saloon at Ormiston, smiling as she poured tea, her dark eyes seductive beneath the heavy fall of her lashes, her hair aglow against the windows with their famous view of his park.

The picture was perfect. Alarmingly so. His heart thudded heavily in his chest, as if it were fighting to free itself, and shake off the shackles of the past eighteen years. As if this fantasy in his mind could somehow become reality.

'Duke, please, you are staring.'

Her soft reprimand made him blink. He realised then that an uncomfortable silence had fallen, the polite chatter from the other two occupants of the room stumbling to a halt. He *had* been staring. It was his observance of her that had brought the faint flush to her cheeks, the glitter to her fine dark eyes.

'Duke!' she said, more sharply than before. 'I am not an object for your study.'

The vicar cleared his throat. Leo sighed and set down his cup. 'My apologies, Mrs Fitzgibbon. I did not mean to be impolite, if indeed I *was* staring. I prefer to think I was admiring the picture you made with the sunlight upon your hair. It was quite… quite…'

'Mesmerising.' The vicar supplied the word, and then cleared his throat again, noisily.

Leo smiled. 'Yes, I believe that is it exactly.'

Miranda looked away, enchantingly disconcerted. 'That is all very well, Duke, but it is rude to stare. I daresay your mama taught you that, and if she did not, then she ought to have.'

He laughed. 'She did teach me that, and several other principles of good manners. Hmm, let me see if I can remember them. Not to chew with my mouth open, not to lean my elbows on the table, never sip from the finger bowl—'

Now it was Miranda's turn to laugh, her expression one of delight and surprise. Clearly she had not imagined the Duke of Belford could be so charming or so playful. He had not, he thought uneasily, felt the need to be either for a very long time.

The vicar was beaming. 'Capital, capital!' he declared. 'Wonderful to see you both getting on so well, your Grace, Mrs Fitzgibbon.'

His observation had the effect of immediately extinguishing the spark between them. The atmosphere became tense, suspicious. Soon afterwards Leo made his excuses and left. Later, thinking back, he did not believe the interlude could possibly have been as comfortable as he had imagined it. And yet, just for a fraction of time, over the tea cups and the laughter, Leo had felt very much at his ease with the Decadent Countess.

Oak House was a pretty dwelling, built in the local brick, and though not large in comparison to the sprawling Grange, could certainly not be dismissed as of no account.

Sophie Lethbridge had sent a carriage for Miranda upon learning she did not have a conveyance of her own. They were to enjoy a chat and Miranda was to meet Sophie's father, Sir Marcus Lethbridge.

Nervously Miranda smoothed her ankle-length skirts. She was wearing a high-necked dress of blue chintz, with long, close-fitting sleeves and a hem ornamented with Spanish trimmings. All very fashionable—flattering without being ostentatious—for Adela had chosen it for her, and Adela was never wrong when it came to good taste in clothing. Strange that she should have such bad taste in other matters!

Sophie was waiting to greet her upon her arrival, and complimented her on her looks.

'I believe you are happier than when I last saw you,' she said with her characteristically breathless rush of words. 'Your colour has returned and you have lost those shadows beneath your eyes. Is it because Leo has taken charge of The Grange? I heard that he had sent his servants there.'

Miranda said nothing for a moment, seating herself in a yellow brocade chair and restraining with difficulty the urge to tear Leo Fitzgibbon's character to shreds.

'Perhaps that is it,' she murmured with a forced smile.

Sophie did not seem to notice. 'Well, Leo can always be relied upon to take charge.'

There it was, that malicious little sting that characterised many of Sophie's artless comments.

The servant arrived with tea and cake, and Sophie fussed about with milk and teacups and saucers. When they were settled again, Sophie asked her if she had become lost yet.

'I beg your pardon?'

Sophie giggled. 'In The Grange. It is very confusing. When we were children we used to play hide-and-seek. Julian knew so many places to hide we could never find him.'

'I can well imagine that!'

'I have had another letter from my brother Jack. He will be coming to stay within the week.'

Miranda smiled and sipped her tea. 'That will be pleasant for you.'

'Oh, he is only coming because Leo is here. He wants to throw me in his way as much as possible. Poor Jack, he will never give up.'

There did not seem much to say to this, so Miranda didn't try.

'When he has come we will arrange a little party, Miranda. Dinner, with some dancing. You must come and meet the neighbourhood families. They are all very friendly, no airs or graces.'

'Not even from the Duke?' Miranda asked.

'Oh, Leo is not so high in the instep as he pretends. If I begin to feel nervous of him, I remember him as a boy, when he fell ill with measles. Quite covered in spots, he was. They do say they were everywhere!'

'Sophie! I quite despair of you ever learning to behave!'

The voice was deep and full of exasperated humour. Surprised, Miranda turned to face the fair-haired man who had just entered the room. He was clearly Sophie's father, and she would have known it even if Sophie had not gabbled an introduction, for there was a strong resemblance. A small man with a lined face, he appeared stern until one noticed the twinkle in his faded green eyes.

Miranda, recalling that she had imagined Sophie's parent to be a harsh and unfeeling gentleman who had kept his daughter at home rather than give her another chance upon the Marriage Mart, quickly revised her opinion. If Sir Marcus kept Sophie from repeating her disastrous season in London, it was only because he cared for her and meant to protect her.

'How do you do, Mrs Fitzgibbon?' His hand was firm, his smile inquisitive. 'Sophie has spoken much of you since her visit.'

'Her visit was much appreciated, sir. The only bright spark in a dark day.'

The smile turned sympathetic. 'I heard you had routed the Bennetts. Was that wise, Mrs Fitzgibbon? They are a large family. One never knows when one of them might pop up.'

'Oh, Papa, there is no harm in them! Nancy is a little wicked, I know, but she has such a droll way with her. And her father—'

'A detestable old reprobate,' Sir Marcus retorted. 'On second thoughts, you are well rid of them!'

'I believe so. Or I did until Pendle came.'

'Pendle has been with the Fitzgibbons since time began,' said Sir Marcus. 'Even Leo is afraid of him.'

'Oh, pooh!' Sophie declared. 'Leo is afraid of nothing. Papa, I have told Miranda that Jack is coming down from London and that we are to have a party.'

'You will come, Mrs Fitzgibbon? You can meet my son and heir, Jack.'

'Yes, you must meet Jack!' Sophie cried.

'But do not expect him to speak much sense,' Sir Marcus added. 'He never does.'

'You are wrong, Father,' Sophie reproved him, a naughty twinkle in her eye. 'Jack knows a great deal about horses and cards and what is good *ton.*'

'You are right, my dear. I stand corrected. Jack knows all that is necessary to a young man of good breeding and comfortable situation!'

The Lethbridge household, Miranda decided upon leaving, was one of the happiest she had ever visited. It made her own difficult circumstances appear all the more stark.

Miranda prevailed upon the driver of the carriage to leave her in the village, saying she would prefer to walk the remaining three miles to The Grange, for it was a fine day and she had some business there. He did as she asked, though clearly reluctantly.

Miranda did indeed have some business to attend. She had not forgotten Thorne, her appropriately named estate manager, and hoped to run him to earth at his home. The Grange tenants had visited her again to remind her of their leaking roofs and damp floors. The running of the house might have been taken away from her for the present, but Miranda could still do something about Thorne.

His house was on the edge of St Mary Mere village,

set apart in its own garden with a high wall surrounding the whole. The gate was locked, and though Miranda rattled it and peered through it to the front door, no one looked out at her from the narrow windows or came to see what she wanted.

Frustrated, she had no choice but to relinquish her plan, and at last turned to go.

Nancy Bennett was standing directly behind her.

Miranda started, not frightened but, firstly, rather surprised the woman could have crept up on her without a sound, and secondly, that she should want to. If Miranda had been Nancy, she would have been too ashamed to come within miles of her former mistress.

'You are bold to show your face to me, Nancy,' she said, following on from her own thoughts.

Nancy showed her teeth, but the smile did not reach her eyes. 'Well, here's a case of the pot calling the kettle black, mistress! Me, bold? I think 'tis the other way around. You owe me and my family wages. We weren't paid in months, and then you turned us out without a farthing.'

'Turned you out?' repeated Miranda in amazement. 'You stole my belongings!'

'They were Master Julian's belongings, and he gave them to us. He appreciated us even if you didn't.'

There was a great deal of aggrievement in her tone, and Miranda wondered again if Nancy believed in her own lies. That would certainly justify her appalling behaviour. Perhaps humouring her delusions made more sense than arguing against them.

'I will give the matter some thought,' Miranda said, in what she hoped was an authoritative voice.

'You tossed us out without our wages, and now you've got the old house full of strangers!'

'They are the Duke of Belford's servants.'

'That were our home!'

Nancy's face had grown hard with resentment. For the first time Miranda felt uneasy. She glanced quickly down the lane and saw only a lone horseman.

Nancy noticed her glance and sneered, 'You don't belong here, you're a foreigner.'

'I am Master Julian's widow.'

'We don't take to foreigners.'

'I have as much right as you to be here, Nancy.'

'I've lived here all my life, I have. Come to The Grange when I were a girl. My family's been there since King Henry's time. The Grange belongs to Bennetts more than it does Fitzgibbons!'

'If you will move aside, I must get on.'

'Not till I'm paid!'

Nancy reached out as if to take her arm, but in that moment another voice, deep and familiar, interrupted them.

'Go home, Nancy. Mrs Fitzgibbon has done you no harm. You have brought your present situation upon yourself.'

Nancy's lips whitened, and she swung around to look up at Belford, her bearing taut with fury. Briefly it seemed as if she might continue to argue her case, but then she evidently thought better of it, for she marched off.

Miranda took a breath, and then another. She felt

oddly shaky, could almost have described herself as all a-tremble, but whether that was from the confrontation with Nancy or her timely rescue by Leo Fitzgibbon she was uncertain.

'Thank you, sir. I do not know if I would have escaped her if you had not come.'

He was frowning down at her. 'You should never have come to the village alone, Countess.'

'I did not realise she would have the effrontery to— to accost me like that. Horrid woman!'

The tremble in her voice seemed to stir him from his anger. Leo dismounted, reaching to take her arm in his strong, steady grip. 'You are shaken, ma'am. Come, let me walk with you back to the village and I will arrange for a conveyance.'

'Oh, no, no.' Miranda managed a laugh as she shook her head. 'I am unharmed, only a little… surprised by her—her belief in what she was saying. Truly, she does not think she was in the wrong, rather that I am. She cannot see that stealing my belongings and refusing to obey my instructions was in any way deceitful or outrageous.'

Leo was gazing into her face, watching the colour come and go, watching the quick, nervous rise and fall of her breasts. His voice, when he replied, was mild and sensible. It did not betray the turmoil he himself had felt when he turned into the lane and saw the two women. He had instantly recognised one of them as Miranda Fitzgibbon and the other as the decidedly dangerous Nancy Bennett, and had thought only of rescue. If Nancy had lifted a hand, had struck at her, before he had reached them…

'Then I will throw you up upon my horse,' he said, blotting out such dark thoughts. 'You cannot walk in your state.'

'No, no, I am able to walk, sir.'

He gave her a hard, disbelieving look, but Miranda did not mind his superior manner today. Everything about him seemed comfortingly familiar and reassuring.

'What did you think you were doing, Mrs Fitzgibbon? I came upon Sophie Lethbridge's driver on his way back to Oak House, and he told me he had set you down in the village. He would not have told me that, but he was very concerned. He has, he said, heard tales of Nancy's rantings against you.'

'Oh.' Miranda was beginning to regain her composure. She put up a hand to brush back an escaping auburn curl, securing it beneath her hat. 'I had only seen the village once before, when I arrived, and I thought I would like to know it better.'

He looked at her as if she had run mad. '''Know it better''? What is there to know?'

'Well, it is very pretty. Have you never noticed? Having lived in Italy so long, I am unaccustomed to English villages, and this one is very fine. I am a—a great lover of the countryside, you know.'

He stared at her a moment more, and then he burst out laughing. Miranda eyed him coldly until he had finished.

'You came to see that rascal Thorne, Miranda! Admit it and have done.'

Miranda's mouth dropped open. 'I will not! And I did not give you leave to call me by my first name.'

'Miranda,' he retorted, 'Miranda, Miranda. It is a very pretty name, far prettier than this village. And as for Thorne, he has been sent packing.'

She was speechless. *He* had sent Thorne packing? How very high-handed of him! And what a relief. After a time, she flicked him a glance up under her lashes. 'You knew, then?' she said bleakly.

'That you were prevaricating just now, or that Thorne was avoiding you?'

'About my problems with Mr Thorne,' she answered primly.

'Yes, I guessed. I doubt Julian himself saw the man above once a year, and then it was only by waiting for him outside the Rose, which you could scarcely do, Miranda.'

The Rose would not have stopped Adela, thought Miranda, but before she could remind him of that another thought popped into her head. 'But, sir, if Thorne is gone what will become of my poor tenants?'

He gave her a look which was a strange mixture of impatience and indulgence. 'You had only to come to me, Miranda, and I would have seen to them.'

Miranda's back stiffened. 'You are very high-handed, sir! They are *my* tenants, and Thorne was *my* man. It was for me to deal with them, *and* him.'

'Miranda—'

'I have asked you not to call me that, sir!'

He stared at her in exasperation and then, before she could utter more than a squeak of protest, lifted her bodily and placed her upon his horse. Miranda, finding herself in such a position, had no time to do more than gasp before Leo swung himself up behind her.

'Say nothing,' he advised her, and proceeded to settle her more comfortably. His arms were ranged either side of her as he gripped the reins. Caging her in, she thought indignantly.

'Do not argue,' he went on, 'do not demand to be set down and do not call me any names—I imagine you know a great many. In short, I intend carrying you back to The Grange and nothing you do or say will prevent me.'

Miranda sat rigidly, furious with such insolent behaviour. Her blood felt as if it was literally boiling in her veins. She stared straight ahead, refusing to look at him, and so did not see the little smile that curled up the corners of his handsome mouth, or the softening in his eyes when he glanced at her. They rode for at least a mile in silence, stony on Miranda's part, amused on Leo's.

'I think you have forgotten we are enemies,' Miranda said at last in the airy voice which no longer deceived him.

'Perhaps I prefer to forget it.'

His voice was close to her ear. His warm breath stirred wisps of her hair and raised gooseflesh on her nape. His voice was doing other things to her, too, but these she did not dare examine. When she had stopped thinking about the timbre of his voice, his actual words registered. She turned to look at him in surprise, and then wished she had not. He was very close. Too close, his eyes so dark a blue that the pupil was barely distinguishable from the iris.

'*I* cannot forget it,' she informed him coolly, forcing herself to remember his insults and his bribes, not to mention his shocking behaviour.

'No, I can see that. You are ready to accept my proposal then, Countess?'

His voice had changed, lost the human quality it had held only a moment before. He was the Duke again, distant, untouchable. Miranda told herself she welcomed the change. *This* was the man she preferred, *this* was the man with whom she chose to deal.

'No, I am not ready to accept it.'

'Perhaps you wish to thank me for coming to your rescue? Coming to your rescue not once, but twice!'

'I had thought I had sent you a note on that head, sir.'

'Pendle does not feel you deserve him, Countess.'

Her eyes narrowed, her slim body vibrating with an anger she struggled to conceal.

'Is Pendle your spy then, your Grace? Does he send you hourly reports? Perhaps that is how it should be. We are engaged in a war, after all, you and I.'

'A war?' he scoffed. 'If it were so, I would have won already. I am a gentleman, Miranda, and I will continue to behave as if you were a lady.'

A fierce hurt burned within Miranda, while on the outside she was working hard to give the impression she did not care.

'I am a man of the world,' he went on. 'I understand you have only the nature you were born with, and are therefore more to be pitied than reviled.'

Miranda forgot to play her part. She was too angry now to be Adela. How dare this creature speak so of her stepmama? What did he know of her, what right had he to judge her?

'If anyone is to be pitied,' she said, 'it is you! I have heard it said you have no heart. Now I have seen the evidence of it for myself. There is no heart in you, sir, none at all.'

He was silent, although he seemed to be having difficulty breathing evenly. 'I act for the good of my family,' he replied at last in a voice completely unlike his usual, calm tones.

'And, I suppose, you are the judge of what is "good" for them?'

Miranda could not know how angry she had in turn made him. How she had stirred that mad recklessness within him, setting free the very emotions he had been trying so hard to subdue since the moment he met her.

'I am aware of what is said of me,' he said. 'That I am lacking that passion attributed to other men. I am not ashamed of my good sense, but neither am I quite as dead to all feeling as *you* believe me. Perhaps it will surprise you to know, Countess, that from the moment I saw you I have wanted nothing more than to kiss you.'

Miranda's head jerked up. She stared into those remarkable eyes and read the truth in them. He wanted to kiss her. But he also thought she was Adela and assumed that she would therefore welcome such advances.

'No,' she whispered.

'Oh, yes, Miranda. Most definitely, yes.'

He swooped down on her before she had a chance

to twist her face and escape him. His mouth closed on hers, slightly off-centre at first, so that his lips slid across hers, settling more comfortably. He made a sound very like a man in deep pain, and his arms closed around her, holding her so firmly she could not move.

And oddly, considering what had just passed between them, Miranda had no desire to move.

His mouth on hers was warm, demanding a response she was as yet too innocent to give, although she did her best. What was more shocking to her even than his kiss were the feelings it engendered. She experienced a sense of abandon, of the world well lost, a hot rushing madness.

And more than that.

A sense of rightness.

'Countess,' he whispered.

His lips trailed along her jaw, nibbling at the sensitive flesh near her ear. It was all very pleasant and exciting, but Miranda's joy in it had gone. His single utterance had snapped her back to cold, harsh reality.

Leo thought her Adela, he believed he was kissing Adela. Not Miranda. Not capable, practical, innocent Miranda.

Leo must have felt her withdrawal. He leaned back, his laugh rough and self-conscious.

'Good God, I appear to have forgotten myself again! It is a hazard of being in your presence, ma'am.'

She heard the apologetic amusement in his voice, but missed the uncertainty. Miranda found herself strangely close to tears.

'I apologise again, and ask that you put my hasty actions down to the temptation set before me.'

'Please…put me down, sir.'

He took a breath to argue, but must have realised the futility of it. Dismounting, he helped Miranda to the ground. As soon as her feet touched earth, she stepped away, face turned from him, hands clasped rigidly before her.

'I will walk with you.' He spoke gently.

'You will not,' she gasped. 'Please go now, sir. I do not need your sort of help.'

'You needed it a moment ago,' he replied, stung.

'Yes.' Now she did look at him and her face was pale, her dark eyes enormous. She seemed young and vulnerable, and Leo felt slightly sick at the memory of what he had done. 'Goodbye, Duke.'

Leo watched her walk away, head high, shoulders and back straight. His loathing of himself filled him. He had behaved like an unprincipled cad, a libertine, a loose fish. Jack Lethbridge had warned him that he was ripe for a fall, but even so Jack would be amazed and disgusted to hear of his friend's behaviour since the Decadent Countess arrived on his doorstep.

Leo was himself all of those things.

He shuddered.

But as he rode slowly home to Ormiston, his disgust with himself gradually took second place to his confusion over Miranda's character. Anomalies he had disregarded at the time now returned forcefully to torment him. When he had met her outside Thorne's gate she had been frightened, yes, but she had seemed…different. Lacking in the pretensions she had previously assumed whenever in his presence. No, she had been different, natural and, not to put too finer point on it, sweet as honey. Then, as they had journeyed towards The Grange, she had changed. She had laughed differently, spoken in the manner of a much more worldly woman...

Was she two women in one? Leo did not pretend to be an expert when it came to the character of the fair sex—no man was!—but he had never before been faced with two such starkly different women in the one delightful package.

Now that he had begun, he recalled other times when similar transformations had occurred. It was all very puzzling and did not help him to unravel his own tortured feelings, or gloss over the fact that he had behaved in a manner far beneath the Duke of Belford.

'Am I going mad?'

Leo drew his mount to a halt and stared hard at the grand gates which led into the winding drive which in turn led to Ormiston. He did not *feel* mad, just a trifle overexcited. What was he going to do? How was he going to extract himself from this tangle and resume the life he had led previously?

With a heartfelt sigh, he kicked his horse into a gallop.

Leo was still no closer to a solution to his problems when he reached the stables. Indeed he was as confused as ever. The groom who came to take his mount increased his confusion by informing him that his sister had arrived at Ormiston.

'My sister?' Leo stared at him blankly. 'I have only one sister and she is in Sussex.'

'No, sir, she has come to Ormiston. She arrived an hour ago.'

Tina at Ormiston? Leo quickened his stride. What was Tina doing at Ormiston? Why should she have left her husband and two young sons to visit her brother? Was there bad news? But this last he all but discarded. Leo's close family, these days, consisted of himself and his sister, and if she had bad news she would hardly be in a state to bring it to him personally.

Still puzzling, Leo reached the main staircase. He had begun to ascend when, looking up, he beheld his sister descending. She was wearing yellow silk, her dark curls coiled upon her head. She was some ten years younger than her brother, a calm and sensible girl who had nevertheless listened to and, when necessary, been guided by her older brother. It had rarely been necessary. Despite having lately been brought to bed of another son, she was blooming. In fact, Leo thought he had never seen her look more lovely. When she saw him she cried out softly in pleasure and surprise.

'You are in looks, Tina,' he said.

But Clementina did not want to hear his compliments. 'Leo, whatever is this about Julian's widow?' she burst out. 'Aunt Ellen has written to me to say she is the Decadent Countess, and either you have lost your wits or else you have tumbled headlong in love with her!'

Chapter Seven

'Are you comfortable?'

Leo eyed his sister, watching her arrange her skirts with impatient tugs.

'Yes, yes.'

'Do you require anything to drink, to eat?'

'No, Leo, I do not.'

'Perhaps you require a cushion?'

Her eyes, every bit as blue as his, narrowed in the manner of a cross Siamese cat. 'No, Leo, I do not require a cushion! I am waiting to hear what you have to say about Aunt Ellen's accusations.'

Leo forced a laugh and was dismayed to find it completely lacking in humour. 'What *can* I say? She is overwrought. She asked me to deal with the matter, and because I have not been able to accomplish it so soon as she likes, she has decided I will not. Or cannot. You know her character.'

'Of course I do,' Tina replied soothingly, keeping a close watch on her brother. 'I also know she is not prone to nervous starts of *quite* this magnitude. Something has thrown her into hips, Leo, and I think you know what it is.'

'There is no need for her to be in "hips", as you call it. I have the matter well in hand.' A picture flashed into his mind of himself and Miranda embracing in the middle of the road, and his voice dried up. He turned to look out of the window.

Tina watched him a moment in silence. She had always considered herself close to her brother, and although her own domestic life had lately expanded to take up most of her time, she still felt as if she knew him well enough to be able to read him now. Leo was worried. Leo was not himself. Leo had been thrown off his usual, controlled balance and he did not know how to deal with it.

'What is this woman like, Leo?'

She watched him gather himself before turning, so that he could face her with his familiar urbane smile. But there was no smile in his eyes.

'What is she like?' Leo repeated. 'Tolerable.'

'"Tolerable", Leo?' Tina raised a slim dark brow.

He laughed, and this time it was genuine.

'Yes, all right, she is more than tolerable. She is a beauty, Tina. But it's not just her appearance. There's a sweetness to her I would never have believed a woman such as she could possess. An innocence, an…an…' He turned away, and suddenly his voice was bleak. 'Oh, God, what can I say? She's a witch.'

'And by the look of it, she's used her powers on you,' Tina said drily. 'Oh, Leo, how could you? I cannot believe *you*, of all people, would fall for such a woman. You cut your eye-teeth years ago.'

'That is just what I have told myself. It doesn't help.'

'Could you…could you…?'

Tina blushed, but Leo, who had turned back and was watching her with interest, read her like a book.

'Could I offer her a *carte blanche?*' he finished mockingly. 'Yes, I suppose I could, although it would be very awkward and she would in all probability make my name as notorious as hers.'

'But you haven't?' she asked curiously. 'Offered her one, I mean?'

Leo shook his head, and now his smile mocked himself. 'No, my dear, I haven't. That does not seem to be what I want, Tina. It would not be enough.'

He looked at her helplessly.

'Oh, Leo, you would not think of…Leo!'

'Marriage? I haven't allowed myself to think of it. I am hoping it will pass, you see. A brief madness, and it is gone. Then I can go back to being myself, marry the Honourable Julia Yarwood, breed a dozen little Fitzgibbons and die a respectable man.'

Tina did not laugh as he had hoped she might. Instead, she stared down at her skirts, her fingers smoothing imaginary creases.

'It may be as you say,' she sighed at last. 'An…an aberration. You are going through some sort of crisis.'

'You do not believe in the family curse then, like Jack?' The question was only half-humorous.

Tina gave an unladylike snort. 'No, I do not.' She hesitated a beat before continuing. 'Do you?'

Leo shrugged. 'I have wondered. There was Grandfather—'

'Odious man!'

'Yes, I cannot imagine myself quite as bad as that. Women as a group are not presently my problem, just one of them. Unless,' he went on thoughtfully, 'it is like the measles, and begins with the one spot?'

Tina seemed to be making up her mind about something, and now she spoke with determination.

'Leo, I have lately thought you have grown far too smug and satisfied with yourself. Probably this was bound to happen.'

'Well, I thank you, dear sister!'

Tina ignored him.

'Yes, this may well be as you say; a madness which will quickly pass. We must pray so, Leo, for all our sakes! In the meantime, you must see this woman as seldom as possible. An obsession cannot thrive if the object of it is not in evidence.'

'By God, you speak as though you are an expert!'

For the first time since her arrival at Ormiston, Clementina smiled. 'Oh, no, Leo, I am no expert.' Her smile faded as she took in her brother's demeanour. 'Are you very unhappy?'

'No, love, I am not unhappy at all.'

But he was, and it pained her to see it. Blithely, Tina changed the subject to her own family, discussing in great detail the latest wonders performed by her new baby son. She did not flatter herself that Leo was particularly interested, but he listened and marvelled and the time passed. It was only as Tina set about the lengthy task of dressing for dinner that she allowed her thoughts to return to Aunt Ellen's letter and the Decadent Countess.

Upon first receiving that letter she hadn't been nearly as worried as she was now. Surprise and amusement had been her chief feelings. It had all seemed so preposterous! Leo? Head over heels with such a woman? But then, as she had read and re-read the hysterical accusations, doubts had begun to disturb her calm certainty. She had remembered that lately, on the few occasions when she happened to see her brother, she had found him frighteningly distant, as though an actual physical shield protected him from the rest of the world.

Oh, he was still affectionate, still her brother, but his feelings were restrained. It was as though he kept himself always on a tight rein. Tina knew that in some men that would be a normal and natural state of affairs, but Tina had known Leo as a young man when he had been a wild and passionate soul.

Although older than she, Tina still recalled the Leo who had set her up before him on his horse and raced with her across the fields. And then been scolded roundly by their mother. When he had come into the title all that had changed. The responsibility had weighed heavily upon him, but he had been determined to bear it with the appropriate stoicism.

Until now Tina had not realised just how much Leo had bound over his true character to his duty. She had grown used to this new Leo, this cold proper man, married to his position as the Duke of Belford. And, with a twinge of guilt, she had been too caught up in her own happiness to delve into the workings of her brother's mind. All, at least on the surface, had appeared calm.

That was why Aunt Ellen's letter had seemed so particularly shocking.

Leo! Involved in a scandal!

Tina had put aside her comfortable domesticity at once, and travelled to Ormiston to see for herself. It had not needed Leo's admittal for Tina to guess the truth—one look at his face was enough. He had fallen into deep waters, and was presently floundering in an unfamiliar sea. Yes, the cold man was mortally wounded, and the Leo she saw now was almost a stranger.

No, not a stranger, she reminded herself. A childhood memory. The Leo of her youth. The cool protective shield hung in tatters, and Tina could almost have been glad…if she had not been so angry.

That evil, hateful woman! No doubt she was enjoying her triumph, playing Leo like a fish on a line. Well, thought Tina, she would have something to say to that!

As soon as possible, she would pay this Countess a visit.

The hall was hardly recognisable. Cleaned and shining, there were pieces of furniture Miranda was sure had not been there before, or else they had been disguised under a heavy coating of dust. She should be grateful, but now that The Grange was perfectly clean and tidy, Miranda felt less like the owner than she had when it was an ill-run mess.

'Good morning, Mrs Fitzgibbon.' As usual, Pendle wore an expression which hinted that he had much to bear.

'Pendle. I'm going to church.'

'To church, ma'am? How are you—?'

'I'm walking, Pendle.'

The look of dawning horror on his face did much to lift her spirits and bring a spring to her step.

The day was a fine one and Miranda enjoyed her ramble along the country lane. The hedgerows were sweet with blossom, while nesting birds flitted about, adding their cheery song to the hum of the bees. It filled her with memories of her childhood, bittersweet thoughts of her mother and the life that might have been.

Her mother had hoped to settle Miranda respectably but happily, with a steady man far different from her own husband. She had died before such a thing were possible, and Miranda had been launched upon her Italian adventure.

Had she thought to find a steady, respectable husband in Italy? No doubt there were many such men, but they had not frequented the Villa Ridgeway. Miranda had occasionally thought of marriage, but as the years had passed, she had resigned herself to being forever the untangler of domestic crises for her financially incompetent father and rackety stepmama.

Loneliness was something she pushed to one side, telling herself she was fortunate, really, to have a home at all.

And then the count had died, and everything had changed. Julian had gently and subtly but firmly taken control of her future. Now she was twenty-four years of age, a widow without ever having been a wife, and the owner of a huge, rundown house. Was her situa-

tion all that much better than it had been in Italy?
Was she any less lonely?

An image of jet hair and dark blue eyes took shape
in her mind.

Would Leo Fitzgibbon assuage her loneliness? He
probably would—and drive her insane in the process!
And yet there were moments when they seemed
strangely suited. Indeed, thought Miranda, it was a
puzzle and not one she was ever likely to unravel.

The church was visible for some distance before
Miranda reached it. A large building for so small a
village, it boldly declared that St Mary Mere must
have been of some import in times past, certainly
more so than it was now. By the time Miranda arrived
at the door, the service had begun, and she crept inside and found herself a quiet place near the back.

The service, though wholesome, was lengthy as the
minister wrestled for the souls of his parishioners. To
distract herself, Miranda took advantage of her position at the rear of the church to peruse the rest of the
congregation.

Sophie and her father were seated at the front, their
fair heads bright in the gloom. There was another gentleman with them, larger in physique than Sir Marcus,
but with hair of a light brown colour. Miranda pon-
dered as to whether this was Jack, Sophie's brother,
newly arrived from London. As far as she could tell,
he wore a fashionable coat and his shirt points were
exceedingly high and well-starched. She was examining the back of his head for any family resemblance,

when she saw him turn his face aside, cover his mouth with his gloved hand, and yawn hugely.

Miranda smiled. She was not alone, then, in finding the sermon overlong. The remainder of the congregation consisted of neatly dressed ladies and country gentlemen, and villagers in their Sunday best. Luckily, there was no sign of Nancy and her large family. Perhaps they preferred chapel.

Her eyes travelled on over the interior of the church and the great many memorial plaques. One of these, on the far wall, was actually carved into the shape of a man in an Elizabethan ruff, his profile stern and hawklike as he gazed confidently into the next world.

His face reminded her, a little, of Leo, although she could not think why. When the service had ended, and she was able to slip over to peer more closely at the effigy, she found some carved words, worn, but one at least was legible.

Fitzgibbon.

Some subtle family resemblance then. Was this stern gentleman the founder of the Fitzgibbon fortunes?

Outside in the churchyard, the congregation were inclined to linger. Sir Marcus had been waylaid by two excessively genteel ladies in tartan shawls, but Sophie Lethbridge hurried over to Miranda, the brown-haired gentleman following at an unwilling trot behind her. As Miranda had guessed, this was Sophie's brother, Jack, lately returned from London.

While Sophie was introducing them, Miranda took a moment to cast her eye over the gentleman. He was an amiable-looking man, and handsome, even if his expression was somewhat vacant. With Sophie and her father as pleasant examples, Miranda had been looking forward to meeting the third member of the family and finding him equally pleasant.

She was disappointed.

Jack Lethbridge's complexion darkened alarmingly as soon as his eyes met hers, even before his sister had finished her introduction. As if he already knew her by sight—or knew who she was.

'Oh!' he said. Then, recollecting himself, 'I mean, how do you do, ma'am?' His bow was small and grudging.

Sophie took instant umbrage.

'Well,' she declared, 'I must say you are not very polite, Jack! Miranda is my friend, I'll have you know.'

Jack looked uneasy. It was an expression ill suited to such an open and friendly continence. However, he stood his ground.

'I always did think you were a bit too free and easy with your affections, Soph. Told you so, more than once. Could get you into bother, one day.'

'Well, really, Jack!' his sister gasped. 'I would never have believed I'd be ashamed of your manners, but I am! Apologise at once to Miranda, or I will…I will never speak to you again!'

Jack appeared shaken by this threat, opening and shutting his mouth like a landed fish. Miranda could see that he was torn between his brotherly duty and his desire to be on good terms with everyone. He was that sort of man. Of course, the reason for his dilemma had already occurred to her.

Jack Lethbridge was Leo's friend, and therefore he must be a privy to Leo's mistaken belief as to her identity. He thought she was the Decadent Countess. She only hoped he had not heard of her escapade yesterday, when Leo had found her outside Thorne's cottage and taken her up on his horse, and...

Well, she could hardly bear to think of it herself without blushing!

But at the moment Miranda was prepared for a conciliatory approach. After all, she told herself, she could well understand a brother's concern for his only sister. Jack was doing what he thought best, and if he were not in serious error his actions would be commendable.

It did not occur to Miranda that Jack's belief that she was Adela, the Decadent Countess, was no different to Leo's, and yet her feelings on the matter were so different! With Jack, the knowledge caused her trepidation and a corresponding eagerness to allay all his fears concerning his sister. In short, to win him over to her side. There was none of the fiery temper and deep inner hurt and anger that the same mistake had induced in her when it was Leo who had made it!

Miranda gave Jack an understanding smile.

'I believe, Sophie, that your brother fears I may have taken advantage of your kind heart. It is not so, Mr Lethbridge, believe me. I am very grateful for your sister's kindness. Indeed, I would be a very mean-spirited sort of person if I were not!'

Jack eyed her suspiciously. 'You understand, ma'am, that I think only of my sister in this matter.'

'Of course,' soothed Miranda. 'Such care does you credit, sir.'

Sophie stamped an impatient foot. 'I think you both must have windmills in your heads!'

But Jack, that easy-going character, was already thawing. 'I dare say I have been somewhat zealous, ma'am.'

'You have been very rude, Jack!'

Jack cleared his throat and smoothed his neckcloth. It was intricately arranged in a creation which must have taken him at least two hours to accomplish. 'Well, Soph, I only ever act in your best interests. You should know that.'

Sophie appeared disinclined to believe anything of the sort, but Miranda assured him again that she understood only too well and that there were far too many unscrupulous people in the world eager to take advantage of the innocent.

'There are, aren't there?' Jack declared, struck by this statement. 'My thoughts exactly, Mrs Fitzgibbon. One imagines the country to be a quiet, civilised sort of place, doesn't one?'

Miranda agreed that all seemed well in the country.

'Yes, but you see it isn't so! All a sham. Worse here than it is in town.'

This struck a chord with Sophie, and she proceeded to tell her brother of Miranda's servants and the manner of their leaving, as well as Leo coming to her rescue. 'So Miranda has had to put up with Pendle for *weeks*,' Sophie ended dramatically.

Jack turned and stared at Miranda in the manner of

one who had just heard that his new acquaintance
wrestled with crocodiles.

'I say!' he breathed admiringly.

'Mrs Fitzgibbon?' Sir Marcus strolled up, smiling,
and after taking her hand and asking how she did,
proceeded to introduce her to the two ladies in tartan
shawls with whom he had been conversing.

'The Misses McKay are the daughters of Admiral
McKay,' he finished.

Miranda supposed by this that she would be considered very ill mannered if she admitted that she did
not know who the good admiral was, and made appropriate noises.

'Julian was a dear boy,' one of the Misses McKay
avowed, her smile at odds with her gimlet eyes. 'The
admiral would have liked him, I am sure.'

'Oh, yes, the admiral would have liked him very
much.'

'As I wrote to his dear mother only last week, Julian understood his duty to the village. He attended
our small church whenever he was in the country. A
common courtesy other members of his family do not
adhere to.'

'Do you mean Leo?' Sophie asked tactlessly.

Shocked by such plain speaking, the Misses Mc-
Kay dissembled. 'Of course, we understand he is a
very busy man. Very grand.'

'Yes, very grand,' agreed the other.

'And yet your church is not at all small.' Miranda
smiled, unable to resist a little mischief of her own.
'Quite large enough for the grandest of men.'

'It was once very important,' said one Miss Mc-

Kay. 'It was part of an abbey which was torn down during the Reformation. The land was then given over to the first Mr Fitzgibbon by Henry the Eighth. He had performed some service for him, I believe,' she ended rather primly.

'One of Henry's ladies was hoping to be his wife,' explained Sir Marcus, 'and Fitzgibbon took her off his hands.'

'Oh, if Henry *had* married her, he would have had seven wives!' laughed Sophie.

'But he did not wish to have seven wives, Sophie, that was the whole point,' Sir Marcus retorted. 'She married the Fitzgibbon, and he was well rewarded for his service to his king. He received the land the monastery had stood upon, and being, I think, an insensitive sort of fellow, proceeded to build The Grange with the same stone. He left the church; I imagine it saved him the trouble of building another.'

Miranda thought the first Fitzgibbon sounded practical rather than insensitive, but couldn't help but laugh at Sir Marcus's sketch of his character.

'It is the Fitzgibbon family's luck,' Jack added, and then looked as if he had said something he oughtn't.

Miranda glanced about, surprised. 'Their luck? Whatever do you mean?'

'Did Julian not tell you?' Sophie was astonished. 'The Grange must stay in the family; it is a talisman of sorts. The Fitzgibbons' good luck piece. Like a very large rabbit's foot.'

'Oh,' Miranda said. 'I see.' And looking from Sophie's surprised eyes to Jack's guilty ones, she suddenly did.

'But you are a Fitzgibbon, so everything is all right,' Sophie went on, quite unaware of the undercurrents circling her.

'I'm sure it will be.'

'You might have noticed the gentleman on the wall inside the church,' Sir Marcus said. 'That is your original Fitzgibbon.'

'I did notice it,' Miranda replied, smiling. 'And I do believe I saw a resemblance to—to the Duke.'

And then, for no particular reason, she blushed.

Her companions eyed her with varying degrees of interest while Miranda attempted to escape her embarrassment by murmuring that it was rather warm.

Sir Marcus saved her by continuing on with his tale of the first Fitzgibbon. 'He lived to a hoary old age, I believe, and died with his head still attached to his neck, which was unusual for those times.'

'And his marriage?' Miranda rallied enough to ask. 'Did it prosper, sir?'

Sir Marcus smiled. 'You will have to ask Leo that, my dear. You have quite exhausted my store of knowledge on the subject.'

The Misses McKay began a conversation between themselves on the extent of their father, the admiral's, knowledge. 'I'm sure he would have known the entire history of our village!' one of them finished triumphantly.

'If he had ever removed here to the village,' the other added with painful honesty.

'Which he would never have done, for he could not bear to live away from the sea.'

'No, he must always have a view of the sea from his window.'

Sir Marcus nodded thoughtfully. 'I believe it is often so, ladies, when a sailor comes to retire on dry land.'

The Misses McKay sighed and said that the admiral had not been particularly happy in his retirement, and, on that sombre note said their goodbyes.

Sophie offered to take Miranda home in their carriage, but she politely refused. Jack Lethbridge gave her a sheepish smile, saying he was pleased to have made her acquaintance.

'You are not at all as I had expected,' he burst out, when they were briefly alone, Sophie being assisted into the carriage by her father.

Miranda bit her lip, but her dark eyes danced. 'I think I shall take that as a compliment.'

Jack, realising his error, floundered in a morass of half-completed apologies, until his father told him to hurry up and stop making a cake of himself.

'Goodbye, Mrs Fitzgibbon,' added Sir Marcus. 'We plan to hold our party soon, and will send out invitations.'

'Yes, yes, you must come!' called Sophie.

Miranda assured them that she would, and waved as they drove away.

The churchyard was all but deserted, and she stood a moment more admiring the church, remembering what she had been told. It was interesting that the Fitzgibbons had been having problems with disreputable ladies as far back as the sixteenth century. Did Leo know the history of his family? She supposed he must. Perhaps that was why he was so wary of troublesome women. Although, Miranda recalled, that particular troublesome woman had brought them much land and glory and, if the Lethbridges were to be believed, their good luck.

Good luck which would be taken away if The Grange were ever to leave family hands.

It partially explained Leo's eagerness to regain the house. Miranda would not have thought him a superstitious sort of man, but possibly his relatives were. Being the head of his family, it would be his duty to please them.

It all sounded very wearing, but did not entirely explain Leo's behaviour towards her.

Miranda allowed herself, briefly, to remember his rescue of her from Nancy in front of Thorne's cottage. The wave of relief she had felt when he appeared, the feeling of joy, when she had looked up into his blue eyes. It had quite taken her breath away, and she was aware that she had gabbled on foolishly for quite some time. And then he had persisted on calling her Miranda.

The sound of her name on his lips! Even now it made her feel quite flushed and uncomfortable. More so than the memory of his kiss, for any man might kiss a woman he thought not quite respectable, and Leo imagined her practised in such matters. Although, afterwards, he had seemed as shaken as Miranda herself.

The problem was, this was all unknown territory to Miranda. Considering the part she was playing, it was an irony not lost on her. She was not at all experienced in kissing, or any other aspect of the relationship that existed between a man and a woman who were wed, or…or close, so to speak.

She and Julian had been married, but there had never been more than a chaste kiss between them. Julian was too ill, and Miranda, although she would have been prepared to do her duty as a wife, had been secretly, guiltily, relieved. Yes, she admitted now, she had been relieved that she did not have to pretend to love where she felt only gratitude and affection.

If he had been well and strong, perhaps she might have grown to love him? Miranda wanted to think so, but in her heart she doubted it.

For no particular reason, Leo Fitzgibbon's face rose before her.

Miranda wondered what he thought of his Fitzgibbon ancestor, who had married at the king's bidding, to a woman he did not love. Probably Leo thought it a canny match, considering what his ancestor gained from it. Leo himself would seek just such a match for himself. Miranda imagined him setting out to find a bride with much the same attitude as he would a new horse.

Now that she had made herself angry again, Miranda felt more comfortable. She dismissed Leo from her mind. Her morning had been pleasantly and fruitfully spent. She had made new acquaintances and, she hoped, at least come part of the way in conquering Jack Lethbridge's suspicion of her. And she had Sophie's party to look forward to! Life at The Grange, she decided, could be very agreeable indeed.

If Leo Fitzgibbon would allow her to enjoy it.

* * *

The Lethbridge's carriage rolled along sedately. Sir Marcus, who had earlier this morning been the recipient of his son Jack's doubts in regard to Miranda Fitzgibbon, had held a thoughtful silence for some time. Jack had been content to allow it to continue, knowing that his father was a safe judge of character and was presently pondering the matter of Julian's young widow. If Sir Marcus decided Miranda was the harpy Leo believed her, the Lethbridges would cut her acquaintance forthwith. If not...

Sir Marcus cleared his throat in preparation for speech.

'It is my opinion that Mrs Fitzgibbon is one of the nicest women of our acquaintance.'

Surprised, Jack said, 'She is certainly very attractive—'

'No, I do not refer to her looks, Jack, although I agree she is very pretty. It is her manner, her character I am concerned with here. She is what is known, bluntly, as a good woman.'

Jack eyed him with a startled air. '"A good woman", eh, sir?'

'Most definitely, Jack.'

Silence again fell, while Sophie, who was not privy to the secret, watched her two menfolk with puzzled amusement. At last Jack released his breath, ridding himself of his struggles at the same time. 'I believe you're right, Father,' he said in his usual amiable voice. 'You know, I feel much better now. I always find it quite exhausting being at odds with people.'

'I know you do, Jack, I know you do.'

* * *

Miranda had only made it as far as the Misses Mc-Kay's residence. A neat, pretty cottage, it stood within an equally neat and pretty garden. The Misses McKay were awaiting her at the gate, eager to usher her inside and refresh her with tea and prune cake.

'The Admiral's favourite! My dear Mrs Fitzgibbon, you simply cannot walk all the way home to The Grange without taking tea with us.'

Although the old ladies were renowned gossips and would probably pump her dry, Miranda still felt it would be churlish to refuse. And she was in no hurry to return home. It would do Pendle good to suffer some slight unease as to her whereabouts—Miranda had found within herself a mischievous quality she had not known existed until the Duke's man came to stay at The Grange.

She was making her way down the path, hemmed in by the two gossipy old ladies, when a horse drew to a clattering halt on the laneway outside. All three turned, and gasped in unison.

Belford sat, handsome if a little windswept, upon his mount. He was obviously startled to see her so cosy with the Misses McKay. Miranda raised her chin and glared back at him, daring him to utter a word of censure. After a moment he pulled himself together, saying in a cheery voice, 'Mrs Fitzgibbon! Miss McKay and Miss McKay. A fine morning to be visiting.'

The elder Miss McKay gave him a reproving look. 'A fine morning to be in church, Duke. I collect you were unable to attend.'

Belford looked startled at her rebuke but, to Miranda's amusement, soon rose to the occasion. 'I was engaged on estate matters, Miss McKay. Unavoidable.'

The lady nodded, grudgingly allowing him the excuse.

'Will you join us for tea, Duke?' her sister asked, fluttering a little, obviously more affected by his presence than her sibling. 'We have prune cake. As we were just now saying to Mrs Fitzgibbon, it was the Admiral's favourite. He would never set out on a sea voyage without an adequate supply of prune cake.'

Leo glanced at Miranda. He could see the glint of laughter in her eyes and knew exactly what she was thinking. She was envisioning the famous Admiral McKay, proud aboard his ship, secure in the knowledge that he had enough prune cake to last those many long months at sea.

His own lips twitched.

She is a witch, he thought. A sweet and delightful witch. The Misses McKay, chronic gossips and notoriously hard to please, had been won over already.

For a second he was tempted to agree to their invitation, to follow them into the cottage and sit with them over their tea and cake. Just so that he could be in her radiant presence a little longer, so that he could share with her another smile... But no, it would not do. He had an appointment, and the fact that the breaking of it seemed suddenly so necessary to his happiness, made him all the more determined not to do so.

'I'm afraid I cannot. Excuse me, ladies. Mrs Fitzgibbon.'

When he had gone, the elderly Misses McKay settled Miranda in their best chair and lavished her with refreshments. A kitten climbed upon her knee and settled for a nap. Listening to their chatter, Miranda felt quite at home, relaxed enough to daydream.

Had Leo really shared with her that brief moment of amusement? His eyes had appeared to be alight with laughter, although his expression had remained politely enquiring. Instinctively she knew he would never laugh aloud in such circumstances, never allow himself to hurt the feelings of the Misses McKay, and neither would she. And yet, Miranda was quite certain, in those brief minutes outside the McKay cottage, she and Leo had been perfectly attuned.

And what of the look on his face when he said goodbye? He had gazed at her as if she were all he held dear, all he had ever wanted. As if he would give anything to stay... Surely she was mistaken in that belief? Surely she was imagining it? Why on earth should the Duke of Belford want her? He hated her, and she had worked hard to make him do so.

When Tina had finally set out to call upon the cause of her brother's turmoil, it was with a very clear idea of what she meant to say. First she would confront this woman, informing her that she knew exactly what she was up to. Not content with Julian, this Decadent Countess was planning to ensnare the far more wealthy Leo in her sticky toils.

Well, Tina would never let that happen. She would do anything in her power to save her brother from that fate. Belford, married to such a woman! He would be the laughing stock of the *ton,* the butt of every joke. She could not abide to see her brother made so ridiculous.

Or so unhappy.

Pendle happened to be in the hall when Tina arrived, and she wasted several moments answering his stilted questions and assuring him she was in the best of health. This news did not seem to please him, judging by the expression on his face, but then one could never tell with Pendle. Tina did not think she had ever seen him smile. Perhaps it was a physical impossibility?

Her cogitations were interrupted by a soft sound above her in the gallery. Turning to glance up, Tina was struck by the sight of a woman gracefully descending the curving staircase. Her auburn hair would have shone bright enough in the shadows, but a single beam of sunlight piercing the gallery windows picked out the colour so that it appeared to burn.

Tina felt as if a hand had reached in and squeezed her heart. Good Lord, if Leo had fallen for *this* goddess…

The woman descended further, beyond the sunbeam, and Tina could see that she was just a woman. Lovely, yes, striking, yes, but only flesh and blood. Her fears receded, and she drew herself up for the coming confrontation.

Julian's widow had reached the hall and now stepped forward, her skirts rustling as she walked, her hand outstretched in a friendly if tentative manner.

'Lady Mainwaring? Pendle said you wished to see me?'

Tina's mouth dropped open. 'Oh, good Lord, is it…can it be…? Miranda!'

Chapter Eight

'I—I beg your pardon?'

Miranda blinked, trying to place the face before her. Dark hair beautifully dressed, a gown made by one of the best dressmakers in London, a woman with deep blue eyes and a smiling mouth…

It came to her then.

Lady Clementina.

Her mind spiralled back. She had been sent to school in Hampshire after her mother died and before her father took her to live in Italy. Miranda had been full of grief and so desperately lonely. She had made few friends, but one of those friends had been Clementina.

Though more than a year older than Miranda, Tina had been kind enough and generous enough to help her through those first difficult and bewildering months. She had never forgotten the kindness of the other girl.

Lady Clementina Fitzgibbon.

Miranda lifted a trembling hand.

'But Pendle said a…a Lady Mainwaring had requested to see me.'

Tina laughed and, reaching out, took Miranda's hand warmly in her own. 'I am married! But at heart, I am still Clementina Fitzgibbon.'

'I am so surprised to see you. And glad, too, of course. I don't quite know what to…' Miranda hesitated as a very nasty thought occurred to her. 'Oh! You are not one of *those* Fitzgibbons?'

Tina pulled a wry face. 'If by that you mean am I related to Belford, then indeed I *am* one of *those* Fitzgibbons. I am Leo's sister.'

His *sister!* If there had been a chair nearby, Miranda would have fallen into it. Of course she should have known, but how could she? How could she have made the connection between Leo and Lady Clementina? And yet, those eyes… With hindsight she remembered that first meeting in Berkeley Square, and how she had thought Leo in some way familiar.

Tina, who had been observing her friend's silent mortification, now made a gentle suggestion.

'Shall we find somewhere to talk, my dear? I believe we have much to say to each other.'

'Oh, of course! I am sorry.'

Miranda lead Tina into the parlour, which had become her favourite room. Now that it was cleaned and had been brightened with new cushions, it was quite cheery and Miranda normally enjoyed sitting and gazing out of the windows at the wilderness of garden.

Today she did not think she was going to enjoy it much at all.

'Now,' Tina said, when she had settled herself in an old but comfortable chair, 'I think you should tell me the story from the beginning, Miranda. *I* know very well you are not the Decadent Countess, although Leo thinks you are. You are no more your wicked stepmama than I am. Whatever possessed you to make him believe such nonsense?'

Miranda looked miserable. 'I don't know how it happened!' she wailed. 'I didn't intend to lie to him. I came to England expecting, I don't know, at least to be treated fairly, if not exactly welcomed with open arms. Julian married me to protect me, Tina. He wanted me to come here and be looked after by your family, to live at The Grange, and to be…to be *safe* again.'

Tina leaned forward, her voice still gentle. 'And you were not safe in Italy?'

'No.' Miranda looked up into Tina's eyes and tried to smile. 'Don't misunderstand me. I love Adela, she is a dear, but it has not been entirely safe for me at Villa Ridgeway since Papa died, and Julian made me see that. He was dying and he wanted to help me, and I agreed. He told me that his cousin would understand, that I could trust him, too.'

Tina nodded. 'But when you came to England you found he had made a complete mull of it, probably thanks in the main to my silly Aunt Ellen.'

'He thought I was Adela!'

'Oh, dear.'

There was a moment of silence, while both women digested the conversation so far.

'You could have told him the truth?' Tina suggested tentatively, watching as the expression on Miranda's face become even more woebegone.

'He was so rude, so…so vile. I did not think he deserved the truth. I wanted to punish him, Tina! Only it has got so that I am trapped by my own lies. I almost told him the truth when he visited The Grange, but then he said such things and I—I did not.'

'I quite see it has been difficult for you.'

'He hates me.'

This was said in so tragic a manner, Tina could have no doubt Miranda's feelings were the complete opposite. But she said nothing. Certainly, Leo did not hate her, but his emotions were as wild and fluctuating as Miranda's. No, Tina was not about to explain to Miranda that Leo was so in love with her he had lost all of his ducal qualities. That would be unfair to Leo, and besides, Miranda probably wouldn't believe it.

The best solution would be for them to sort it out themselves…with some little help from Tina.

But it would take careful planning.

'Perhaps you are both equally at fault?'

'Perhaps.' Miranda sighed, and wiped a tear from her cheek. 'I am so sorry you have become involved in this, Tina. Please, go home and forget about me. I imagine I will have to sell The Grange to your brother anyway. I have no money, and Mr Ealing at the bank has said there is a delay in sending me Julian's funds. I love this house, and I know Julian wished me to stay, but I fear I cannot hold out much longer. I will have to agree to the Duke's terms.'

'Leo has…' Tina swallowed and began again. 'Leo

has offered to buy The Grange from you on condition that you return to Italy?'

'Forever, yes.'

'I see.'

Miranda eyed her friend nervously. 'The terms were generous. It was the way in which your brother delivered them that was insulting.'

'I can imagine.'

'Oh, please, Tina, I do not want to set you against him! He was only doing what he thought best.' Miranda's passionate defence of the Duke's character surprised herself as much as Tina. If she had ever believed him capable of influencing the bank against her, she did not now.

Tina nodded briskly, masking her anger. 'Yes, I'm sure he was. Don't worry, my dear, I do not hate him. I never could.'

'And I suppose he was thinking of The Grange being the Fitzgibbons' luck,' Miranda went on. 'Jack Lethbridge explained that to me.'

'More superstition. I do not believe it, and I'm quite sure Leo does not either. Did Jack Lethbridge tell you there is a tale to go with it?'

'Only that the first Fitzgibbon married to please his king and was handsomely rewarded.'

Tina smiled. 'Do not be fooled by the cold facts, Miranda. If it was not a love match to begin with, then it very soon became one. Our Fitzgibbon ancestor was not a sentimental sort, quite ruthless in fact, but he was a model husband. It would seem that Fitzgibbon men are inevitably drawn to disreputable woman, or those with questionable reputations. There is clear evidence of history repeating itself more than once over the years. Perhaps that, more than anything else, was why Aunt Ellen dispatched me here post haste!'

Miranda blushed a vivid red. 'As my disreputable status is merely assumed, I cannot see a problem.' Her stern voice was quite at odds with her burning face.

'Legend does have it that the Fitzgibbon family began with a woman and will end with a woman.'

'Your family name seems to have rather a lot of legends attached to it,' Miranda replied primly.

'We do, don't we?' Tina smiled. 'Miranda, should I tell my brother the truth?'

Miranda's eyes widened alarmingly and she shed her primness in an instant. 'Oh, no! Please, do not! I could not bear it if he were to know that I…oh, Lady Clementina, I beg you…'

Tina sighed. 'Very well, Miranda, you need not beg. I will not tell him if you do not want me to.'

'You…you will keep my secret?'

'Yes, I will keep your secret. Now…' she rose to her feet '…I must leave you, but be assured I will come and visit you again.'

'Will you?' Miranda smiled her relief. 'I am so glad.'

'Are you lonely here, my dear?'

'N-no. I have made some friends—the Lethbridges, you know, and I have taken tea with the Misses McKay—so I am not lonely.'

'Quite gay to dissipation, in fact?'

Miranda gave a chuckle. 'Oh, no, I would not like to be dissipated. I saw quite enough of that in Italy.'

Tina took the hand that Miranda stretched out to her. 'Don't worry,' she said gently. 'Everything will be all right.'

'Yes, yes, of course it will.'

When Tina had gone, some of the confidence and certainty she so effortlessly carried about her remained behind. Miranda felt so much better for her visit that she determined to tackle the vast depths of the linen cupboard, and set about the task at once.

Tina was not so enlivened. She rode slowly home from The Grange, deep in thought. She was turning over in her mind all that she had learned. In particular she was concerned with Miranda's financial straits and Leo's possible connection. The notion of Leo threatening Miranda was not a happy one; Tina did not like to think of her brother being such a man. But neither could she imagine Miranda being dishonest about the situation in which she presently found herself.

Mr Ealing was well known to Tina. For as long as she could remember, the Fitzgibbons had dealt with that particular bank. It would be a simple matter for an influential client, like Leo, to have a word in Mr Ealing's ear. This would place more pressure upon Miranda, ensuring she agreed to his terms. Or cast her into flat despair, and subsequently into Leo's arms!

Yes, it was all very neat and clever, but was it Leo?

Tina had reached the gates leading to Ormiston. The vista was inviting, and on impulse she asked the driver to set her down so that she could walk up to the house. As she walked she thought over her afternoon visit.

It had turned out quite differently from what she had imagined. Really, it was astounding that the woman she had set out to confront, the woman painted so black by her aunt, should be none other than Miranda.

Miranda had been one of Tina's fonder school memories. Tall and striking, Miranda had appeared cold and stand-offish when she first arrived, but Tina had seen the misery lurking in her dark eyes. It had not taken the clever Tina long to discover that Miranda, though unemotional and practical on the outside, was as soft as marshmallow on the inside.

Tina had taken her under her wing, and by the time she had left school, her protégée had quite settled in. And now their paths had crossed again, and, if she was not very much mistaken, Miranda once more needed her help!

Tina's steps faltered. She paused under a huge old ash tree, facing the house.

This new development altered matters considerably. It was no longer so surprising to Tina that her brother should be in love with Julian's widow, despite Miranda's best efforts to convince him she was every bit as bad as he imagined her to be. Perhaps what was more surprising was that Miranda should have fallen for Leo when he had, by her account, been so extremely objectionable, indeed quite unlike his usually level-headed, polite self. But fall for him she had, if Tina was any judge of the matter.

So, what was to be done?

She could leave them to it, allow the tangle to unravel itself. The trouble with that solution was that it might not unravel itself in quite the manner she wished it to. The two of them might very well argue beyond any hope of reconciliation and part in bitterness.

No, that would not do at all. Tina, having seen Miranda again, had decided she would do very well as a sister-in-law. Certainly a country mile better than that cold prig Julia Yarwood! Yes, Leo would be very happy with Miranda. She would make him more human—look at what she had already achieved! He was almost like the old Leo.

Surely there was a way in which this muddle could be resolved to everyone's satisfaction?

'Tina? What are you doing?'

Leo's voice brought her head up. He was standing at the library window, gazing down at her in a puzzled fashion as she stood beneath the boughs of the grand old tree.

'You have been standing there a full ten minutes. Are you asleep?'

Tina laughed and shook her head, strolling on until she stood directly beneath his window. Leo grinned down at her, so like the boy he had once been that her heart ached. She determined right then and there that she *would* secure his happiness with Miranda, even if she had to tie them up and lock them in a room together to do it!

'I was thinking, Leo,' she said airily. 'Something to which you may be unaccustomed.'

'And here I thought you were just wool-gathering.'

'I have been to see Julian's widow.'

The smile faded from his face.

'I need to speak to you, Leo.'

'That has a serious ring to it, Tina.'

'It is a serious matter.'

Leo acquiesced. 'Very well. Come to the estate office. If you have serious matters to discuss, Tina, then that is the place to do it.'

Miranda was deep in the cavernous linen cupboard, surrounded by teetering piles of musty, moth-eaten household stuff. It was a humbling experience, but Miranda was not one to be browbeaten, even if the task before her appeared immense.

So far the pile of objects to be discarded was twice as large as that to be kept. Apart from the normal paraphernalia, she had found torn bed-curtains, a blackened warming pan, and a mouldy night cap which, from the amount of gold thread embroidery upon it, might have belonged to King Henry himself!

'Miranda?'

Miranda gave a violent sneeze. She knew that voice! Knew it as well as her own...

'Miranda? Come out. I wish to speak to you.'

What was *he* doing here? And to see her in such an unflattering state! *Go away, go away!* Miranda held her breath, as if by doing so she might turn invisible.

'Miranda? Please.'

There was a hint of laughter in his voice, and Miranda knew it would be reflected in his eyes. Like quicksilver in a summer blue sea.

Slowly, unwillingly, she extracted herself from the linen cupboard.

Her hair was a wild and dusty tangle, the skirts of the faded old dress she was wearing were filthy and her sleeves had been rolled up to her elbows in a businesslike manner. In short, she was a sight.

She could tell that Leo was enjoying her discomfiture hugely.

'What are you doing here?' she asked him sharply.

'I'm sorry,' he said in a penitent voice which fooled her not at all.

Miranda sneezed again, and blew her nose on her handkerchief.

'Bless you,' Leo murmured. He made it sound like a caress.

'Pendle should have told me you were here.' She forced herself to remain indignant.

'Don't blame Pendle. It was *I* who should have warned you but, you see, I've run tame in this house since I was a boy. I forget that things have changed.'

That wasn't strictly true. Leo had not wanted to wait for Pendle to be sent ahead with a message, knowing that in all likelihood Miranda would refuse to see him. He had run up the stairs, impatient as the boy who had once been a constant visitor, and eager to set to rights the shocking and mistaken belief under which his Countess was labouring.

And, in an about-turn which had enflamed his passions still more, Tina had encouraged him to go! She had completely reversed her opinion after meeting

Miranda. 'You know what these gossipmongers are, Leo. As usual they've got it wrong… Go and speak to her, sort it out. She's quite as keen as you to be on good terms…'

Miranda had grown uncomfortable beneath his steady regard. She brushed at a stain on her sleeve and gingerly picked a cobweb off her shoulder. 'I believe some of the objects in this cupboard belonged to your earliest ancestors,' she said in Adela's airy voice, slipping into her disguise.

Leo laughed. She flicked him a flirtatious glance from beneath her lashes and found him so handsome her breath caught in her throat.

'I can well believe it!' he replied. 'Have you found any skeletons yet?'

'Why, are there skeletons?'

He sobered slightly. 'Probably. My earliest ancestor was no saint, by all accounts. Quite a black sheep.'

'The one who built The Grange?'

He looked into her dark eyes, bright with curiosity, and smiled. 'Yes.'

'I've met him,' Miranda said, and then blushed. 'I mean…he's on the wall inside the church. He looks a little like you.'

That flirtatious glance again, an invitation if Leo had ever seen one. He stepped closer. 'I assure you I am no black sheep,' he said lightly, but with an underlying note of seriousness. 'Although you may well think differently after my recent behaviour. Miranda…I have come to plead my innocence. My sister tells me you have had dealings with Ealing at the

bank in London and may believe me to be the cause
of a delay in your funds.'

Miranda's eyes grew big. 'Oh, no, I...that is, sir, I
thought...but then I knew...I'm sure you would never
do such a thing.'

Her sentence, though hopelessly jumbled, aptly and
delightfully conveyed her feelings. Leo took another
step closer.

'I hoped you knew that I would not. But, Miranda,
I know I have said, and done, things that could only
give you a very negative impression of my character.'

That was true enough, but strangely now that he
was humbling himself to her and giving her the
chance to tear his former actions to shreds and abuse
him as abominably as she had wished to time and
time again, Miranda did neither. She no longer wished
to. Instead she gave him a quick, shy smile, picked
another cobweb off her shoulder, and changed the
subject.

'Your sister is very nice.'

Leo had been holding his breath. Now he released
it, puzzled and more than a little relieved.

'Yes, Tina is very nice. She tells me that you, madam, are not nearly as bad as you have been made
out to be.'

'Oh, I am quite as bad,' Miranda replied dully, remembering her lies.

Leo's heart sank, but almost at once he rallied.
'Surely that is for others to judge?'

Miranda gave him a direct look, searching his eyes.
'You judged me harsh enough, sir, at our meeting in

Berkeley Square. I will not soon forget your treatment of me.'

Inside, Leo squirmed. He, too, remembered clearly what had been said in the drawing room at Berkeley Square, and how badly he had handled that first, disastrous meeting with Julian's widow. His voice now was a little stiff. 'Possibly my actions were rather precipitous.'

Miranda almost smiled. 'Are you apologising, Duke?'

Was he? Leo asked himself in surprise. He so rarely felt he had anything to apologise for, because he so rarely allowed himself to be placed in a situation where there was a need to do so. But he was aware, uneasily aware, that in Miranda Fitzgibbon's case he had erred. Tina had told him to make a clean start with his Countess, and that was what he must do.

'I am sorry if my actions caused you pain, Countess,' he said, and gave a formal bow.

She said nothing in return, when he had been sure she would be unable to resist the urge to gloat. Instead Leo found himself captured by a wonderfully warm and smiling gaze. It filled him with a powerful longing to sweep her into his arms, a longing he had rarely been overcome with before. She must have read the thought in his own eyes, for her smile wavered and she stepped back to put a safe distance between them.

'Pendle can arrange these matters for you.' Leo gestured impatiently at the linen cupboard. 'That is what he does best.'

The warmth had begun to fade in Miranda's dark eyes, and now it vanished altogether.

'I do not want Pendle to "arrange these matters" for me, your Grace. I call such behaviour high-handed and arrogant. The Grange belongs to me and it is mine to arrange as *I* wish.'

'And I call that very ungrateful of you, Countess,' Leo retorted, stung.

Of course, he was right, but that did not make the situation any less awkward and frustrating. Now it was Miranda's turn to be stiff.

'I'm sorry if I sound ungrateful. Of course I am grateful for your help, your Grace, but sometimes I cannot help but wish Pendle elsewhere. I cannot believe that you, yourself, don't sometimes wish him elsewhere!'

Leo sighed. 'He means well.'

'Does he? You are more charitable than I then, your Grace—'

'Stop calling me "your Grace"!'

Miranda widened her eyes. 'What am I to call you then?'

'Anything but that.'

Several sobriquets instantly occurred to her.

He read that in her eyes, too. 'No, Miranda. Call me Leo,' he said quietly.

That look was back. She knew it was *that* look because it frightened her, a little, while at the same time filling her with an almost irresistible longing to swoon into his arms and forget all that had gone before.

'Leo,' she whispered.

He drew her into his arms and she suddenly understood what the authors of Adela's favourite penny novels meant, when they wrote of how the hero took the heroine in a masterful embrace. But, practical creature that she was, Miranda found she could not sustain this romantic fog for long.

'You will make your clothing all dusty, Leo!'

Leo laughed. 'I don't care, Miranda. I'm going to kiss you now.'

Satisfied with this answer, she returned his embrace, and his kiss, with enthusiasm.

'Miranda, sweet, sweet Miranda,' he whispered, and kissed her again.

Oh, this was right. So right. How could she ever have thought it wrong?

And yet it was wrong! Leo was under a serious misapprehension as to her true identity, and she must clear the matter up. Now!

Trembling and breathless, Miranda pulled a little away from him, though still clasping her arms about his neck. He looked surprised and a little wary, and opened his mouth to speak.

Miranda placed her fingertips across his lips. 'Hush, Leo. I have something to tell you. I am not as you think me. I have done something very bad and very foolish, and—'

A loud and persistent coughing coming from directly behind them prevented Miranda from saying any more. Leo released her, slowly and reluctantly, and turned with resignation to face his faithful butler. Pendle, seeing the expression in his master's eyes, bowed rather lower than usual.

'Your Grace, I beg your pardon. I was not aware you were here.'

'No, indeed, Pendle, how thoughtless of me not to have informed you.'

Pendle appeared to think this answer quite in order. 'Do you require refreshments, sir? I have had some of your favourite claret brought down from Ormiston.'

'A little early for me, Pendle,' Leo replied coldly. He turned back to Miranda, regret warring with his annoyance. 'I'm sorry, Countess. This tête-à-tête will have to wait until tomorrow. Will you do me the honour of taking dinner with my sister and myself at Ormiston tomorrow night? I am sure Tina will be very disappointed if you have a previous engagement.'

Miranda, swallowing her disappointment—and her secret relief—at not having been able to complete her confession, smiled. 'The only previous engagement I have, sir, is with this linen cupboard and that I can quite happily forgo!'

He smiled back at her, a smile so warm she felt as if her insides were melting with joy. 'Until then,' he said softly, and turned to follow Pendle.

Miranda leaned back against the cupboard door, afraid her legs would give way. He loved her...he must, to apologise and to kiss her so and then to ask her to Ormiston. A pity Pendle had interrupted them just then, but Miranda was more determined than ever to explain to Leo what she had done and why. To throw herself upon his mercy.

It was very clear to her now, and, if she was honest, had been for some time, that he was not the arrogant and heartless man she had thought him on first acquaintance. That being so, she was sure he must forgive her when he knew the whole. And with Tina there to back her up, the matter should be speedily resolved.

Miranda sighed deeply.

Her eyes turned dreamy.

She had never been in love. She had been very fond of Julian, but she had not loved him with the kind of love she had always dreamed she might one day experience. Now she found herself thinking of the Duke of Belford in a manner that could only mean she was inordinately fond of him. Did she love him? She wanted him to think well of her, she wanted him to look at her with that look in his eyes, and hold her close, and kiss her. Yes, that too.

Of course, before any of her dreams could come true, she must tell him the truth…

No, everything would be all right. Leo would be understanding and reasonable, he would forgive her.

A little shiver ran through Miranda. A premonition, perhaps.

She ignored it.

Leo galloped his horse home, more pleased with himself than he had been for ages. She hadn't believed him capable of influencing Ealing, not for a moment, despite what Tina thought. Indeed, Tina had thought better of Miranda than she had of him, her own brother! Tina had waxed lyrical about Miranda for some ten minutes, and Tina was normally a good judge of character.

Leo could hardly believe it. Should he begin to trust what his own heart was telling him? Was it possible that that unreliable organ had been right all along?

Miranda was a sweet woman, a lovely woman. Miranda had forgiven him at once and denied she had ever believed him capable of dealing with Ealing behind her back. She was nothing like the woman portrayed by the rumours. She was…

His thoughts drew to an abrupt halt, like a coach and four which has been travelling a clear, straight road and has come unexpectedly upon a fallen tree.

What had she said, just before Pendle interrupted them? Something puzzling.

I am not as you think me. I have done something very bad and very foolish.

She had certainly sounded very contrite. Maybe even a little afraid? As if he was bound to disapprove of whatever it was she had done. Well, she had had no reason so far to think him capable of level-headed and fair-minded consideration, had she? He had been anything but either in his dealings with her.

Whatever the 'something' she had done was, Leo determined to forgive her. Probably it was nothing. Yes, he would forgive her at once, without hesitation. He would show her that he could be as magnanimous as she, when it came to accepting apologies.

But still the doubt remained, like a small, dark shadow on the bright sun of his new-found happiness.

Chapter Nine

Miranda had slept well and deeply, and arose with a smile on her face. Her conscience might not be completely clear but it soon would be. It was as if, in her heart, she had already confessed and Leo had forgiven her.

Everything would be all right, she was certain of it!

Perhaps it was Lady Clementina's arrival upon the scene which had given her this sense of certainty. The knowledge that she had a friend in the enemy camp. She imagined she had Tina to thank for Leo's unceremonious arrival yesterday. It was only fair she repay Tina's confidence in her by making a clean breast of her deceit.

Lay the Decadent Countess to rest.

Sun poured in through the old mullion windows, shining like melted butter upon the uneven floorboards. A warm fire was burning in the hearth, while hot washing water steamed in a jug, a fresh towel folded neatly beside it. Everything was so very dif-

ferent from her first weeks at The Grange. Despite
Pendle's, and his master's, high-handed behaviour,
she had to be grateful for the changes they had
wrought. Miranda knew she was not secure yet, but
this morning she felt almost content.

Esme tapped on the door, peeped in when told to
enter, and with growing confidence carried Miranda's
tea and toast to the table by the bed.

'Thank you, Esme. It is a marvellous day, is it not?'

'Aye, ma'am.'

'How is your brother, who works in the stables at
Ormiston?'

'Very happy, ma'am. The Duke is a good master.
My brother says as he's always got a kind word for
his servants, even the lowest of 'em. When old Dis-
hart, the groom, were poorly, he even paid for a doc-
tor!'

Esme's eyes were quite round with wonder.

Miranda felt the warmth inside her grow. It was
pleasant to hear such things about the man one loved.

And she did love him. Miranda was sure of it now.
It was as if, during the hours of sleep, her uncertainties had been resolved. Her hopes and dreams of a
settled and happy life were beginning to take on the
hard, crystal shell of reality.

When Esme had gone, Miranda quickly completed
her *toilette,* donned a white muslin gown and went
downstairs. She felt eager to get on with things, and
to occupy herself during the hours until evening. Her
invitation to Ormiston—she felt a tingle of apprehension and excitement—loomed over her. But, in the
meantime, she must write another letter to Mr Ealing,

demanding an explanation of his tardiness, that he right matters as soon as possible. Once she had the monies due to her, she could employ her own servants. She could be rid of Pendle.

As if conjured by her thoughts, Pendle appeared in the hall, his face as pinched and sour as it always was.

'Madam—'

'Not now, Pendle, I am busy.'

He seemed somewhat taken aback by her abruptness. Miranda was herself surprised by the aura of confidence which enveloped her this morning.

'Madam, there is—'

'I am going to spend the morning at my desk, Pendle. See that I am not disturbed.'

'Normally I wouldn't disturb you, madam, but you have a visitor.'

Miranda turned and frowned. Pendle pursed his lips apologetically, but Miranda saw the triumphant flare in his eyes.

'A visitor?'

'A Mr Harmon, madam. Mr Frederick Harmon from London. He says you are acquainted with him.'

Pendle spoke the name as if he were swallowing pips, but Miranda was too surprised to notice.

'Oh! I did not expect—' She caught herself, assuming a calmer demeanour. It would not do for Pendle to think her rattled—Pendle did not respect the meek or the muddled. 'Bring him to the parlour, Pendle, and I suppose we had better have some tea and cake.'

'This early in the morning, madam?'

'What do *you* suggest then, Pendle?'

Pendle drew himself up. 'As it is the height of bad manners to visit anyone before ten o'clock, I suggest he receive no tea and certainly no cake, madam!'

Miranda smiled, and then she giggled. Remembering herself, she bit her lip, but it was too late. Pendle looked as if he had received a severe shock.

'Send Mr Harmon into the parlour,' Miranda said, composed once more. 'We *will* have tea, but definitely no cake.'

'Very good, madam.'

Miranda closed the door on Pendle's bowing figure, and then closed her eyes. She had dared to laugh at the pompous Pendle. What terrible revenge would he exact of her? No pudding for a week? No bedtime stories? Miranda giggled again, holding her hand over her mouth to stifle the sound. Really, sometimes she thought Pendle was more like a duke than Leo!

Her head cleared abruptly.

What was Frederick Harmon doing so far from London? The last time she had seen him, at Armstrong's Hotel, had been the evening Leo burst in upon them and accused her of entertaining men in a private parlour. Miranda remembered, with mortification, how she had stumbled over her words. But she had nothing with which to reproach Mr Harmon. He had been kindness itself and she had felt very comfortable in his company. Indeed, she had found herself treating him much as she would Adela.

Perhaps, she thought suddenly, he had had another letter from Adela and wished to share it with her? Was it bad news? Miranda admitted that she had been a little surprised that she had so far received no letters

from her stepmama. She had been about to write a
letter of her own, following the one to Mr Ealing.

A discreet tap on the door heralded Mr Harmon,
and Miranda hurriedly composed her features into a
polite mask of greeting.

Despite her fears, Miranda could not help but notice that Mr Harmon was dressed rather splendidly for
a sojourn in the country. His double-breasted jacket
was padded at the shoulders, and severely nipped in
at the waist, his waistcoat was a bright concoction of
greens and yellows, while his shirt points were very
stiff and very high.

Miranda, who could not remember him being so
elaborately dressed when she last met him, thought
he must lately have come into money. Being used by
now to Leo's quiet elegance, she wished he had spent
his funds in some other manner. She could not know
this splendid display was entirely for her benefit.

Mr Harmon, obviously believing himself the epitome of high fashion, strutted into the room with a
beaming smile upon his face. The smile was enough
to convince Miranda he brought no ill tidings, and
she allowed him to take her outstretched hand.

'Mrs Fitzgibbon…Miranda,' he said and, stooping,
pressed his lips fervently to her flesh. 'I am so sorry
for imposing upon you. As your manservant has already conveyed to me, I am very early.'

Miranda forgot her damp hand. 'Did Pendle tell
you that? He is usually more subtle.'

'No, no, he merely grimaced. I read everything
from that.'

Miranda laughed. 'You must not take it personally,

Mr Harmon. He grimaces at everybody. He is the Duke's butler and has been loaned to me until I find servants of my own.'

It was said in a light-hearted manner meant to put him at his ease, but Mr Harmon did not take it so. His smile vanished and he frowned in a worried fashion.

'Mrs Fitzgibbon, I hope you are not in some sort of difficulty? I have had another letter from Adela, and she feared you might require my assistance, so I—'

'No, no, it is nothing serious, I do assure you! *Have* you had a letter from Adela? I wish she would write to me. I miss her. Is she well? Tell me what she says.'

Mr Harmon took the seat she offered, smoothing his tight sleeves and carefully crossing his legs. His hair had been arranged into a Brutus, which was meant to disguise the encroaching bald patch on the top. Miranda bit her lip and told herself firmly she must be tolerant. It would not do to laugh at a gentleman's pretensions. Mr Harmon had been kind enough to come all this way to give her Adela's news, and therefore she must treat him as Adela did—as a friend.

'I am surprised she has not written.' Mr Harmon was speaking. 'Unless she thinks…' He hesitated, as if doubtful whether or not he should complete the thought.

Miranda waited politely, while Mr Harmon deliberated.

He was only pretending. Frederick Harmon knew

very well the lines he meant to say, and how he meant
to deliver them!

Since their meeting in London, he had been carefully formulating a plan which would enable him to
gain some power over Miranda. Enough so that she
would allow him to speak for her, as her friend and
adviser. He had also made numerous enquiries. One
of the discoveries subsequent to those enquiries was
of an old Fitzgibbon legend concerning The Grange.
Superstition said that if The Grange were ever to
leave the Fitzgibbon family's hands then they would
go into a decline.

Slide into obscurity.

Being a rather superstitious man himself—he had
been known to throw salt over his shoulder at the least
provocation—Frederick Harmon had no difficulty in
believing that Leo would subscribe to this legend. The
Duke, he thought, must be quite desperate to recover
The Grange.

And Frederick would relish being in a position to
deny it to him.

It was all consistent with revenge. Mr Harmon was
not an overly intelligent man, but he was cunning and
he was an opportunist. More than anything he wanted
to do Belford an ill turn in repayment for the one
Belford had done him, or so he thought of it. He told
himself that he could have made Sophie Lethbridge
happy and she would certainly have made him happy.
Belford had therefore prevented two lonely people
from finding marital bliss.

That Sophie was an heiress had very little to do

with it—and so he had told himself so many times that he almost believed it.

Now the time had come for him, through Miranda, to repay Belford. If Belford wanted The Grange, then he would have to deal with Harmon. He would have to humble himself to Harmon. The picture that conjured was extremely pleasing.

'Forgive me.' He spoke at last. 'I had meant only to visit you, see that all was well, and then leave. But now…under the circumstances, I feel I should explain a little more of why I am here. My cousin Adela fears you are in some danger from Belford.'

The effect of his words was not quite as he had hoped. He had meant to give a brief account of a probable dastardly plot by Belford to evict her from her home, so that he, Belford, could reclaim it. Freddie had then imagined her gasp of horror, her demands to know all, and then, her pleas for assistance. Which he would gladly give.

Miranda *did* blink in startled amazement, and when she spoke her voice *did* hold a note of outrage. But it was outrage directed at Frederick Harmon rather than Belford.

'Danger? I do not understand you, Mr Harmon. The Duke of Belford has offered me nothing but kindness.'

Considering the scene Mr Harmon had witnessed in London, this quite rightly confused him. Miranda had an expression on her face of high dudgeon, a lioness protecting her cub…or her lion king.

Mr Harmon swiftly revised his plans. It appeared that Belford had wasted no time in paying court to his cousin's wife—'turning her up sweet', as Mr Harmon called it. The dastardly plot idea was useless then, she wouldn't believe it. But Freddie was yet to meet a woman in the first flush of love who completely trusted her beloved or the emotions he inspired. Who was not vulnerable to a little manipulation?

He rallied, giving Miranda his most sorrowful and sincere smile.

'Yes, he is good at dissembling. But I'm afraid the truth is that Belford is a libertine. ''A loose fish'', as our dear Adela would say. It is not generally known, and I can see from your expression you find it difficult to accept but, believe me, it is so.'

He leaned closer to deliver the *coup de grâce,* and watched his victim's eyes grow still wider. 'I have heard it said he has a particular weakness for redheads.'

Miranda, who had listened to this recital in stunned silence, now spoke.

'Mr Harmon, I am finding this very difficult! I have never met a gentleman more—more gentlemanlike than the Duke!'

But even as she said the words, Miranda knew they were not altogether true. Leo had been very *un*gentlemanlike on several occasions since she had made his acquaintance. Miranda had put this down to his believing she was Adela and, more recently, to his having developed a tenderness for her. In short, he was in love with her. Now everything she had thought solid fact was shifting and shivering like quicksand.

Was it possible, she wondered in dismay, that Leo treated all women in such a way?

All redheads, that is.

Mr Harmon, observing her growing disquiet, resumed injecting his poison.

'What, has Belford never held your hand a little too long, or tried to kiss you?' he demanded. 'Knowing him as I do, I would be very surprised if he had not!'

Miranda's eyes widened, her mouth opened to argue in Leo's defence, but the words that came out were not the ones she expected.

'You know him well?' she whispered. 'I—I remember that evening at Armstrong's he seemed to know you. I—I had forgot.'

Freddie knew he had her. But instead of crowing in triumph, he softened his voice still more.

'Yes, I know him well, although he does not like to admit to it. We were at school together, but he is too high in the instep to acknowledge me now. He was always…unreliable, when it came to the fair sex. He would have been sent down, if it were not for his family's influence. These days, it is said among the *ton,* even among his friends, that he has no heart. My dear, do not allow his clever manners or his sincere address to persuade you differently. He feels no pity, and what he wants he will have. He sees it as his right.'

Miranda lifted her hand to her lips, as if to stifle a cry. What had Julian said to her in Italy? *The Fitzgibbons are determined to have their own way and usually do.* The words could have been expressly written for Leo.

Mr Harmon was still speaking.

'I said that Adela had written to me. She fears you will fall under Belford's spell. That you will be hooked like a pretty little fish, landed, and then discarded for the next catch. Believe me, Miranda, I am reluctant to tell you this, for I think it must give you pain, but it is so.'

Miranda did not see how incongruous Mr Harmon's story sounded. Confused and confounded by all that had passed since she returned to England, Miranda placed herself in Mr Harmon's hands. At this particular moment she was remembering all her dreams and all the bright confidence in the future she had awoken with this morning, and how it now appeared to be leaking away, leaving her with a sensation of cold emptiness. A lifeless husk, in fact.

How could he do this to her?

'I don't believe it,' she whispered.

But even as she protested, her practical voice was reminding her that everything the Duke had done and said could easily be read another way. Mr Harmon's way. And if that were so, then all he really cared for was to conquer her.

And yet…her honesty compelled her to admit that even if he was so wicked, the blame must be partially hers.

Considering the game she had been playing with him, the lies she had led him to believe, how could he think other than that she would not be adverse to a little dalliance herself? She had willingly received his kisses on more than one occasion. She had even kissed him back!

Yes, she was also at fault.

And yet, for Miranda, those moments had been very special. How could it have been so different for Leo? She struggled briefly with the painful and bewildering possibility that the words and kisses they had exchanged had been nothing to Leo but meaningless little markers on his road to seduction.

'I am sorry.' Frederick Harmon was leaning even closer to her, his brown eyes filled with sympathy. 'It is my fault. I have come too late. You have already grown a *tendre* for the Duke.'

It was the sympathy that did it.

Miranda's head came up. She swallowed her tears. Pride was the thing. He…no one…*he* must never know how badly he had hurt her, how easily she had fallen in love with him. He must never realise his victory over her. As far as Leo knew she was the Decadent Countess—worldly, flighty, tough. And so she would remain.

'No, indeed, sir!' Miranda replied bracingly.

Mr Harmon sat back hastily, disguising his wince with a thoughtful frown.

'The Duke has been kind to me, but I have no special regard for him. Although I am very grateful to you for having warned me, Mr Harmon. I shall take special care not to allow such—such feelings as we have discussed possess me.'

Mr Harmon nodded as if he believed her, while he was mentally rubbing his hands together. Belford had ruined his happiness, now with any luck he had ruined

Belford's. And there was still the matter of The
Grange to be contested. Oh, yes, this was a happy
day!

A maid brought tea and Miranda concentrated on
the familiar ceremony of pouring and serving. It
seemed to help. The pain receded to a dull ache.
When they were settled again, she asked quietly after
Adela and listened, with a polite smile, as Frederick
Harmon lied about the letter he had never received.

'I am glad she is well and happy,' was all Miranda
said when he had finished.

Frederick Harmon, realising his visit had came to
an end, rose to his feet. 'I am putting up in the village,
at the Ivy and Rose. If you wish to contact me there,
Mrs Fitzgibbon…Miranda, I am at your service.'

Miranda smiled and nodded as if she understood
his hint, but Frederick was almost certain she did not.
He clarified the matter.

'You may wish me to mediate between you and the
Duke on the matter of The Grange. To stand between
you, as it were, if things become uncomfortable.'

Miranda looked surprised. 'I had not thought…but
I am not selling The Grange, Mr Harmon. Did you
think I was?'

'No, no, I just thought… Well…' and he laughed
with pretended relief '…I am glad you feel so settled
here that you plan to stay. Still, if you should need
me for any service, however small, I will be remaining at the Ivy and Rose for several more days. I am
due a little holiday and have never been to this part
of the country before. May I call on you again?'

Miranda could hardly refuse him; indeed, he had

been very kind. She could not blame the bearer of the bad news for the news itself. 'Yes, of course, sir, I look forward to a future visit. Goodbye.'

He took her hand, squeezed it gently, then took his leave.

Miranda stood in the hall for some time after he had left, her thoughts filled with unpleasant images and unhappy imaginings. No, she decided, continuing on with her previous thoughts. It was not Mr Harmon's fault this had happened. And she could not blame Adela for trying to protect her, Adela who, in her own ramshackle way, loved her.

If it was anyone's fault then it was Leo's, for simply being what he was. Certainly not the man of her dreams, not any more.

Rather the man of her nightmares.

What now? She was engaged to dine at Ormiston tonight, and she had promised herself she would tell Leo the truth. Should she continue with that plan and listen to his scornful laughter? Or should she play along with his belief that she was the Decadent Countess? Turn his game end upon end, and punish him for the terrible hurt he had caused her? Wait until the right moment, and then inform him she had known of his intentions all along, and was only likewise amusing herself. And that, after all—sorry!—she was no longer amused and no longer interested.

It was tempting.

Oh, yes, it was very tempting.

Pendle coughed behind her.

'You seem to be coming down with a cold, Pendle,' Miranda said coolly. 'I will have Cook prepare you a remedy.'

'Yes, madam.'

His meek reply so surprised her, Miranda turned to stare, but Pendle was already making his back the way he had come.

Jack Lethbridge was dawdling along the country lane on his favourite horse. He had enjoyed a large and hearty breakfast, a joke with his sister, and his father had complimented him on his taste in riding boots.

All was right with Jack's world.

As he approached the village of St Mary Mere, something caused him to glance up. Before him was a small and picturesque humped-back bridge straddling a small and picturesque stream. In the background rose the village, through which Jack had been about to ride, but that was not what caught his eye.

There was a man standing upon the bridge gazing down into the water. It was a gentleman Jack knew well.

Freddie Harmon!

This realisation came as a most unpleasant shock. So unpleasant, in fact, that Jack drew up clumsily, causing his horse to rear and whinny and almost unseat him. The gentleman on the bridge turned to discover the source of the disturbance, and Jack saw that he was not mistaken, although he had briefly felt sure...hoped he must be.

Raising his beaver top hat, Frederick Harmon nodded in Jack's direction, giving Jack ample time to take

in the details of his dress, before strolling nonchalantly away.

Jack watched him go, feeling, as he afterwards said,
'damned sick, all that bacon and sausage churning
inside me'. Harmon in St Mary Mere! It was unthink-
able, it was beyond belief. Could he have imagined
it? But no, he had not even been thinking of Freddie
Harmon when he recognised him.

Jack turned and rode away, his mind an exhausting
whirl of speculation. But one thing at least was very
clear.

He must speak to Leo, and at once.

Leo was engaged with estate matters when he received Jack's urgent message, and soon joined him in
the library, where any notion that this was one of
Jack's starts was quickly dismissed.

'What in God's name is it, Jack? You're as white
as a sheet!'

Jack gulped several times, but was only able to
reply after a restorative glass of Leo's excellent
brandy.

'I've seen him in the village, Leo! Large as life, he
was, standing on that bridge. You know the one.
Pretty, made of stone.'

Leo had no more patience with Jack's meanderings
than he had with his Aunt Ellen's.

'Who have you seen, Jack?'

But Jack was in no state to be hurried. 'And do
you know, Leo, I saw it plain as I see you now. He
was wearing *my* waistcoat! Not mine…I don't mean
mine, I mean the one I had made up for me by Kip-

plington, in Bond Street. You remember? Cost me a small fortune. And now he's got the exact same one! I'll ask for my money back, so I will. Fair turned my stomach to see *my* waistcoat on that man. Thought I was about to cast up my accounts—'

Leo could restrain himself no longer. 'Who, Jack? For God's sake, pull yourself together and tell me!'

'Harmon!' Jack gasped, and flopped down into a leather chair. The two dogs sprawled by the fireplace lifted their heads. 'Freddie Harmon. He was standing there on that bridge large as life! Almost fell off m'horse!'

Leo stared at him. His first reaction was to reject what his friend was telling him.

'No,' he said firmly. 'You must be mistaken. Why would Freddie Harmon come here? He knows he has no friends in this part of the country—the reverse, in fact—and he could hardly believe Sophie would look kindly upon him after what he did. Even *he* is not such a fool. No, Jack, it was someone like Harmon, that is all.'

'It *was* him, Leo. *Believe* me.' When the Duke still appeared unconvinced, he added, 'Send one of your grooms to ask at the Rose and see if I'm not right!'

Leo paced closer to the dogs and their tails thudded on the hearthrug. 'But why would he come here?'

Jack rose to pour himself a second glass of brandy. 'Lord, *I* don't know. I would have planted him a facer last time, if you hadn't stopped me.' Then a solution suddenly occurred him, and so pleased was he that he spoke it without thinking. 'To see the Countess! They were pretty thick in London. I told you how it was at the time, and you went to see for yourself. Remember?'

Jack turned to Leo as he spoke and then wished he could have pulled the words back. But it was too late. They hung in the air, and Leo's silent, pensive gaze had a stricken quality.

With an effort, Belford shook his head. No, he thought, she would not...would *never*... But even as he rejected the idea of Miranda and Freddie Harmon being connected in some way, her words of yesterday came sombrely into his head.

I have done something very bad and very foolish.

'Leo?' Jack was watching him.

Leo forced himself to assume the mantle of the Duke. His voice, when he spoke, was calm and level, his demeanour mildly enquiring. No one would ever know that, inside his cool exterior, his happiness had become a writhing, molten mass of doubt.

'I find the idea of Harmon visiting the Countess almost as difficult to believe as his coming to renew his addresses to Sophie.' His voice went on. 'But I agree I must send a groom to discover if it *is* Harmon you saw on the bridge, and, if it is, what he is doing here.'

'I say,' Jack blurted out helpfully, 'you're very sure it ain't him, Leo! I'm almost persuaded myself, except I saw him with my own eyes.'

When the groom had been dispatched, Leo turned Jack's thoughts to more pleasurable matters, and they conversed easily for some half an hour on subjects of which he could not afterwards recall a word. Jack would never have guessed how desperately his friend wanted him to be wrong.

When the groom returned, however, it was to report that, yes, it was Frederick Harmon at the Ivy and Rose, and that he had told the landlord he was very friendly with the new Mrs Fitzgibbon up at The Grange, and would be visiting her. 'And it were said,' the groom muttered, red as a beet, 'in the sort of way a man could not mistake. As if this Harmon and the lady were better 'an friends, sir.'

Leo thought he made no movement, but the groom must have sensed something for he turned an even deeper shade of red.

'Thank you, Mitchell, that will be all.'

The door had hardly closed on the poor groom when Jack shook his head and declared, 'Damn shame! I thought she was a lady. Fooled my father, too, and she'd have to be a knowing one to do that. He called her a "good woman". Doesn't even call my mother that. Sophie's fond of her too. Don't know how I'm going tell them this latest news.'

'Then don't.'

He looked up and found Leo smiling at him, but it was a strange, humourless smile. The smile of a man about to run another through with his sword.

'What do you mean "don't"?'

'Just that. Our beautiful harpy fooled my sister, too. So much so that Tina issued an invitation for her to dine with us this evening. I will deal with her then. Don't worry, Jack, you will have nothing to explain. By tomorrow morning, the Countess will be packing in readiness to return to her villa in Italy. We will never see her again.'

Jack nodded dubiously. 'That a good thing, Leo?'

'Oh, yes, Jack. That is a very good thing indeed.'

But Jack, watching the white, strained look about his friend's mouth and eyes, did not think Leo was being entirely honest with him.

Chapter Ten

Ormiston had been built in the Palladian manner. A rectangular, somewhat austere house, with a central portico, it was far different from the jumble of styles which made up The Grange. Miranda could not help but wonder, as her carriage drew up before the great house, what it would be like to live in such a place.

To be mistress of such a place.

The subsequent pain in her chest felt very real, but she reminded herself that because she had never actually had Leo's love in the first place, it had never been hers to lose. She repeated this to herself as she climbed one of two curving exterior staircases to the main front door.

Surely a man like Leo was not worth mourning, and to do so would be an insult to herself and all womankind?

Miranda continued to climb, her chin held high. She was looking her best and she knew it. After Mr Harmon's visit, and a good cry in the privacy of her bedchamber, she had reappeared with a new resolve.

Now, after several hours sorting through her wardrobe and primping at her dressing table, she had turned herself into a young woman of style and sophistication. And something more. There was an air of mystery, an elusiveness about her. Leo may look and covet, but he could no longer touch and he would never have!

And, thus, it was in this frame of mind that she was greeted by Lady Clementina in a central hall which was a wonder in pink marble.

For a moment Miranda forgot her humiliation and other grievances, and could only gape at her surroundings.

Tina, looking very fine in a red velvet gown with a low décolletage, and with her dark hair sprinkled with pearls, laughed at her guest's astonishment.

'Yes,' she said, 'it is rather amazing, isn't it? I can't imagine what my ancestors were thinking when they ordered all that pink marble!'

'They were certainly enamoured of columns. It is quite breathtaking.' Above her, painted birds cavorted and dived on the domed ceiling, their plumage more brilliant than that of any flesh-and-blood bird she had ever seen. There was an exotic feel to Ormiston which was quite strange in an English country house, and yet Miranda found herself liking it.

'For some reason it reminds me of Italy,' she murmured.

'My Fitzgibbon ancestor who built the house spent some time in that country,' Tina replied. 'The marble was brought from there. Come, Leo is in the saloon.'

Miranda followed her, feeling rather light-headed.

She had expected Ormiston to be grand, but not this grand. Somehow the beauty of the house made Leo's perfidy so much worse, like an ugly chip in an exquisite piece of porcelain.

'You do look lovely tonight.' Tina's voice was bright as she examined Miranda's silk gown and the matching ribbon in her hair. The silk was a blue-green colour, reminiscent of the deeper parts of the ocean. It suited Miranda very well, accentuating the auburn of her hair and the pallor of her skin.

Although perhaps, thought Tina, she was a little *too* pale tonight, and a little *too* serious. Whatever her inner qualms, however, Tina was far too experienced in her role as hostess to allow her bright smile and polite chatter to falter.

'We will make but a small party tonight. I had thought we might ask some of our neighbours, but Leo insisted that you alone must be our guest. Our special guest.'

She squeezed Miranda's hand as she spoke, and Miranda could not mistake her meaning. Tina was hoping that she and Leo had made up all their differences—or were about to—and that soon she would be congratulating them on their coming nuptials.

Despite her resolution to be strong, Miranda's eyes flooded with tears. They were tears of anger, she told herself furiously, turning away and pretending to examine a large bowl of summer roses, no doubt picked this morning from Ormiston's extensive gardens.

When she spoke in reply her voice was pleasingly cool and without inflection.

'Your brother is very kind, Lady Clementina.'

Tina hid her surprise. 'So formal, my dear! I thought we had got past that stage? You must call me Tina, for I shall certainly call you Miranda. We have a long history, you and I.'

'If you wish,' Miranda murmured. From being too pale, her face was now a little flushed and her eyes, when she turned them briefly upon Tina, were glittering as if she had a fever.

Tina wondered if she were ill, but again did not say so. She had had high hopes for this evening, yet already the doubts were creeping in. Leo, too, was behaving strangely. Yesterday he had returned from The Grange raving of Miranda's sweetness and sharing with his sister his touching and tentative hopes for the future.

He had been so unlike the urbane, confident man she had grown used to, almost…well, almost vulnerable in his uncertainty.

Today he had been busy on estate matters, and she had had no chance to speak to him until a few moments before Miranda arrived. He had looked particularly handsome in his formal attire, and she had hurried to his side in a bubble of delight. She had been missing her husband and sons dreadfully, but if by travelling to Ormiston she had been the instigator of Leo's happiness, then it had been worth it.

And then he had looked up at her and smiled, and it was as if, like a child's balloon, she had brushed against something spiky and her joy had promptly popped.

For Leo's smile was not the smile he had worn yesterday. It was not even the smile she had grown used to since he came into the title. No, this was something altogether more brittle. And when she looked into Leo's eyes, she understood why. Something lurked far back in the blue, something which reminded her, shockingly, of the hurt and bewilderment of a wounded animal.

'Leo—' she had begun softly, her heart contracting, but it was already too late. Miranda's carriage had arrived, and the naked pain she had surprised in Leo's eyes had been replaced by a polite, questioning smile.

The evening, for good or for worse, was underway.

Despite Tina's friendly chatter, Miranda had felt the other woman's disquiet. Lady Clementina had been her friend and her mentor, and Miranda was sorry that she would be disappointed by tonight's outcome. She could only think that Tina did not really know Leo, that perhaps her eyes were blinded by the worship a younger sister might feel for her older brother.

It was not for Miranda to enlighten her.

'Miranda?' Tina gestured to the saloon doorway, puzzlement in the blue eyes so very like her brother's.

With an unconscious straightening of her back, Miranda followed her over the threshold.

Again, she couldn't help but stare. The saloon was lavishly decorated, a study in white and gold. Large mirrors reflected the glitter of numerous candles, giving Miranda the impression of a hundred stars, captured purely for the Fitzgibbons' pleasure. Velvet curtains of rich gold covered the bank of windows on the south wall—though one or two remained uncovered, giving a view of the park—the sumptuous cloth looped up with white tassels.

In the midst of this grandeur, Leo stood completely at his ease, glass in one hand, the other in his pocket. As the two women entered, he set the glass on to a small gilded table, and walked towards them.

Miranda had herself under control. The Adela persona had slipped over her own like a well-worn shoe. She could, she told herself, watch his approach with little or no emotion. And if her heart was beating a little quickly and her palms were damp, well that was only the mildness of the evening.

'Miranda.' Leo's soft, deep voice was suddenly as familiar as her own. If voices had a colour then Leo's would be golden brown, rich and smooth.

'Your Grace,' Miranda replied sweetly, and gave a curtsy. When she straightened he kept her hand in his. He was smiling at her. At least, Miranda corrected herself, his mouth was smiling. His eyes were as cold as the marble in his grand hall.

What had happened to the warm, seductive man who had kissed her yesterday? Where was the libertine against whom Mr Harmon had warned her? Why was he hiding himself beneath this chilly exterior?

'You look very beautiful this evening,' he was saying, but there was no feeling in his words. It was as if he were reading a script…no, not even that, for an actor would have to at least pretend emotion. Leo showed none.

Nevertheless, Miranda gave a gay little laugh. 'Thank you, your Grace. I would prefer to be remembered for my fashion sense than for my *good* sense.'

Tina winced at the false laugh as much as at the archness of the words that accompanied it. Hastily she took a step into the breach. 'I have informed Miranda that she is our special guest tonight, Leo.'

Leo had not taken his eyes off Miranda, and although the girl was fiddling with her gloves, she was very aware of him. Tina had to repeat his name again before he heard her.

'Perhaps you would have preferred a larger party, Mrs Fitzgibbon?' Leo finally responded, but not as his sister had hoped. 'This is hardly fair on you, is it? You are the sort of woman who needs a large audience.'

Tina gasped—Leo's rudeness was not even subtle. And yet, when she expected Miranda to cry out in protest, the girl jutted her chin belligerently, gave that horrid little laugh, and gazing straight back into Leo's eyes, replied,

'Of course! I like to play to an audience. The larger the audience, the better. It is so dull when one knows everyone at a party. There is no sense of conquest, no sense of adventure. As you know, Duke, I am an adventuress at heart!'

Leo went pale with anger. Tina, her gaze darting from one to the other, felt her spirits take another dip. This evening was not going at all as she had planned. That Leo and Miranda had had some sort of falling out was an understatement. Had Tina been made of weaker stuff, she might have excused herself and hurriedly retired to her bedchamber, but Tina was not yet prepared to concede defeat.

It was her brother's happiness at stake here, after all!

'I believe Mrs Mullins is ready for us to be seated in the dining room,' she said in a rallying voice. 'But first I would like to show you something, Miranda.'

Miranda turned and followed her without a word.

The 'something' was a large, dark portrait. If it were not for a brace of candles on the mahogany table beneath it, the subject matter would have been indistinguishable from the shadows. The candle light, however, picked out the face and figure of a man.

He was dressed in the Elizabethan style, with padded doublet and a high neck ruff. His greying hair was cut close to his head, his nose prominent, his expression harsh. The resemblance to Leo was even greater than it had been in the effigy on the church wall. Especially with the eyes. The eyes in the portrait looked black, but Miranda knew they were blue, a dark piercing blue. He gazed down at her as if at any moment he would demand to know what she was doing in his house.

'This is our famous ancestor,' Tina murmured beside her, pleased by her absorption. 'The one who built The Grange. He was King Henry's man, and later his daughter, Elizabeth's. I thought you might like to see him in the flesh, as it were.'

'Not a man to be crossed, Countess.' Leo's voice was right behind her, and although Miranda kept her eyes on the portrait, she was intensely aware of him.

Tina smiled. 'Yes, rather a bully by all accounts. This is his wife.'

Miranda turned from Fitzgibbon, and found herself

facing a far smaller, far more intimate portrait. A woman with a pointed face, matt pale skin, and large dark eyes. Her hair was tucked under a jewelled cap, one long strand tumbling naturally over her white breast.

The colour of her hair was a deep, rich auburn.

'Oh,' Miranda said.

'Yes.' Tina's voice was dry. 'The Fitzgibbons have a weakness for redheads. Is that not so, Leo?'

Miranda experienced a hot wave of anger. Tina could not know that she had repeated almost exactly Mr Harmon's words of warning.

'To our cost,' Leo said. His hand closed on her bare shoulder, his fingers very warm on her cool flesh. Miranda jumped. His touch seemed to sear her, shaking her to her very core, and giving the lie to all she was planning to say and do this night. He had felt her reaction, and he would know now how he made her feel. Well, it did not matter. He would never be able to turn her feelings for him against her—she wouldn't allow it.

She loved him, but he didn't deserve her.

'The dining room is this way.' Tina broke the awkward moment.

Leo dropped his hand, and Miranda released a quiet, shaky breath. As she followed Tina, she felt a strong urge to glance back over her shoulder, to look again upon the two portraits. Tina's inference had been clear enough—the past was to repeat itself. But Tina didn't know that Leo was every bit as bad as his ancestor. Worse! At least *he* had been faithful to the one woman he loved. Leo was incapable of loving one woman, let alone being faithful to her!

In the dining room, Mrs Mullins had done them proud. The silverware was gleaming, the best crockery was laid out, and candles burned in the many sconces throughout the room. Leo, noting all this, wondered that it left him so unmoved. After that one moment of intense anger, when Miranda had more or less agreed to his summation of her character, he had felt very little.

The arctic winter that had held sway over his emotions for so many years had returned. For him, spring and summer had been brief indeed, numbered in mere weeks. He didn't want to remember the madness that had come upon him, only that he was now in a situation from which he must extricate himself at any cost. It would not do for the Fifth Duke of Belford to be thought of as a lovesick fool and that, he very much feared, was exactly how he had been behaving.

Luckily—better late than never!—he had now come to his senses. The illusion was broken. His eyes were open, and he had seen the true Miranda. Now it was up to him to drive her back to Italy, where she belonged, so that he need never see her again.

Tina was making conversation, still 'flogging a dead horse', as Jack would say. Miranda answered when she felt like it, but most of the time she appeared bored. Awaiting the entertainment, Leo supposed. Well, he would give her entertainment!

His sister had just finished commenting on how nice it was to be spending time at Ormiston, and how comfortable it was to know people and be familiar with them, having grown up with them.

'Do you think so?' Miranda asked, a frown marring her smooth brow. 'I find I become bored very quickly. I am always needing new faces and new places. Only the new is exciting.'

Tina didn't seem to know what to say to this, but Leo wasn't surprised by her answer. It was exactly what he had expected. She was tantalising him, hinting that she had never meant to stay long at The Grange, and awaiting his next offer.

'I wonder you don't move on to greener pastures,' he said in a bored voice.

'I would,' Miranda replied. 'Sadly, I am as poor as a church mouse. But then, you know that, Duke.'

'Are church mice different from ordinary mice?' Tina was growing desperate. 'I have often wondered.'

'All mice are despicable and destructive little creatures.'

Miranda glared at him—he saw the fury in her eyes—and then she laughed, and the door through which he had had a momentary glimpse of her soul was closed again.

The meal was delicious, but Leo could not enjoy it. The talk grew desultory at best, even Tina appeared to have given up. The two women rose from the table and left him to his brandy, and where normally he would have forgone such tradition, tonight he was glad to be alone.

That dress, the colours of it swirling around her, as if she were swimming beneath the sea. Naked, beneath the sea. He imagined her white skin and long, auburn hair as she moved languidly through the shadowy depths. It was surprisingly easy to imagine, but then his mind had been particularly active in the fantasy arena since he met the Decadent Countess.

Leo had seen her as both the hard sophisticate and the sweet innocent, but now she was different again. There was something unreachable about her tonight, as though no matter what he said or did, he could not touch her. Perhaps he had never touched her, not really.

The kisses they had exchanged were no more than a game on her part, while they had served to suck him deeper into self-delusion. He had believed what he wanted to believe, seen what he wanted to see.

But now he had shaken clear of the dream, and stepped into the cold light of day.

Jack was right, she and Harmon were a team. No doubt they meant to fleece him and then depart The Grange for greener fields. Well, they would learn he was a very lean sheep indeed!

Leo reached for his glass and drank the brandy in one swallow. He was surprised to see his hand trembling, and squeezed it tightly into a fist. No weakness. Tonight he had set himself the task of sending his Countess off, far away from St Mary Mere. He had told Jack not to worry, that he would do everything necessary. He, Leo, had allowed this situation to develop, and now he must fix it.

But it would be interesting to see just how far his Countess would be prepared to go.

'Miranda, I must speak plainly with you.' Tina's blue eyes were almost as hard as her brother's, and she leaned forward intently. 'What is going on? I thought…I believed… Was everything not resolved yesterday?'

Miranda shook her head, hands clasped tightly in her lap, face turned toward the windows. They were back in the saloon, and the large, splendid room seemed to echo about them. Someone had lit a fire, and she and Tina sat before it in straw silk chairs, drawn up in an intimate half-circle.

'I don't understand.'

Miranda bit her lip. She did not want to hurt her friend, but how could she possibly tell her of her brother's true character? Better that Tina should hate Miranda than that she should be disillusioned with Leo.

'It is a matter between the Duke and I,' she said quietly. 'I cannot say more than that.'

Tina let out an impatient sigh. 'You have had a tiff.'

'If you like.'

'Can you not make it up with him?'

'Perhaps.' *No, never.*

'I wish you would, Miranda! If you mean to draw daggers at each other all night, then I would much rather leave you to it. I am sure I will have indigestion after sitting through that meal with the two of you.'

Miranda said nothing. She was now very quiet and subdued, and far from the bright, brittle person she had appeared to be in Leo's company.

Tina eyed her thoughtfully. 'Do you mean to go on pretending you are Adela for the rest of the evening?'

'I think I must.'

Tina sighed. 'Then I think it best if I *do* retire now. I am rather tired, and I do not enjoy conflict when I am tired. Leo will join you soon. Unlike me, I am sure he can hardly wait for the next round!'

'Oh please, do not…Tina!'

But it was too late. Tina had risen and, deaf to all entreaties, left the room. Miranda had jumped up as if to follow her when she heard muted voices from out in the hall, and the next moment, to her dismay, Leo appeared in the doorway and closed the door firmly behind him.

He was watching her like a hunter his prey.

For an instant she felt trapped and alone, but there was now no alternative but to conclude the drama she had been playing. Miranda, turning to Adela for strength and inspiration, strolled to a small table upon which a number of pretty objects were displayed.

'My sister has retired.'

'Yes.'

Miranda heard him approaching and tried to remain calm and composed. He would kiss her, she supposed, and pretend to be enamoured of her. Her plan was to play along with the game for a little while, and then simply tell him she was bored with him. She wanted to hurt him as he had hurt her, although she did not expect it would have the same catastrophic effect.

How could it, when he had no real feelings? No heart?

'Tina was a little disappointed by this evening,' Leo went on in that cold, steady voice.

'Oh?' Miranda made herself turn. 'And has this evening been a disappointment for you, too, Duke?'

'No, Countess, I am not disappointed. It is always best to know where one stands.'

She gave him one of her direct looks. 'Of course.'

But his voice was thoughtful as he went on, as if he had been giving the matter a great deal of contemplation.

'One should never expect too much, that is the trick. If you do not expect too much, then you can never be disappointed. Those of us who are used to the ways of the world can shrug our shoulders when things do not go as we planned.'

'And have things not gone as you planned, Duke? I am sorry to hear it. Perhaps I can help them take a more agreeable turn?'

She sounded breathless, the words forced out of her. Miranda had never thought it would be so difficult to lead him on, to play the flirt. Even though he deserved everything that was coming to him, she felt soiled by her part in it.

'Perhaps.' He laughed, one of his abrupt laughs. 'Do you know, Countess, sometimes I think you are a chameleon. You are one thing one moment, then another the next. How do you do it?'

'Chameleons are very ugly creatures,' Miranda replied airily. 'I would hate to think I resembled anything with eyes that swivel all about. Surely you are more practised at compliments than that, Duke?'

'Oh, I am practised at many things.'

His voice was cold, but his eyes were bright with emotion. Was it anger? Just for a second, Miranda was fooled into thinking he really cared, and then she remembered his reputation and her broken heart, and put aside her doubt.

She pouted like a spoiled child. 'I did not think an evening with you would be so dull, Leo. You have not even kissed me yet. You always kiss me, every time we meet you kiss me. Why do you not kiss me now?'

Leo smiled, looking even more like his ancestor. He reached out and caught her chin, turning her face this way and that, as though he were inspecting it for flaws.

'You are very lovely,' he said dispassionately.

In a moment, she thought, he will make his move. In a moment the game will be over.

'I wonder…is your hair really that colour?'

Miranda froze. His intimation was clear, but still she questioned it, not quite believing she had heard him aright. 'I beg your pardon?'

'Your hair, Countess. The colour. Is it your own?'

He had done this to her before, turned the tables on her, caught her unawares. Her bewilderment was almost comical.

'I ask,' he went on smoothly, 'because although I have a weakness for redheads, I am particular as to the colour.'

'Particular?' she repeated impatiently. 'Does it make a difference?'

'Very much so! I do not like cheap imitations.'

Again there was danger in the smile he gave her.

Miranda stilled, every particle of her being alert. She moved to pull away from his hand, which was still loosely holding her chin, but he prevented her by sliding his other arm about her waist. Their embrace was anything but amorous as they stood close, breathing fast, she glaring and he mocking.

'Of course this is my natural colour,' she said at last.

He ran his fingers up into the gleaming mass, dislodging numerous hair pins, so that the heavy tresses came down about her shoulders. He bent closer and appeared to breathe in the scent of her hair.

'What are you doing?' she asked in astonishment.

'I am testing the merchandise, Countess, and I can now say that, though you are many things, you are not a cheap imitation.'

'Thank you.' Her voice shook only slightly as she tucked a tickling curl behind her ear. 'I am glad I am up to your high standards. Now let me go.'

Briefly she thought he would, as he ran his thumb back and forth across the shining strands he still held. And then she realised he was teasing her, for he laughed softly and repeated, 'Let you go? No, Countess, I won't let you go, not yet. You've asked me to kiss you, and I want to. I think, after all you've put me through, I deserve a kiss.'

All *she*'d put *him* through!

Now when his arms closed around her, all gentleness had gone. Her body felt moulded to his, a part of him, not separate at all. As his lips closed over hers she was aware of every hard, masculine inch of him. He kissed her with, if not quite brutality, then certainly a determined thoroughness.

Tears filled Miranda's eyes. This was different than

before. She did not know how or why, but the tingling emotion that had always filled her previously when he kissed her was missing. What he was doing now was teaching her a lesson.

Miranda struggled, pushing against his chest, but nothing seemed to do any good. And then, just when she thought she could bear it no more, he drew back a little and, breathing hard, stared down into her face.

Her mouth was red and swollen, and there were tears in her eyes and on her cheeks. She looked young and angry and frightened. But, worse than that, she looked betrayed.

Leo, whose intention, he supposed, had been to show her he cared no more for her than she did for him, was ashamed. Before he could remind himself that this emotion was all pretence on her part, he had bent and, with a groan, begun to kiss her salty eyelids.

'Oh, Miranda,' he breathed. She gave a little hiccup, and he followed the line of her tears, using his tongue to lap them up in a manner which made her feel quite giddy.

Gasping, lips parted, Miranda waited. And was not disappointed. Leo's mouth closed on hers once more, but although urgent, this was a far different kiss from the last one.

This time her lips softened beneath his, responsively, eagerly, and her arms crept about his neck. Leo felt the ice inside him melting, a thaw of monumental proportions. And he knew that he had been wrong. Nothing had changed. She still held him in thrall and, no matter what she did or said, his heart was bound fast to hers.

If she knew it, she would ruin him.

He rested his cheek upon the top of her head and took a deep breath. 'I hope that has made up for some of this evening's disappointments.'

'I believe it has,' she murmured, equally breathless. Her arms were reluctant to let him go, the fingers of one hand playing with the silky hair at his nape.

'Miranda?'

'Yes?'

Should he say it? Probably not. But he was going to. He couldn't help himself. Possibly she knew it, too, for her voice had held all the reluctance of one about to be told something they did not wish to hear.

'I have known Frederick Harmon for years. He's a bad sort. Leave him.'

She went rigid. 'L-leave Mr Harmon?'

'Yes. I don't care what he's been to you. I don't want to know. I won't ask. Just leave him, now, to-night.'

Very calmly, she said, 'Well, that is very tolerant of you, Duke. You are accusing me of being Mr Harmon's...of monstrous things. I suppose now, to top it all off, you will offer me a *carte blanche?*'

He tried to read her eyes but they were blazing with so many emotions he didn't know where to start. Leo had wanted to see how far she would go in her quest to push him to the highest price. Now he thought he knew just how far that was. Something cold ran through his blood, something pitiless.

'I want you, I won't deny it. What price do you place upon yourself, Miranda? Remember, I may be a wealthy man, but I am not a fool. Yes, I will make an offer. Do you want it in writing, or will a hand-shake do?'

She appeared to sway slightly, and then she had jerked free of his arms. 'I know very well what you are!' she cried, and stood facing him, panting slightly, her hair a halo about her, her face flushed and so angry that despite himself he was struck dumb with admiration.

Why was she insulted? he wondered. How could one insult a woman such as the Decadent Countess? Had he not given her the answer she wanted? Was she not after his money after all?

Miranda didn't notice his confusion. She was blinded to everything by her hot mist of fury and triumph.

'I knew it!' she burst out. 'It *is* true. Mr Harmon told me, and yet I hoped… But you are the worst of men. Do you really think you can buy love with your money? Do you imagine you can blacken a good man's character because you are a Duke? I hate and despise you. I would never stay with you, not for a year, not for a minute. Nothing you could say would tempt me. Nothing!'

By now Leo had recovered himself. She had all but offered herself to him, and then, when he accepted that offer, turned around and humiliated him.

She was even worse than he had imagined.

'I wish to leave,' Miranda announced in a choked voice. 'I will walk if necessary, but I will not spend another moment in the same house with you.'

He ran a hand through his hair and closed his eyes. Suddenly his distaste for her, and himself, was more than he could bear. He wanted to get drunk...very drunk.

'Yes, I quite agree,' he murmured, and moved to ring for a servant. 'But there is no need to walk, Countess. You shall leave as you came. I trust it is clear that I never wish to see you again?'

'And I never wish to see you again!'

She had never seen him look so bleak. 'I will, of course, pay for your passage home to Italy, and will deal with The Grange. Whatever else you may choose to think of me, you may trust me to send on any of your belongings which—'

'You are mistaken.' Her tone was icy. 'I am not leaving The Grange. Be quite sure that I will remain there until my dying day. Please remove your servants from my home, I neither need them nor wish to be further beholden to you. In fact, render me an account of their wages, and I will settle it as soon as possible!'

He laughed.

God rot him, he laughed.

Miranda walked past him, her head held high. She told herself that, although it had not quite worked out as she had planned, she had more or less achieved what she set out to. He had made his offer, and she had refused him. There was an end to it.

Why then did she feel no exhilaration, why did she feel no self-congratulation on her success? In short, why did she want to sink down and cry?

Above her, the painted birds silently fluttered. Miranda did not notice them. She did not notice the pink marble. She passed a footman in a smart blue uniform as if he did not exist, and descended towards the smart carriage, which was waiting at the bottom of the steps.

Lonely darkness encircled her, and the vehicle lurched into motion, turning to make its stately way down the drive.

Yes, she would rejoice in this moment all her life. She would remember again and again the look in his eyes when she told him what she thought of him.

With a heart-wrenching sob, Miranda buried her face in her gloved hands.

Leo stood at the window and watched her go. He had never felt so wretched before in all of his life. The knowledge that she had played him for a fool was bad enough, but worse even than that was knowing that, in the end, he'd forgotten his pride, his position, everything, and been willing to sacrifice it all to her.

And she hadn't wanted it.

He turned away and reached for the brandy.

'Do you think that will help, Leo?'

Tina stood in the shadows, watching him. She was still dressed in her red velvet gown, although she had let her hair down. It lay in a gleaming dark cloak about her shoulders. She looked like the little sister he remembered. Perhaps that was why he spoke to her so patiently.

'If I drink enough of it, I should think it will help. Go to bed, my dear, and let me get on with it.'

'Leo, what is the matter? You were so happy yesterday, and I thought that… What has gone wrong?

And don't try to flummox me, for I am wise to your ways!'

He moved to pour a glass and, lifting the cut crystal, swirled the brandy against the light of the tall candles.

'I was duped, Tina. Your wise and clever brother was duped. That is all. Now, if you will leave me—'

But instead of leaving him, Tina took several steps into the room. 'Oh, Leo, how could you? It was nothing…a little subterfuge. You could have overlooked it, surely? The fault was as much yours as hers!'

Leo turned to stare at her.

Tina hesitated, trying to read the expression on his face. 'Leo? What did you say to her? Perhaps I can mend it—'

'Mend it!' he cried, clenching his fingers about the glass until his knuckles turned white. 'How can you *mend it?* The woman is every bit as bad as she has been portrayed. Worse! Jack came to me this morning with the news that a certain gentleman has arrived in the village, and that gentleman is a particular friend of the Countess. They were together in London, and now they are together here. What is there in such a tale not to understand?'

Tina frowned and shook her head. 'But I don't understand. Miranda would not… You are mistaken, Leo.'

Leo sighed and came to take her hand. 'I know it is painful to learn one has been lied to, Tina. Believe me, I know. Forget Miranda. Go home to your family. I will deal with my problems in my own way.'

'Oh, Leo!' Tina snapped, and pulled her hand

away. 'I know you mean well. Only... What *has* that silly girl done!' She hesitated, glanced at his puzzled, ravaged face, and then seemed to make up her mind.

'There is something I am going to tell you. Brace yourself, Leo, for if you are feeling foolish now, you will feel much worse presently!'

Chapter Eleven

Miranda had not slept well. Most of the night, she had lain with her eyes open and staring into the darkness, wishing she had never met Leo Fitzgibbon, Duke of Belford. The few times she had managed to fall into a restless slumber, she had dreamed in lurid colours and twisted shapes, and had been glad to wake again.

No, it had not been a good night for Miranda, and the day to come didn't promise to be any better.

The letter to Mr Ealing remained to be written, but the urgency had gone. What did it matter if she had to live on burnt toast and break the ice on her washing water every morning? Who would care? Certainly not Leo. He had made that plain last night.

He had not even cared when she abused him, not really. All he had wanted was for her to be gone from his house. Probably he already had another victim lined up. Well, she could comfort herself with the thought that, although they may never again meet face to face, Miranda would always be a presence here at The Grange, a reminder of his one failure.

Each time his eyes strayed in this direction he would remember, perhaps feel a sting of regret, wonder if maybe he allowed his one chance of happiness to slip by. He would—

Miranda stopped herself.

Considering the way in which things were presently going, she did not even know whether or not she'd have a home next week, let alone grow old and grey here. Leo, the new Leo she had so recently unmasked, would seek revenge. And what better way to revenge himself than to destroy her one chance of a settled, happy, safe life?

She didn't believe it.

Not in her heart. That was the trouble. Whatever her mind told her, she just couldn't believe that he would ever hurt her. The conflict was tearing her in two.

Pendle tapped politely on the door. 'You sent Esme to fetch me, madam?'

'Yes, Pendle, come in.'

His entry into the parlour was almost tentative. He did not look at all intimidating this morning, his usual sour expression twisted into something almost, but not quite, resembling a smile.

Now that Miranda paused to deliberate, she realised Pendle's behaviour had changed. It was as if her laughing at him had reversed their roles in some way. Instead of treating her with his usual disdain he seemed almost in awe of her.

Well, that aside, she had a speech prepared and it must be said.

'I did want to speak to you, Pendle. I have decided I can manage quite well now without your help. Assemble the Duke's other servants and prepare to leave.'

Pendle blinked. 'I beg your pardon, madam, but I fear you grossly overestimate Esme's abilities. You must realise that—'

'I am not in a state to argue with you.'

'I can see that, madam,' he replied with some of his old panache.

Despite her present grim situation, laughter bubbled in her throat. Good God, was she going mad? The thought sobered her.

'Do as I have asked, Pendle. The time has come for you to return to Ormiston where you belong. The matter is out of your hands. No arguments, Pendle.'

'No, madam.'

'Well—' she smiled her relief '—it is for the best, you know, and—'

'I mean, "no, madam", I will not go.'

'Pendle, please—'

The sound of a horse outside caused her to stop abruptly. Miranda clicked her tongue in annoyance. She did not want to see anyone; she was not up to seeing anyone. She only hoped it was not Tina come to plead her brother's case, or heap more abuse on her.

Pendle peered towards the window and then said in a smug voice, 'We will be able to ask the Duke himself to decide on the matter, madam. I believe he has just arrived.'

All her thoughts spiralled down to one, single word.

No!

Miranda sprang from her chair in a singularly unladylike manner, startling Pendle into scuttling to safety behind a spindly-legged table. She went to the window and leaned close to the numerous small panes, her breath clouding the glass. Was she dreaming? But no, while *she* might be capable of hallucinating, Pendle was not. It was definitely Leo.

Gripping the sill, she stared wide-eyed. His face was set and grim beneath his top hat, and pale from lack of sleep. The fact that he was perfectly turned out in a dark blue riding jacket and fawn breeches, with Hessian boots polished to a mirror-like gleam, seemed suddenly and terribly incongruous. He should be wearing black armour and waving a sword!

Perhaps she made some movement for, as he dismounted, Leo looked in her direction.

Miranda jumped back. Memories of last night, the current expression of tired fury in his face, her pain and humiliation, *everything* swooped down on her. As far as she could see there was only one option.

Flight.

She spun around, and almost knocked Pendle over, who had followed her to the window.

'No,' she wailed. 'I cannot speak to him!'

'M-madam?' Pendle actually stammered.

'I will not speak to him, Pendle! Do not ask it.'

'But, madam, the Duke…'

'No, Pendle!'

And with that, Miranda turned and bolted.

Leo should know that her wounds were still too painful and raw. How could she bear to have such fresh hurts pressed and prodded? He should have the sensitivity to realise! But, of course, there was the rub. Leo Fitzgibbon had no sensitivity. He had nothing but cold, heartless, ruthless, arrogance.

Miranda had reached the top of the stairs before the ridiculousness of her action occurred to her. This was *her* home. If she did not wish to see the Duke of Belford, then she need not. She could send him away, or better still, she could ask Pendle to send him away.

And yet Pendle was Leo's servant, loyal to Leo. Why should he protect her privacy from his real master? Miranda groaned and clutched her head, slumping against the wall in the upstairs gallery. Why had he come anyway? What more could they possibly have to say to each other?

Didn't he know it was over?

'Where is she?' Leo's voice echoed from below. He sounded as though he was speaking through clenched teeth.

Miranda stilled, her heart battering against her ribs so hard it seemed to be trying to escape.

Pendle's voice was stout but a little high. Remembering Leo's expression, she could understand his alarm. 'Your Grace, Mrs Fitzgibbon is not able to see you just now.'

Miranda took a ragged breath. Good old Pendle. She would never doubt him again.

'Not able to see me!' Leo shouted. Though, thought

Miranda, shouted was too polite a word for it. He roared. 'I don't believe it, Pendle! I know she's here. Fetch her at once. I want to speak with her. I want to ask her why she lied to me. She is no more a countess than I am!'

He knew the truth about her. Tina must have told him. Even as she cringed, Miranda could not in her heart blame Lady Clementina. Leo was her brother and her first loyalty was to him. However, the truth coming out had complicated an already mind-bogglingly complex tangle.

Or had it simplified matters?

Down in the hall, Leo was still ranting like a man possessed. At least I will no longer have to pretend to be Adela, thought Miranda. I can be Miranda now, I can be myself. The acknowledgment was comforting, and gave her back the courage which for a moment had deserted her. With a silent prayer, Miranda stepped up to the gallery railing and peered down into the hall.

'Your Grace.' Pendle was actually wringing his hands. 'Please, you must go. Go home and recover yourself. I will tell her—'

Leo prowled back and forth like a large caged beast.

'I will not go home! I want to speak to her now! I want to know why she did not tell me the truth when she had numerous opportunities to do so! I want to take her by the neck and—'

'I did not tell you the truth because I was afraid of just such an outburst as this.'

He stopped in mid-stride, so abruptly he might well

have been shot. He looked up, and his blue eyes were blazing. She stood in the shadows, but her face was clear enough, a pale, lovely oval as she gazed down upon him.

Leo felt something deep within himself catch and hold its breath, as if time itself had stopped. When he spoke his voice was hoarse with emotion.

'And do you think you do not deserve to be abused, madam, after what you have put me through?'

'I think it only fair you suffer as you made me suffer with your rudeness and arrogance.'

'Oh, it is *I* who am rude and arrogant, is it?' he burst out in evident disbelief.

'For goodness' sake, stop shouting! What must the servants think?'

'I don't care what they think. They are my servants anyway.'

'Yes, and you can take them away with you. I don't want your help anymore. I do not need it. I am sure Mr Harmon will assist me in engaging the services of replacement staff.'

His face went a violent red. She thought he was going to fly up the stairs at her, he was so enraged. Instead he gave a heartfelt groan and drove his hands into his hair.

'You are driving me mad!' he said.

Miranda raised her eyebrows. It was strange, but the angrier Leo became the calmer she felt. 'You are certainly in the throes of madness, but whether it was I who caused it is open to speculation.'

Pendle made a sound and tottered towards a chair, but they both ignored him.

Leo, who was looking up at her again, appeared to lose some of his wildness. When he spoke it was in a harsh but much more moderate tone.

'I can only think that it amused you to pretend you were something you were not. That you thought to teach me a lesson in some childish, ill-considered manner.'

'As it amused you to try and drive me from my home, in between pestering me with your unwelcome attentions.'

An echo of his previous rage kindled in his eye, but he mastered it. 'You alter our past history to suit your own purposes, madam.'

'We have no past history. Go away, I do not want to see you today. I do not want to see you any day.'

He stared at her a moment longer, but even he could hardly drag her screaming down the stairs. With a muffled curse that brought stinging colour to her cheeks, he turned and left as abruptly as he had come.

Leo did not go home.

He could not face his sister, not yet. She had told him not to come, that it would be best to wait a day or two and allow Miranda to cool down and reconsider. Had he listened to her? No, he had not. Patience no longer seemed to be one of his virtues.

When he had learned last night that Miranda was not, after all, the Decadent Countess, he had wanted to ride immediately to The Grange, though it was past midnight. He had wanted to drag her from her bed and shake her until her teeth rattled.

Tina had prevailed upon him then. Perhaps she had

thought that waiting would cool his hot head? If so, she had been mistaken. The long hours had only increased his sense of grievance, for he kept remembering more and more instances of her perfidy. Until, when he set out this morning, his anger had been near ungovernable.

As he rode swiftly towards his objective, he had thought that he would find the necessary words when the time came. He had never lost his temper before he met her—he was famous for his forbearance. He was confident his good breeding would enable him to give her the sort of polite but freezing set-down she deserved.

But as soon as Leo had stepped over the threshold all breeding, good or otherwise, had failed him. In short, he had become a raving lunatic.

He groaned aloud.

He had behaved in a manner that was an insult to his name and position. No one who had seen him this morning could possibly recognise the urbane and tranquil Leo Fitzgibbon. Was Miranda right? Had he run mad? Well, if indeed he had, it was her fault. She had driven him past sanity. He did not think he would ever be sane again! Unless…unless he could have her.

Leo sighed and slowed his stallion as he accepted the painful acknowledgment.

He wanted her.

Even last night he had wanted her, even then, when he had believed her totally ill suited to partner a man in his position. But still he would have pigheadedly gone against all good sense and good advice, and married her. Done anything, just to be with her.

Why could he not have told her so this morning when he had the chance, instead of once more abusing her so thoroughly? And if somehow, overnight, she had found it within herself to forgive him…why would she want to align herself with a lunatic, be he a Duke or otherwise?

The point was moot—she wouldn't forgive him.

How could she, after his treatment of her since she had arrived in England? She was Julian's widow and, according to Tina, a girl of gentle nature making the best of a difficult position. She had come to him for his help and support, just as Julian had advised her. And what had he done?

'Oh, God.'

Leo could hardly bear to recall what he had done. It did no good to remember that Tina had shared the blame equally between himself and Miranda. If he had behaved better, then she would have been able to disclose the truth to him sooner, and last night would never have happened. Instead he had driven her into a corner, and she had fought him valiantly with the only weapons she had in her possession.

No, she would never forgive him now. And he could not even warn her against Harmon—God knew how such a man had got his hooks into her!—without her believing he had some ulterior motive.

Leo lifted his head. Perhaps he could do some good in that quarter, after all. He looked around him, as though coming out of a dream, and realised he was not too far from the village. He would visit the Rose. If he could no longer help Miranda directly, then he would do so indirectly.

It was time he and Mr Harmon had words.

* * *

It was close on midday when Sophie Lethbridge called at The Grange.

Pendle came to inform her of it, and appeared a good deal recovered from this morning's episode. Miranda, less well recovered, replied that, yes, she was at home to Miss Lethbridge, and it was only the Duke who was forbidden entry.

'If you do not begin packing now, Pendle, you will not reach Ormiston before dark,' she added, as he turned to leave.

Pendle cleared his throat. 'I think after this morning I must ask you to allow me to remain a little longer, madam. I would prefer his Grace regained his good humour before I resumed my duties at Ormiston.'

She took pity on him. 'Very well, but only a little longer, Pendle.'

'Thank you, madam.' It was heartfelt.

Miranda's mood lightened. She even found a smile as Sophie entered the parlour. Ever the optimist, she hoped that in Sophie she would find a true friend, one who would not judge her as harshly as Leo for her foolish and ill-considered behaviour.

'Sophie, how do you do?'

They were the only words she was able to utter for several minutes.

Sophie began to speak, her words falling over each other in their hurry to get out. She caught Miranda's hands in hers, squeezing them so tightly it was almost painful. Miranda, secretly wondering if it was her fault all her neighbours had run mad, managed to make soothing noises while at the same time struggling to make sense of the garbled recital.

It went something like this.

'Jack has said that that dreadful Mr Harmon is here and that you are his friend! More than his friend, although I cannot...I will not have it so. Tell me it is not true, Miranda, for I cannot believe you would encourage the attentions of such a man? He is vile. Jack says that if it is true, then we may no longer be friends, and that, besides, you are leaving The Grange to return to Italy. Oh, please say you are not going! Why are you returning to Italy? Jack says that Leo has sent you away because you are ''not as you ought to be'', but he will not tell me more. He can be so stupidly stubborn sometimes. Oh please, please, answer me, for I cannot bear to be held in suspense any longer!'

Miranda, who had turned pale and then pink in turn during Sophie's speech, found her voice.

'I will answer you, Sophie, if you will but give me a chance to do so! Firstly, I am not going back to Italy. No one is sending me anywhere. Secondly, you say that your brother has told you that Mr Harmon is here in the village? Does he too know Mr Harmon? Were they also at school together? Oh, Sophie, then you must know about Leo?'

Sophie gave her a curious look. '''Know about Leo''? I do not understand you, Miranda. We all know about Mr Harmon! He is a terrible man. How could you possibly be his friend?'

The girl was almost in tears. Sophie might be a trifle flighty, but Miranda had never doubted her respectability. If Sophie said that Mr Harmon was terrible, then he was.

Miranda sat down abruptly on the sofa.

'Mr Harmon is a relative of my stepmama,' she explained. 'He has come to visit because he is concerned for me, that is all.'

Sophie shook her head, and arranged herself neatly on the sofa by Miranda's side. A solitary tear slid down her cheek. She searched in her reticule with trembling hands and found a small scrap of lace.

'He is a horrid man, Miranda. It is *his* fault that my season was a disaster. He made up to me, you see, and when Jack learned of it, he warned him off. Jack had known him at school, and he was very bad even then. But when he told me I did not believe it, or rather I thought it did not matter. Mr Harmon made me feel that I could change him. I could save him. That, without me, he would sink into the pit. They were his words, Miranda, ''the pit''!'

'I see.' And she did. Such romantic nonsense would appeal to a girl like Sophie.

A second tear had joined the first. Sophie mopped at them ineffectually. 'I was very silly. I thought it was all right to do such things, because he loved me and I loved him. Of course, it all came out. I was lucky, because he had not quite persuaded me to run off with him, not yet. In a day or two, I might well have done, because there is something very appealing about running for the border. Leaving all behind for love. Riding pillion in the snow…though of course one could not be sure it would be snowing. It would depend upon the time of year one went, I suppose.'

She sighed and shook her head.

'Jack and Leo made certain there was no scandal, although really it was Leo who did everything. Jack was so angry he could hardly speak, which is most unusual for Jack, and just shows you how deeply he felt the whole thing. Don't you agree?'

Miranda hardly knew whether she agreed or not. She sat staring at the other girl as she dabbed at her eyes, and for a time was quite unable to reply. She felt that she should strongly refute such allegations. That she should explain that Mr Harmon had been nothing but kind to her and that she would no longer listen to such accusations.

But she didn't.

Apart from the fact that she had no reason to doubt Sophie was being completely honest with her, something in the other girl's recital struck a chord in Miranda. There had been moments when she was with Mr Harmon when she hadn't quite believed him either.

'Do you mean to say,' she said, 'that Mr Harmon is the sort of man who would make up to a young girl in order to marry her for her fortune?'

Sophie gave a watery giggle. 'You don't mince words, do you, Miranda? Yes, he is.' She stopped, struck by a new thought. 'He has not been trying to make up to you, too? I did not think of that. Perhaps you will be glad I have warned you, even though Jack told me that I must not speak to you any more, or come to see you, or be your—your friend, because of Mr Harmon. But I do so much want to be your f-friend, Miranda.'

Sophie's lip wobbled, and then she burst into noisy sobs.

This time it was more difficult to comfort her, though Miranda did her best, reassuring Sophie that she was still her friend and had not been made up to by Mr Harmon. Although he had been pretending to be respectable, and it now appeared that he certainly was not. Perhaps, in hindsight, Mr Harmon's lack of respectability was not so surprising, considering that he was Adela's cousin.

'He came to see me because my stepmama asked him to,' Miranda went on, when Sophie was quiet. 'She was worried about me.'

Sophie gulped and her eyes flashed angrily. 'You make him sound almost chivalrous, but he is not, Miranda! Oh, I am so glad you do not like him either. I'm so glad we can still speak to each other and see each other and be friends!'

Miranda patted her hand, and wondered if Sophie was up to more questions. The ravages of her tears had almost faded already, and apart from a slight pinkness about the eyes, she seemed remarkably pretty for a girl who had just cried her heart out.

'Sophie, I must ask you something.'

'Oh!' Sophie straightened herself, smoothing out her skirts and touching at her hair. 'All right, I'm ready.'

'Sophie. Is Leo a loose fish?'

Sophie's mouth opened in a perfect O.

'Is the question too blunt? I have not shocked you?'

Sophie shook her hand. 'No, I am not shocked.' And indeed she did not appear shocked, only thoughtful. 'I believe I do know what a ''loose fish'' is, because I have heard Jack use the expression, so I can answer your question. No, I don't think he is. He has had love affairs, of course. He is quite old, you know. But he has never been the least bit ungentlemanly, and Jack would never have wanted me to marry him if his character was in doubt. Jack may be silly sometimes, but he is a very good brother. Why? Do you think he is one?'

Miranda took a deep breath and shook her head. 'No, I don't. I can't believe now that I ever did. Perhaps I didn't believe it, not really, although I tried very hard to.'

Memories of last night flashed into her mind, but Miranda forced them back. No, she would save the self-flagellation for later.

'Why did you believe Leo was a—a loose fish, Miranda? Did he tell you so himself?'

Miranda met Sophie's curious green eyes. 'No. Mr Harmon told me he was. I think he did it because he believed that I…that I would repeat what he said. He wanted to cause a fight between us.'

'Well, isn't that just like him! He hates Leo, you know. He'd do anything to made Leo uncomfortable.'

'Was Mr Harmon very angry with Leo and Jack for spoiling his runaway marriage to you?'

'Oh, prodigiously!'

Perhaps that, then, had been his reason for the mischief he had made. Miranda felt oddly calm and collected, which was a strange thing to feel when she had just ruined her entire life because of a pack of lies told to her by a fortune-hunter with a grudge.

Sophie rose to her feet with a bounce.

'Do you know, I feel so much better! I knew Jack could not have it right. He even told me that you were not a proper lady!'

'He has me confused with someone else,' Miranda replied with an effort. 'I am sure he will soon tell you that himself.'

'If he does not, then I shall certainly tell him he was wrong, don't you worry! Oh, Miranda, I nearly forgot. How silly of me. I wanted to give you this.'

She reached into her reticule and removed a card. On it was printed an invitation to the long-awaited Lethbridge party. Miranda took it from her very carefully, almost as if she were afraid it might bite.

'Oh, Sophie,' she breathed, 'I don't know if I can—'

'Don't you dare refuse, Miranda! You cannot allow Mr Harmon to spoil everything. You will come, and Jack will be there, and of course Leo, and…and everyone, and it will all turn out very nicely. No one dares to misbehave at a Lethbridge party.'

Miranda stared at her friend in wonder, and then she laughed. 'I believe you are right, Sophie. No one would dare.'

'There, you see,' cried Sophie, a gleam in her green eyes. 'You are feeling better already!'

Chapter Twelve

As Miranda turned from sending Sophie on her way, she found Pendle hovering about behind her and making rather alarming faces.

'I will see no more visitors today, Pendle. In fact I want no more visitors, ever!'

'I'm sorry, madam, I would grant your wish if I could, but unfortunately you have Mr Harmon awaiting you in the garden.'

Miranda stared in a manner more bewildered than angry. 'What is Mr Harmon doing in the garden?'

'He was in the house, madam, but when he heard Miss Lethbridge's voice he became quite agitated, and scampered through the side door into the garden.'

'Scampered?'

'Yes, madam. That is the only word I can think of which properly describes his movements. I thought it best to leave him there until Miss Lethbridge had left. Perhaps he is a little touched in the upperworks, madam.'

Miranda made a tart reply. 'Why not? Everyone else seems to be.'

'Yes, madam,' said Pendle, with feeling.

'Very well! I will go and see him in the garden. And, Pendle?'

Pendle leaned toward her, his manner most subservient, while at the same time alert for new instructions.

'Don't allow Mr Harmon into The Grange again. He is no longer welcome. Do you understand?'

'I do indeed, madam. Neither the Duke nor Mr Harmon are to be allowed admittance to your presence.'

'Exactly, Pendle.'

Miranda made her way into the garden. It had clearly been a wilderness for years, but new growth had turned roses and flowering shrubs quite rampant. She paused a moment to enjoy the sunshine and the mingled outdoor scents, thinking it was a little like the garden in a fairytale. Only there was no chance of a prince cutting his way through this wall of thorns to wake her with a kiss.

As if he had been awaiting the chance to pounce, her head was suddenly full of Leo. A fog of despair all but took her breath away. What a fool she had been! How could she have taken the word of a man like Harmon over someone like Leo? All along her heart had been trying to tell her the path she should take, but she had ignored it and followed another.

Now she would pay the price with a lifetime of unhappiness.

Even this morning, when he had come ranting to her door, she might have salvaged the situation. She might have… Well, thought Miranda, perhaps not. Leo had wanted to murder her. A bright flicker of anger stirred the murky depths of her misery. He had been very rude. As if it had all been her fault, when anyone could see that the bulk of the problem was his.

If Leo had not made that arrogant assumption in the drawing room in the house in Berkeley Square, none of the rest of it would have followed. If he would once apologise for… He *had* apologised. He had apologised when he came to see her and she had been sorting in the linen cupboard. And then he had kissed her, and she had thought, foolishly as it happened, that everything would be all right.

Tears stung her eyes.

'Blast and damn it!'

The exclamation was so in keeping with her own thoughts that for a bizarre moment Miranda believed she must have spoken aloud. And then, of course, she realised that she had not and that the voice had belonged to Mr Harmon.

He was stooped over beside a huge mound of roses, tugging furiously where his trousers had caught upon a particularly vicious thorn. His violent action was causing the rose flowers to fall in a cascade of white and pink petals all about him.

'Mr Harmon?'

The trousers came free with a faint but ominous ripping sound. Mr Harmon straightened and adjusted his apparel with a couple of angry tugs. His hair, usually so carefully arranged, was rather unkempt, a lock falling across his forehead, a couple of rose petals decorating his crown. He smoothed it impatiently. He looked very cross, almost a stranger. As Miranda watched, he reset his features by the same mechanism of tugs and adjustments into the amiable gentleman she had always believed him to be.

'Miranda!' he cried, as if he had not been playing tug-of-war with a plant, and strolled towards her. He meant, she supposed, to take her hand and kiss it in his usual manner. As Miranda waited, she supposed she should be angry with him. He had stolen her happiness because of his own vendetta against Leo. Had he known she was in love with the Duke when he did it, or was it simply that he didn't care? Whatever the extent of the damage, he had knowingly caused it.

She *should* be angry.

Instead she felt a sort of irritable impatience. Mr Harmon was, on reflection, not a man worth hating. He was a figure who clearly longed to be in the limelight, but the fact was he would always be one of the lesser performers. She no longer liked him, no longer trusted him, but neither could she hate him as he probably deserved.

Mr Harmon captured her hand but, when he bent to press his lips to her knuckles, Miranda quickly withdrew it and placed it behind her back. He stilled and looked up at her, his brown eyes suddenly very sharp as they examined her face. Like a fox that has been caught robbing a nest.

In a moment the impression was gone, and he was smiling benevolently once more.

'Your garden is absolutely blooming, Miranda. For some reason it puts me in mind of the lines of a poem

I once read. If you have no objection, I will recite them to you.'

'I do object. This is neither the time nor place for poetry, Mr Harmon.'

He smiled, but his eyes remained watchful. 'Surely there is always a time and place for poetry, my dear?'

'I am not ''your dear'', and I have heard some very unpleasant facts about *you,* Mr Harmon. I think you know what they are.'

Frederick Harmon looked pained. 'Ah, I understand. Believe me, if it was up to me, Miranda, I would not have spoken. I do not believe in telling malicious tales. But it appears that others are not so scrupulous, and if I must defend my honour, then I must.'

Miranda opened her mouth to cut in on this bold avowal, but Mr Harmon held up his hand to prevent her and, other than shout above him, she had perforce to listen to what she expected to be a tissue of lies.

'Sophie Lethbridge appears to be a sweet girl. Her face, her manner, her smile, all inspire one to believe she is as good as she is beautiful. I did believe, and I gave my heart to her. Alas, she is not as she appears. That lovely face hides a serpent. Imagine my despair when, instead of honouring her promises to me, she jilted me most cruelly? And the reason? Because I was not rich enough for her! She may have held some small regard for me, I do not know. Certainly she did not love me as I loved her. But she had no qualms about sacrificing our love at the altar of Mammon.'

He had worked himself up into quite a state. Perhaps part of him believed what he was saying, but

Miranda was quite sure Sophie would not recognise herself in the tale he was telling.

'If anyone worships at Mammon's altar then it is you, Mr Harmon,' Miranda informed him coldly. 'Once I might have listened to you and accepted your lies, but now I see you are a scoundrel. Miss Lethbridge wants you gone from the neighbourhood, and so do I.'

He gasped and appeared shocked to the core, but again Miranda wasn't deceived. At least, she told herself, he had been useful in educating her in the detection of cads. She would never be quite so gullible again.

'Miranda, I beg of you! Adela will be heartbroken if she hears you and I have fallen out. She is quite depending upon me to—'

'Did you really receive a letter from Adela?' Miranda asked, not really expecting to hear the truth.

Mr Harmon did not disappoint her. 'Of course I did! She is very concerned. She begged me to watch over you. How can I tell her that you have taken the word of others over mine and sent me from your side? Miranda, you are in danger and they are all in cahoots against me. Once I am out of the way, you will be at their mercy. There will be no one to watch over you.'

Miranda bit her lip. There was really nothing amusing in what he was saying, and yet she felt like laughing in his face. Too much drama in the one day, she supposed. It had made her light-headed.

'Then you had best write back to her, telling her that I am perfectly well and happy, and that I have relieved you of the onerous duty of ''watching over me''.'

'Miranda, please—'

'Goodbye, Mr Harmon.'

He wanted to say more, and may well have done so, but Pendle appeared behind him and stood waiting in ominous silence to escort him on his away. Mr Harmon, spying him there, turned his gaze from Miranda to her servant and back again. His expression changed, hardened, the easy friendliness dropping from him like the rose petals in his hair.

'Very well,' he said. 'I will go. Once again Belford triumphs. But it will not always be so.'

'Come, Mr Harmon, this way.' Pendle spoke in his most superior manner, his mouth twitching as though he had drunk vinegar. Quite like his old self.

When they had gone, Mr Harmon stalking crossly ahead of the relentless Pendle, Miranda did not immediately follow. She preferred to linger amongst the overgrown shrubs and flowerbeds. It was peaceful here, and her thoughts wandered sadly through the maze of her life since she left Italy.

She looked about. Perhaps there had once been a maze here too, in the flesh, as it were. And Elizabethan knots and bowers, where lovers could sit and make their plans, and steal secret kisses. No doubt Fitzgibbon and his wife had strolled together, hands clasped, and dreamed of founding a dynasty.

A pity such happiness would never be hers and Leo's.

Mr Harmon had done what he had come to do. He had destroyed any chance of her finding happiness.

Nothing she could possibly say or do would ever restore her to Belford's affections. He would never forgive her now, and she could not blame him for it.

Mr Harmon had almost reached the Rose. He was footsore and weary, and neither had improved his temper. He had gone to The Grange hoping for at least a glass of ratafia and a piece of cake, and instead he had been turned out like an unwelcome tradesman.

It was too bad.

He had travelled to Somerset with such high hopes. He had spent considerable sums of money, which he could ill spare, on new clothing, as well as coach fare, inns, et cetera. In his most optimistic moments, he had dreamed of vanquishing Belford and himself winning Miranda's hand. She was not wealthy, of course, far from it, but she owned the house and land that Belford coveted.

What a triumph if she chose him over the Duke!

But he was generally a practical man—he had to be—and he had known it was unlikely Miranda would marry him. It had been enough that she considered him a friend, and would have in time, he was sure, come to lean heavily upon his advice. How he would have enjoyed burrowing, like a tick, into Leo's skin, itching infernally but always just out of reach. He could have driven Belford beyond the limits of his famous caution, and maybe even made himself a small fortune in the process.

But now it was over. All that time and effort, not to mention credit, wasted.

Sophie Lethbridge, that Jezebel, had put her dainty

foot in it, and Miranda had judged him, and sent him away. He did not think she would ever be persuaded to change her mind—he had seen that inflexible look before in too many women's eyes.

No, it was over and he'd best leave before things got nasty. He might rusticate on the continent for a month or two. There was a place he knew on the French coast that was pleasant and cheap, and the weather was a damned sight better than in London.

So thinking, he entered the narrow lane behind the inn and strolled briskly towards the outside staircase leading to the back door. He had put one foot on the bottom step when a voice hailed him.

'Mr Harmon, is it?'

Mr Harmon glanced up and found himself looking into a pair of cunning dark eyes in a face rather like a hefty slice of raw beef. The woman gave him a wink, which startled him considerably.

'I beg your pardon?' he said in chilly accents.

She was unimpressed, and answered saucily. 'What, are you hard of hearing, Mr Harmon?' She leaned toward him conspiratorially. 'I'll speak up, will I?'

He blustered. 'What is your name, woman? What business do you have with me?'

'My name is Nancy, but I'm no street walker, Mr Harmon, if that's what you're thinking.'

She appeared to be amused by the thought, which irritated him even more. 'Well, be on your way, then!'

'Not just yet, sir. I heard you was a friend of her ladyship up at The Grange. You might be able to have a word to her for me. You see, she owes me and my family wages. Before she come we never had no complaint. Her husband, Master Julian, he was a fine gentleman. But her ladyship, she's hard as nails. We're poor folk, Mr Harmon, and we need those wages.'

Her words suggested she was seeking his help and compassion, her tone did not. Frederick Harmon knew a spiel when he heard one. He gave Nancy a long, hard look. 'Be on your way, old woman.'

Nancy's cheeks flushed bright red and her resemblance to a slab of meat increased.

'"Old woman", is it! I'm not old, no more old than you, Mister London-gent…I *don't* think! I know what you're after. Maybe I'll have my owed wages from you, what do you think of that?'

Frederick Harmon laughed sourly. 'I pay no one else's debts. Certainly not Mrs Fitzgibbon's!'

Nancy raised an eyebrow with interest. 'What, have you fallen out with her ladyship? Well, here's news.'

Mr Harmon suffered her laughter, and her perusal of his person, with what dignity he could muster. 'If you will excuse me,' he began, but she caught his arm in a surprisingly powerful grip—or perhaps not so surprising, going by the breadth of her shoulders.

'No, I won't excuse you. She owes us wages. That's our house, we lived there longer than she's been alive. We want our house back and, failing that, we want to be paid what we're properly owed.'

'Do you?' Mr Harmon muttered, looking down at her grubby hand on his new jacket, which he expected he would have to sell when he reached London. The knowledge strengthened his anger, and he drew himself up to his full height and glared down into her sullen countenance.

'Do you, indeed? Unfortunately, Nancy, I cannot help you. If you want to remove Mrs Fitzgibbon from your house you had best burn her out of it like a rat in a haystack. There, *that* is my advice to you!'

Nancy stared at him, her eyes narrowing. He expected her to start screaming, or at least offer a threat or two. She did neither. She smiled, which was just as unnerving, and disclosed a checkerboard of white teeth and black spaces.

'Why, thank you for that advice, Mr Harmon,' she said, releasing her grip on him. 'I won't keep you no longer.'

Mr Harmon hurried into the inn without looking back, wincing at the echoes of her laughter. He had not meant it, he told himself. That bit about burning her out. It had been said in the heat of the moment, because he was already cross with Miranda, and having his plans ruined, and then to be accosted by such a person. He hadn't liked the look of her at all, though she was probably bluffing, and it was hardly his fault if a madwoman took an offhand comment as an instruction to...

It might be sensible if he caught the first available coach back to London. Just in case something happened. None of this was turning out as he'd hoped; indeed, he was most disappointed with himself for having so wrongly read the situation.

Mr Harmon had reached the narrow, creaky staircase that led up to his room, when another voice halted him. It was deep and familiar, and the icy shiver that ran up his spine briefly prevented him from turning.

'Harmon. At last. I have been waiting for you.'

Slowly, unwillingly, and hoping Belford had not noticed his momentary lapse, Mr Harmon looked to his left.

Belford was leading idly against the doorway into the downstairs parlour, a tankard of the landlord's best in his hand, and a look on his face which bespoke retribution.

'What do you want, Belford?' he blustered, his hand gripping and ungripping the banister. 'I am busy. I have a coach to catch. I will not be delayed.'

Leo pretended to be surprised. 'What, leaving already, Freddie? Wasn't the country to your liking?'

'If you must know, sir, I find it damp and cold and utterly disagreeable!'

A cold light gleamed in Leo's eyes. 'Well, well. Perhaps you need a helping hand, Freddie. You see, I've come to send you on your way.'

'I do not require any help,' Mr Harmon replied sulkily.

'And to warn you,' added Leo, as if he had never spoken, 'that if you show your face in my part of the world again, I will very likely flatten it. Do you understand?' He smiled, but there was no mistaking his seriousness.

Mr Harmon experienced a wave of self-pity. Everyone seemed to be against him. Had he not one friend remaining? 'I said I was leaving, Belford. What more do you want?'

'And if you have taken advantage of Mrs Fitzgibbon in any way, shape or form, I will pursue you wherever you go, and I will not be happy until you are completely ruined. Do you understand that?'

Harmon's cheeks flushed. 'You are very violent, Belford! Quite lacking in the gentlemanly qualities for which you are so famed. I wonder if Mrs Fitzgibbon knows what you are really like? I think you will find she prefers men of refinement over bruisers. You are a brute, Belford. Go and bully someone else.'

Leo appeared to consider his words. '"Brute", am I? Perhaps you are right. Perhaps, at heart, I *am* a brute. I find it strangely liberating being rude to you, Freddie. Beware we do not meet again, or I may liberate my fists as well as my tongue.'

Frederick turned to mount the creaking stairs with as much dignity as he could muster.

'Oh, and Harmon?' Leo was smiling grimly up at him. 'If you're not gone in half an hour, I'll come up and help you pack.'

Leo's smile became genuine as the footsteps quickened into a half-run before an upstairs door slammed. He felt an immense sense of self-satisfaction. He had seen off the dragon and rescued his lady love. Now all that remained was to sweep her up into his arms, kiss her, and live happily ever after.

His smile faded, turned rueful.

Unfortunately real life was not a fairytale. A happy ending was not obligatory, even for a duke.

The note from Tina had arrived as dusk was blurring the landscape around The Grange. A bird called

from the shadowy copse on the hill, a mournful cry
that exactly suited Miranda's mood.

Since Mr Harmon had gone, she had tried to re-
capture the urgency she had once felt to make The
Grange into a proper home, but it seemed to slip
through her fingers. Like the mist in the hollows about
the house where the moat had once been.

Esme, as though sensing her mistress's malaise,
had brought a vase of flowers to place in the parlour.

'There we are, ma'am,' she had declared, her thin,
young face full of pleasure. 'That will cheer things
up for you.'

'It will indeed, Esme. Thank you.' She hesitated,
glancing to the door. 'Is Pendle still here?'

'Yes, ma'am.'

'He hasn't packed and left then?'

Esme shook her head.

Pendle had persisted with his stubborn stance. He
was here on the Duke's instructions and could only
leave if ordered to do so by the Duke. 'And,' he reminded her primly, 'as I have been forbidden to allow
his Grace into your house, madam, it is unlikely he
will be able to give me those orders, even if he wishes
to.'

'Very good, Pendle,' she had replied with more
than a little exasperation. 'You have it all worked
out.'

'I only do as I am told, madam.'

'Do you, Pendle? I wonder.'

With a smile and a bob, Esme left her, and the
Pendle question was no further resolved. The scent of
the flowers filled the room, heavy and sweet. The par-

lour had become very cosy, a refuge from the worries of the world. Miranda tended to retreat here when she needed to be alone, to think.

Thus she had come here when she received Tina's note.

The sight of it had briefly lifted her spirits, but when she read it she found the contents kind and apologetic, but certainly not the inspiring message of hope she had wanted them to be.

My dear Miranda,

You will know now that I háve told Leo the truth about you. I would come to make my apology in person, but I do not believe you will want to see me just yet. My reason for betraying your trust was my brother's confusion and unhappiness. I hoped that once he knew you were not Adela the trouble between you would be resolved. I was wrong, and for that I apologise. Please see it in your heart to forgive me—and him. Leo feels as badly as I do about this matter. I know he will not rest until we are all comfortable again.

Your friend, Tina

Miranda sighed and laid the note aside. Leo was a gentleman who felt deeply his position as the Fifth Duke of Belford. Of course he would not feel comfortable until he had resolved their differences. Then, and only then, could he relegate her, and these last weeks, to the past where they belonged.

An unpleasant episode to be forgotten.

Probably he would give her a cool, courteous nod in passing, or, if absolutely necessary, exchange a few words with her if they met accidentally. But no more. She could not expect more.

And yet, God help her, she did!

Would they live so close, only a few miles apart, and yet be so far away? How could this hurdle be got over? How could she make him fall as in love with her as she was with him? He had been about to, she was sure of it. That day when he came to her here at The Grange, there had been something in his eyes.

For some reason her mind kept circling back to the past, the long-ago past, when the first Fitzgibbon had been coerced by his king, and possibly his own greed, into marrying a woman he did not love. Was there a message for her in that story? Did those long-dead lovers look upon her now, and wish her to find a happiness to equal their own?

Despite all the odds, their lives had worked out well.

Why, oh, why could she and Leo not find a similar conclusion to their sorry tale?

Chapter Thirteen

The night was still, everything and everyone sleeping. Except one.

A bulky figure crept around the side of The Grange, keeping to the deeper shadows against the house, ducking once or twice beneath the shelter of an overgrown bush. But there was no one to see or hear, and soon the intruder reached the side door and, with a brief manipulation of the lock, silently entered.

The old house slept on.

The bulky figure paused, but there was no sound, and soon it moved on hushed feet up the stairs, towards the family bedchambers. There was no hesitation in its steps, no confusion as to which direction to take—it was obvious that here was someone who knew the house very well.

'She has no right.' The words were a mere breath of sound. 'If I can't have The Grange, then no one will.'

The intruder reached a door in the dark corridor and halted. It fumbled with something—a bundle of rags held fast under one arm—and then a spark flared. Smouldered. Caught. The acrid sting of smoke filled the air.

A firm, determined wrench on the door latch and the portal swung open. There was no sound here, either, apart from the faint whisper of someone's sleeping breath. The intruder came closer and stared at the bed. The curtains were drawn, but within them Miranda slept on, unknowing and unaware of the danger.

The bulky figure gave a soft, triumphant laugh, and bent to place the smoking bundle of rags against the covers at the base of the bed. It waited briefly, watching the smoke increase, seeing the first bright flicker of hungry flame, and then backed out of the room as silently as it had come.

Down the stairs the intruder went, on swift, sure feet, only to pause. A glance in the direction of the kitchen…the larder. Temptation there, and the sudden thought, *Why not? 'Tis only right I take what should be mine.*

In a matter of moments the outside door had opened once more and the bulky figure slipped out and ran. There was a faint patter of footsteps across the lawn, a murmur of laughter, and then the heavy silence resumed.

Miranda was the first to smell the smoke.

She was dreaming of Leo and the night she had dined at Ormiston. Only this time the birds that were painted upon the domed ceiling had come to life and were flying about the room. Pendle appeared to inform them that dinner was served. And then Leo took her hand and they both soared into the air.

She woke, disoriented, staring into the cave of her bed curtains. And coughed. For a moment she did not know what had woken her, only that there was a peculiar smell and her eyes and nostrils stung. An urgent drumming began in her skull.

There was a strange light beyond the bedcurtains. A flickering, dancing light.

As she stared, flames licked up the fabric at the end of her bed and, with a sudden, frightening ferocity, began to spread to the canopy.

Smoke! Fire!

At last realisation flooded her.

With a loud shriek, Miranda hurled herself out of her bed, fighting through the curtains. The room was burning. Fire was consuming the base of her bed; smoke poured upward. And the fire had a voice; it seemed to roar.

Avoiding the burning bedding, Miranda edged about the wall towards the door and found it ajar.

The corridor was already hazy with smoke. More of it drifted over the gallery railing and down into the well of the hall, where a lantern shone eerily through the gloom. In a moment her desperate cries had brought numerous servants, in various states of undress, stumbling to her rescue. They milled about aimlessly, until Pendle took charge. The fact that he was wearing a ridiculous nightcap whose drooping end kept falling over one eye, and a pair of scruffy bright green slippers, appeared to have no effect whatever upon his authority.

Miranda had thought the flames too entrenched to put out, but Pendle soon dealt with them, ordering the servants as they went about smothering the fire and soaking the bedclothes with water. The conflagration resisted briefly, but it was no match for Pendle.

When the flames had been extinguished to Pendle's satisfaction, one of the servants was placed on guard, just in case a wayward spark reignited. The room looked blackened and singed, and smelt sickeningly of smoke, but apart from the destruction of the bed-curtains and bedcovers, no serious damage had been done.

It could have been so much worse.

If Miranda had not woken and smelled smoke, if the fire had burned more quickly, then the house could have been well alight before anyone realised, and with no possibility of its being saved.

And not just the house.

Miranda's own life would have been lost.

Oh, yes, she thought, it could have been much worse. She was grateful, really she was. And yet now she had this further burden weighing down her already burdened shoulders.

It might have been the final straw, if she were not so angry.

'How could it have begun?' she asked, more to herself than Pendle, trying hard not to stare at his bizarre nightcap.

'A stray spark, madam,' he answered promptly. 'I

will question the servants, there is some simple explanation.'

But Miranda did not believe that. Besides, there was something in the way he held his mouth which made her think he was keeping secrets from her. She fixed him with a hard look. 'You think someone lit it deliberately, don't you?'

'I cannot say, madam.'

'Can't or won't! If you are holding something back from me in the mistaken belief that I am a helpless female, Pendle, I will—I will never forgive you.'

He paled, but his eyes did not waver. 'I do not now, nor ever have, believed you to be a "helpless female", madam.'

There was obviously no more to be done with Pendle, or the house, until morning. The smell of smoke remained strong and rooms would need to be thoroughly aired out, but in all they had been very lucky. Miranda sent her household back to bed with unstinting thanks, and retired herself to one of the spare bedchambers. But she did not sleep. She could not.

The mattress was comfortable enough, the bedding was fresh and aired, the room was clean and welcoming. None of those things was stopping her from sleeping. It was just that there were too many thoughts revolving in her head.

Who could have attempted such a crime, and why would Pendle not share his suspicions with her? Was it possible that the perpetrator was someone Pendle wished to protect?

An image fluttered into Miranda's mind, but she

dismissed it instantly. Leo would never stoop to such base behaviour. He was a gentleman, and although he occasionally lost his reason where she was concerned, that did not mean he would turn arsonist. No, the perpetrator must be someone with a grudge against her. A hatred so deep that he would stop at nothing in his quest to revenge himself upon her.

Mr Harmon?

It was unbelievable that Adela's cousin should so resent what she had said to him. He had deserved it, after all, and there had been an expression in his eyes that told her he knew it. The game had been up, and he had left accordingly. She could not imagine him returning with such viciousness in his heart, intent on doing her harm.

However, there was *one* other person who was a perfect fit for the picture she had just drawn. Nancy. For some reason Nancy Bennett believed The Grange was hers by right of her family's long association with it. And Nancy was more than capable of viciousness, maybe even of harming Miranda.

Yes, Miranda decided, with a yawn, she would speak to Pendle about Nancy in the morning.

On the verge of sleep, Miranda jerked awake again.

She had forgotten that tomorrow night was the Lethbridge party. Would Leo be there? After all that had happened between them, she was less than thrilled with the notion of coming face to face with him. And yet, despite Leo, and despite what had happened tonight—or perhaps *because* of those things— she had no intention of missing the party.

Maybe he would not come. Maybe he had already returned to London and had resumed his life there. In a month or two she might read in the newspaper of his engagement, and think a little sadly of what may have been. But, of course, by then she would be over him and happy in her solitary life.

The image she had created was unbearably depressing. Miranda closed her eyes and, finally, slept.

'Pendle? What in God's name are you doing here at this time of the night? Or is it morning?'

Pendle straightened a little more, his voice lowered in respect for the sleeping household. 'Your Grace, it was imperative I come, despite the hour. I apologise for waking you.'

Leo shrugged. 'I was not asleep,' he said.

Pendle paused, as if expecting some further explanation, but when there was none forthcoming he launched into his own story in regard to the events that had occurred at The Grange.

'There has been a fire, sir. I came myself because I do not believe it was an accident. I believe it was deliberately lit.'

Leo listened, his eyes narrowed, his face blank. But Pendle was not fooled. He knew his master well, and he knew when he was angry.

At the moment he was very angry indeed.

'I don't think you have turned out at this hour to tell me something you could have informed me of in daylight, Pendle.'

'No, sir. I admit to you that I am more than a little worried.'

'No one was injured in this fire?' Suddenly Leo was very much awake, sitting stiffly upright in his chair.

'No, sir, everyone is well.'

No doubt that was true—Pendle did not tell untruths—but there was something in the older man's eyes that turned Leo's heart to ice.

'Miranda is not hurt?' Leo's question was sharp.

Pendle shook his head, but again that anxious expression clouded his eyes.

'Than what, man? In God's name, what is it?'

Leo felt odd. As if the world around him was receding behind a dark film. Pendle's voice came from a distance, the tone soothing, but nothing could camouflage the damning nature of his words.

'The fire was started in Mrs Fitzgibbon's bedchamber, sir. The bed was alight and she escaped just in time. Some charred rags were found at the base of her bed. I believe a person set them alight in the hope that… I believe, sir, that whoever did this wished the lady ill.'

'Wished her dead, you mean?'

Pendle eyed him uneasily. 'Yes, sir, that is what I mean.'

Leo nodded. He felt damned strange. He swallowed. Miranda, dead? What would be left him then? The Duke of Belford with his large estates and pure-bred horses and twenty thousand pounds per annum. Suddenly the idea that that was all his life meant seemed unbearable. The knowledge pressed down upon him, crushing him, choking him.

Miranda. He needed her, he wanted her, he could not live without her.

And it had taken his nearly losing her to make him realise it.

'Pendle?' His voice was harsh and strange; he cleared his throat.

'Yes, your Grace?'

'Who did this?'

Pendle shuffled slightly, then straightened his already ramrod-straight back. 'Whoever did this deed knew their way about The Grange, which, as you are aware, is a veritable maze. In darkness a stranger could break his neck. I had thought it might be Mr Harmon, but...'

Leo gave a faint grimace of reminiscence. 'Mr Harmon left this afternoon for London. I saw him off myself.'

Pendle was not unduly surprised.

'Was anything stolen, Pendle?' Leo's head seemed to be clearing. He was thinking again. The horrid moment had passed.

Pendle moved to shake his head, and then hesitated. 'Now that you mention it, sir, there were some items missing from the larder. I had a need to visit the kitchen after the upset with the fire—my stomach, you know—and I am almost certain there was a ham, and a cheese, which were no longer there. I can confer with Cook tomorrow.'

'And what do you deduce from this midnight feast, Pendle?' Leo asked quietly.

'There is only one person, to my knowledge, who is familiar with The Grange and who would be unable to resist stealing food, your Grace.'

'Exactly! I believe if I were to ask in the village tomorrow, I would find the entire Bennett family well provisioned.' Leo's eyes glittered. 'Do nothing further in the matter. *I* will deal with Nancy.'

'I would leave it to you, sir, but...' Pendle shifted uneasily from his military stance. If he had been a lesser man, one might have said he wavered.

Leo watched him curiously. 'What is it, Pendle?'

'Mrs Fitzgibbon is an intelligent woman, sir. By morning she will have concluded for herself that Nancy was the culprit.'

'Very well, I will send her a note to the effect that I am handling the matter.'

Pendle shifted again. 'She may not take such a note in the spirit in which it is intended, sir.'

'I see.' Leo frowned, eyeing his butler with malevolence. 'I collect you are referring to my recent visit.'

'Your Grace was rather...forceful.'

'I was angry, Pendle! She has a powerful effect on me.'

'Indeed, sir.'

Leo's eyebrows rose. 'You seem to have grown very protective of the lady, Pendle.'

Pendle cleared his throat. 'It has been a unique experience receiving orders from Mrs Fitzgibbon, sir. I can only say that returning here to Ormiston will be very tame indeed.'

'Pendle, you ungrateful wretch! If I had known you would transfer your allegiance so easily I would not have sent you. What must I do to tempt you back, eh?'

'Oh, I will return, sir. I will be glad to. I fear I am too advanced in years to remain in Mrs Fitzgibbon's household for too long.' He gave a delicate shudder, but Leo was not deceived. Pendle had found his match and was revelling in it.

Despite his lack of sleep, Leo rose at his usual early hour. His sister was still abed, and he had no intention of waking her until he had dealt with this new, urgent problem.

He wondered, with a faint sense of depression, if this was how he would spend the remainder of his life. Protecting his lady love, but secretly, and never receiving the recognition he deserved. A faithful and loving admirer, but at a distance.

It did not sound a very satisfactory occupation. Leo did not think he would be able to remain at a distance for very long. Nor did he intend to. He meant to claim the lady as his as soon as possible—she would be safe in his arms. It was just exactly how he would accomplish this task that still eluded him. Surely there must be a way to return himself to her good graces? He did not think he lacked the will.

Leo realised now that Miranda was the woman he must spend his life with—he supposed in his heart he had known it since the moment he saw her. But it was last night, when he had feared for her life, that everything had become so brutally clear to him.

Still, first things first...he had Nancy Bennett to deal with.

Shrugging off his pensive mood, Leo found pen and paper and sent off a brief note to The Grange.

Miranda, too, had risen early, had finished her tea and toast and was sitting at her dressing table, her auburn locks spilling wildly about her, when the missive was brought to her by Esme.

She had woken with the realisation that whoever had lit the fire in her house had known it well. When cook sent word that there were items missing from the larder, the final piece in the puzzle had clicked into place. And it had spelled Nancy.

She had the answer, but what was she to do about it?

Her mind only half-concentrated on what she was doing, Miranda broke the seal and spread the single sheet before her. The words struck her with some force. Her breath caught in her throat.

My dear Mrs Fitzgibbon, I intend dealing with the matter of last night's fire, therefore there is no need for you to concern yourself. Belford.

Miranda's hand was shaking as she searched out a pen and paper of her own, and her letters were not nearly as well formed as usual. When she had finished she hastily folded the paper and, ringing for Esme, sent the girl off without delay.

* * *

Leo had finished his breakfast and sent for his horse when he received the news that his groom had returned from The Grange, with a reply to his letter to Miranda. Somewhat surprised—he had not thought a reply was necessary—he tore it open. It was short and to the point.

Your Grace, as generous as your offer of assistance is, I must decline it. Miranda Fitzgibbon.

Leo stared at the words for some time, amused and exasperated. 'Generous', he noted, had been underlined twice, and it was not difficult to picture the expression in her magnificent eyes as she had written it.

Leo felt his mouth twitch into a smile. Still, he had no intention of being dismissed like an interfering schoolboy. Miranda must learn that when Belford made up his mind to do something, then there was nothing more to be said. He had been the head of this family for far too long not to know exactly what was best for it. Even his recent bout of irrational behaviour had not changed that.

Leo dashed off a hasty reply, before setting out for the village as he had originally intended.

Time had passed. Miranda had dressed and was downstairs in the library, writing the long-delayed letter to Mr Ealing, when the groom from Ormiston arrived yet again, carrying a reply to her epistle. When Esme brought it in, her eyes curious, Miranda pounced upon the folded paper and tore it open with all the eagerness of a starving animal finding a parcel of food.

Her eyes skimmed the bold pen strokes.

'Oh!' she cried angrily. 'It is too much!'

Esme, craning her neck, ventured, 'Bad news, madam?'

'Yes, it is bad news. Very bad news. I wrote to the Duke to tell him I could not accept his offer, and now he says he refuses to allow me to refuse. Of all the arrogance! As if he has anything to do with what I can or cannot do. And then he says, if you please, that he is the head of the Fitzgibbon family and I must obey him. As if that is an end to it!'

Esme's eyes widened and her cap threatened to fall down over her eyebrows and hide them completely.

'Well, it is not an end to it. I know who lit that fire, and I will deal with them in my own way. Fetch me the groom who brought this letter, Esme. I will have his horse off him.'

'H-his horse, madam?'

'Yes, his horse, for I am not walking to the village today, I am riding. Go on, do as I say.'

'You do not wish to send another letter, madam?'

'No, Esme, I do not!'

'Should I press your dress, madam? The one you said you wanted to wear to the Lethbridges' party?'

'Yes, yes, very well, Esme, but fetch the groom!'

Esme closed the door softly behind her. Pendle was lurking about in the hall and came swiftly towards her, almost as if he had been laying in wait for her.

'Everything all right, Esme?' he asked quietly.

Esme managed a jerky nod. She was still very much in awe of the Duke's butler. 'Yes, sir. At least…the mistress says she wants the groom's horse, so's she can ride to the village.'

Pendle's mouth grew pinched. 'Why does she want to ride to the village, Esme?'

'I don't rightly know, sir, but I think it's because of the letter the Duke sent to her. She was very cross with the first one, and now he's sent a second one and she's crosser than I've ever seen her.'

Pendle didn't answer for a moment, his rather colourless eyes staring into hers, then he sighed. 'Very well, Esme, fetch the horse. I see no way out of it. She will walk if you do not. I think I know where she is going.'

He did indeed know, and with any luck Leo would also be there. Just in case, though, Pendle would arrange for a third party to journey to the village. He wondered, as Esme hurried away, why he had had the misfortune to be at the beck and call of two such powerful and headstrong personalities. It was almost more than any butler—even one of his calibre—could bear.

The door to Nancy Bennett's cottage opened unceremoniously to the chill morning air, and someone entered. Nancy turned, expecting to see one of her disreputable family, and at the same time opening her mouth to shout abuse…and goggled at the sight before her.

The Duke of Belford was standing there, large as life and immaculate in his riding jacket and breeches, the top of his dark head brushing against the ceiling beams.

'Nancy! Just off out? Stay a moment. I wish to have a word with you.'

He sounded almost jovial, but his eyes, a very cold blue this morning, slid knowingly over the remains of the ham and the few crumbs of cheese—Nancy had eaten most of it last night upon her return.

She watched him warily, wondering if it were possible that he knew, that she wasn't as clever as she had thought herself after all. And when he turned his gaze back on her, something in it chilled her more than winter.

'You've done a very bad thing, Nancy,' he said, and though the words themselves were not particularly frightening, his tone of voice was.

Her usual cockiness rose to her aid. 'I haven't done anything, sir,' she retorted saucily. 'I don't know what you mean.'

'Oh, but you have, Nancy. Fortunately, the fire at The Grange was put out before it did too much damage.'

The chagrin was in her face before she could hide it. Leo stepped closer, very big in the small space, and Nancy found herself shuffling backwards. She glared up at him like a wild animal in a snare, hating him and yet terrified of what he might do to her.

'I've done nothing,' she said boldly. The words spilled out of her, full of corroding bitterness. 'I don't know about any fire. Not that I'd care if The Grange did burn down. That was *my* home, and now she's there. I've as much right to it as her. The Bennetts have lived at The Grange since King Henry's day. 'Tis said...' She swallowed hard as Leo stepped closer but refused to be silenced. ''Tis said the king left the house to *us* and not the Fitzgibbons!'

Leo's eyes widened in blue fury. 'Is that why, Nancy? Is that the reason you tried to kill Mrs Fitzgibbon? Have you honestly deluded yourself to such an extent?'

Nancy trembled before his wrath. 'My father told me it were so!'

Leo stepped still closer, crowding her.

'Do you really believe that? The king gave my ancestor The Grange, Nancy, and I have the deeds to prove it. I think you did this thing for your own wicked reasons and you are using your father's ramblings as an excuse. All this time with my cousin Julian you have believed you can do whatever you wish, and when Mrs Fitzgibbon put a stop to that, you wanted nothing more than to take out your spleen on her. That is the truth, now, isn't it?'

Nancy shook her head. 'She should have gone when I told her to,' she managed, but now there was guilt and fright in her eyes.

'You are an evil woman.'

''Tisn't so,' she breathed, edging behind a stool. 'I have a right—'

'You have no right,' he retorted, and an anger so violent gripped him that his self-control teetered on the edge of an abyss. The thought of Miranda, trapped, crying for help that never came, the fire all about her, was demanding he punish this woman in a like manner. He stepped closer still, and watched Nancy's eyes dilute with terror.

'Mrs Fitzgibbon is under my protection,' he informed her in a soft and deadly voice. 'You will not try and hurt her again, you will not go near her again. Ever.'

Nancy swallowed. Her head bobbed up and down in a jerky nod, her chest rising and falling in genuine fear. 'Don't hurt me, sir,' she whined.

He loomed over her and she flinched, burrowing further into her corner. The hands she held up before her shook like leaves in a storm.

It brought him to his senses. As much as he would have liked to take an eye for an eye, that was not his way. Slowly, inch by inch, Leo regained control over his anger. When he was sure of himself, he spoke again.

'You will leave this village now, this morning, and never return. And if you do return, Nancy, then I will send you to Taunton Gaol, and there you will rot. Do you understand?'

Her mouth opened and shut, but when no words came out she nodded her head.

Leo's smile was grim. 'Good. We understand each other. Now pack your things and leave.'

It took Nancy all of two minutes.

The cottage door was ajar. Miranda hesitated, wiping her palms on her skirts, but there was really no option, so she ducked her head and stepped through the low doorway. Her eyes narrowed in the sudden gloom.

The single room was dirty and untidy, but among the odors of damp and smoke and unwashed clothing lingered the unmistakable smell of ham.

'She is gone.'

Leo's voice brought her head around, and she saw that he was sitting in a chair by the window, looking strangely at home despite the squalor. The sunlight slanted across his face, and Miranda could see that he was smiling in that self-satisfied way that so ruffled her.

'Gone?' she repeated.

'I've sent her off with instructions never to return. I decided banishment was preferable to gaol. There is the matter of proving she lit the fire, and then I did not imagine you would enjoy divulging your private concerns to the justice any more than I. Don't worry, if she returns, I will take the necessary action, but somehow I do not think she will.'

'But I wanted to speak to her!' Miranda wailed.

His smile did not waver. 'I have spoken to her for you, Miranda. You can put her from your mind.'

He seemed so pleased with himself, so…so smug! Just as he had been when he tried to bribe her, and when he had sent Pendle to torment her. She wanted to shake him, to rattle some of that conceit out of him. Instead she gave a little cry of frustration and stamped her foot.

'*I* wanted to do it. It was *my* house that she tried

to burn down, it is *me* she hates. You had no right, Belford, no right at all!'

He eyed her blankly, as if realising for the first time that she may see his help as other than a blessing. And then he sighed. It was a deep sigh, the sigh of a man who has reached the end of his rope. 'Oh, Miranda,' he murmured. 'You do not make it easy, do you?'

Her eyes flashed. 'I do not understand you. First you write me an insulting letter, ordering me to allow you to take charge, and now you say I am being difficult!'

Leo ran a distracted hand through his hair. 'I did not know that I ordered you to do anything of the sort.'

'Perhaps such insolence is normal for you, sir, but I run my own affairs and have done for years. I certainly do not need your interference!'

He straightened, a hint of turbulence finally ruffling the calm blue of his eyes. 'Interference? I had thought I was saving you the trouble of embroiling yourself in a difficult and dangerous situation. As head of the family it is my duty to attend to these matters. I must say, madam, you have a strange way of expressing your gratitude.'

'Oh, have I!' she retorted, cheeks flaming, eyes brilliant, her hair catching the sunlight in a myriad of reds and golds. 'And how should I express it then, sir? I think I have been most forbearing, under the circumstances.'

Annoyance had turned rapidly to anger. Leo felt

the now familiar beginnings of loss of control. 'You may not be the Decadent Countess, Miranda, but by God you do a good imitation of a harpy!'

'How dare you!'

'I dare, oh, yes, I dare. You have driven me to madness. You have turned a calm and rational man into a raving lunatic. I have done things, said things, of which I thought myself incapable. You have much to answer for, by God.'

'So it is *my* fault?' she gasped in disbelief, stepping closer still.

'Yes, it is!'

He glared back at her, chest heaving, their faces but inches apart. And then, slowly, the anger drained from his eyes, leaving them once more a tranquil blue. Miranda watched his mouth, straight and hard and white with fury, begin to relax into its habitual curve. And she realised that he was looking at her with *that* look.

Her heart began an uneven journey around her chest and she listened with some trepidation as he began to speak.

'I don't want your gratitude, madam.'

'Don't you, Leo?' she managed breathlessly.

'No, Miranda,' he replied firmly. 'I want much more than that. It's true, what I said. You have rocked every basic belief I have held in myself. You have stripped me bare of all I thought I was. I don't know if I like it, certainly I am no longer comfortable, but I think, in time, I will be a better man because of it.'

'And I have done all of that?' Miranda asked softly.

'All of that and more.'

She managed a smile, but her gaze was sombre. 'Leo, I have thought and thought, and I believe if I had only been honest at the very beginning, all of these…misunderstandings might have been avoided.'

'Ah, so you accept all of the blame?' he teased.

She opened her mouth.

'No, no, my love,' he murmured, sliding a warm arm about her waist, 'you cannot take it all. We must allow for my part. Come, we will make our peace in the time-honoured tradition.'

'Will we?' Miranda's voice was very nearly breathless with longing, and she found that her own hands had crept over his shoulders.

'I love you, you know,' he said, and uncertainty flickered behind the confidence and humour in his eyes. He wasn't as sure of himself as he liked to pretend, not where she was concerned anyway.

Her own heart melted. 'Oh, Leo, I love you, too.'

'Do you?' He sounded relieved.

She laughed, she couldn't help it. Happiness filled her, and the bleak surroundings of Nancy's cottage took on a decidedly rosy glow. 'Weren't you going to kiss me?' she reminded him softly.

Leo reached out to cup her face, his fingertips smoothing her stubborn jaw, his thumb following the soft shape of her lips. He gazed down at her with such a warm, wondering expression most of her doubts vanished in an instant. He loved her. And his love for her had taken the man famed for his cool

good manners and shaken him completely off balance.

What more proof did she need?

But one doubt did remain, and in her usual practical, straightforward manner, Miranda voiced it.

'Leo, are you sure it is me you love, and not the
Decadent Countess? I know I was playing a
part…some of the time, at least. How do you know
which is me and which was she?'

He stroked her cheek with a thoughtful air. 'How
do I know I love you? I love the Miranda who is
courageous enough to take on a duke and teach him
a well-deserved lesson. I love the Miranda who would
consider living in a rundown house with one servant
and refuse to give up. I love the Miranda who can be
calmly practical when it is necessary, and yet whose
mouth is warm and passionate against mine. Is that
you, Miranda?'

Miranda smiled up at him, her heart full of joy.
Bending his head, Leo set his lips very carefully to
hers.

It was a pledge rather than a kiss of passion. A
conclusion to the long weeks of turmoil. Still, thought
Miranda, it was very nice and they might have remained there longer, but for the interruption.

The familiar sound of throat-clearing just beyond
the door.

Reluctantly, Leo set her from him. 'Pendle,' he said
in a voice which was more resigned than aggravated,
'what are you doing here?'

Pendle peered fastidiously around the door, nose

wrinkling at the chaos within. The sight appeared to cause him actual physical discomfort, for he flinched and gripped the doorjamb for support.

'My apologies, sir, but I did not want any harm to come to Mrs Fitzgibbon.'

'I see.'

'There was a letter arrived from Mr Ealing, madam. As you can see, it is marked urgent, so I took the liberty of carrying it with me.'

Miranda took the envelope from him with a frown and opened it. 'Well!' she gasped at length. '*That* is why Julian's monies were delayed.'

Leo raised an eyebrow.

'Nancy Bennett and her father had made a claim upon The Grange. They swore that Julian had left all to them. Mr Ealing did not believe it for a moment, but he felt obliged to make an investigation. He didn't tell me—he says he didn't want to worry me.' Miranda glanced at Leo, her expression conveying what she thought of that.

'And?' Leo said, trying not to smile.

'It was all nonsense. Mr Ealing says he will now go ahead and send me a draft. I do not need to impose upon you any more, Duke.'

Now Leo did smile, directly into her eyes. 'I enjoy it when you impose upon me, Miranda.'

Pendle sniffed.

Leo gave his butler a long, searching look. His eyebrows rose. 'You are somewhat dishevelled, Pendle. Did you walk?'

'No, sir.' Pendle grimaced horribly. 'I rode.'

'You rode? On a horse?'

'No, sir. There was no horse at The Grange. I was setting out to walk when a—a tinker arrived. I believe he had come to sell beads and needles and other trinkets. For a small recompense, he allowed me to ride upon his cart.'

Leo stared at him a moment more, but the image of the fastidious Pendle in such a situation was too much for him. He threw back his head and roared with laughter.

Pendle, rather pink, ignored his master as best he could. He turned stiffly to Miranda. 'You are not harmed, madam?' he inquired politely.

Miranda, gazing from one to the other in wonder, shook her head. 'But thank you for your concern, Pendle.'

'I am very glad, madam. Now, if you will forgive me, I think I shall leave The Grange and return to Ormiston. I believe I have reached the limit of my endurance.'

Leo gave another hearty laugh.

Miranda managed to retain her composure. 'Please, feel free, Pendle. I quite understand.'

'Do you, madam? That I very much doubt!'

Chapter Fourteen

The long-suffering Pendle had only just left The Grange, when an unfamiliar but modish carriage pulled up to the front door. Miranda and Esme exchanged puzzled glances, as they watched the footman jump down to hand out the vehicle's occupant.

'This is it? I have seen better ruins in Italy!'

A droll voice, full of world-weary sophistication and yet with an underlying hint of mischief, drifted towards them. Miranda's eyes widened in wonder and amazement as a small woman in a blue, fur-lined cloak stepped down from the carriage.

'Adela?' she whispered.

'Ah, there she is, my stepdaughter!'

Adela, the Countess Ridgeway, made her elegant way up the steps towards Miranda. The rich swish of her skirts was very loud in the silence and, when she tipped back the hood of her cloak, her dark hair shone with a trace of silver.

'Dear Miranda. I came all the way from Italy to find you—*so* exhausting—and then found you had already left London, and disappeared into the wilds of Somerset. It was too, *too* vexing. But, you see, I have at last found you.'

'Adela! I did not expect—'

'I know you did not expect me to visit, my dear, but I was worried.' Hazel eyes examined her frankly. 'Although now I am here, I see you are perfectly well, blooming, in fact. I wrote to Freddie, you know, and told him to visit you, but he has never replied to any of my letters. What could I do but come and see for myself?'

Miranda hugged her, tears pricking her eyes. 'You are very kind to come all this way, but you can see I am quite well.'

'Yes, in fine fettle, as your father would have said.'

Miranda laughed with a little catch in her voice, and led her stepmama inside. Adela glanced about with interest, at the same time unfastening her cloak and slipping it nonchalantly from her shoulders.

Esme caught her breath, her eyebrows promptly vanishing under the brim of her cap.

Adela was wearing a very fashionable, but very sheer, gown over very little at all. Miranda was certain that, for a moment, as Adela turned about, she glimpsed her stepmama's limbs through the gossamer cloth.

'Adela, we are in the country,' she reproved. 'You cannot wear such things here.'

Adela smiled and tossed her glossy head. 'Why not? I have a reputation to maintain, after all.'

And suddenly Miranda remembered exactly how

appalled Leo had been when he believed her to be Adela.

She had been aware of this impediment to her happiness with him, but she had thought Adela far away in Italy. An impediment was not so serious when it was far away. Only now Adela was here, at The Grange. How could Leo possibly marry her when the Decadent Countess was right here in Somerset? He would recoil at the very idea, just as he had recoiled when he believed Miranda to be Adela.

And what was the alternative? That she never see nor speak to Adela again? That from henceforth she pretend Adela did not exist? Miranda knew she could not agree to such a thing. She may disapprove of Adela, but she also loved her, and Leo would break her heart if he forbade her contact with her stepmama.

Adela was speaking. 'Your house is nicer inside than out, darling, but it is still too cold for me. I could never live here.'

Miranda cast her a bewildered glance. 'No?'

'No, Miranda. I have not come to stay with you. Is that what you thought?' she asked, with an intelligent glint in her eye. 'I was worried about you, so I have come to set my fears at rest. Are you happy?'

Miranda smiled. 'I am. I am very happy. There is a man who... I think I am in love, Adela!'

'You only think it?' Adela replied, but she was smiling too. 'What is his name?'

Miranda stiffened her spine. 'It is the Duke of Belford.'

Adela's eyes widened and then she laughed. 'Oh

no, not the proper, frozen Belford whose heart is ice? But, my dear, that is a triumph! I see I have been concerned for no reason. I can return to Italy forthwith.'

'Oh, but won't you stay for a little while, Adela?'

Adela smiled and patted her hand. 'It is too cold for me here. I am afraid I prefer the warmth, darling. And I am to marry again. A nice man, a widower. You would like him, for he scolds me just like you. I find I cannot live on my own, Miranda. Oh, I did try! Truly, I did. I did all the things you suggested, I made all those little economies you listed for me. But it would not do, Miranda. Life became insupportable. So I have offered the Villa Ridgeway up for sale, and I will marry Guido and move to Rome. I think I will be happy in Rome with Guido.'

And she said it with such contentment, Miranda could not doubt her.

'But you *will* stay a little while?'

Adela smiled. 'I will stay a week, Miranda. Long enough to frighten your beloved with the thought that I may remain permanently to make his life a misery.'

Miranda tried to frown. 'You are very naughty, Adela.'

'Well, dear, they do not call me the Decadent Countess for nothing!'

Oak House was a blaze of light, a beacon in the soft twilight. Miranda, approaching in the carriage, felt as if she were nearing a long-sought-after goal. The end of a journey.

She had worn the gold dress. It was made of silk, one of Adela's more extravagant purchases, and the heavy cloth whispered about her. It was rather low cut, too, daring for Miranda. Adela had insisted she wear it, but where as once Miranda might have hesitated, she no longer did.

She realised then that she had grown in confidence since she arrived in England. Her tribulations had strengthened her. Besides, tonight she *wanted* to be daring. She *wanted* Leo to admire her. To burn for her as she burned for him.

Perhaps there was a little bit of the Decadent Countess in her after all.

'No, darling, I will not come with you,' Adela had told her, with a shrewd glance. 'I do not want to frighten your Duke away so soon.'

Guiltily, Miranda had been glad that she would have a chance to break the news to Leo first. And her stepmama had seemed quite happy to be left toasting her feet before the fire.

Thinking of Leo now, Miranda felt her heartbeat quicken. He loved her, there was no doubt about it, and she loved him. But there was more to it than love. She needed to know how he would react when she told him Adela was at The Grange, no matter how short the visit might be. She needed to believe he would put aside his own prejudices for her sake, because of his love for her. She needed to be able to speak freely and honestly to him, without forever fearing the consequences.

Miranda sighed. It seemed even true love had its complications.

Sophie, pretty in a gown of white muslin with pink rosebuds in her hair, met Miranda at the door and pressed her fingers in a warm greeting. 'Jack,' she said firmly, with a glance over her shoulder, 'here is Miranda.'

Jack gave her a sheepish look. 'Oh…oh, yes, Mrs Fitzgibbon. So glad you could come. I—I fear I might have—'

'Mistaken me for someone else?'

Jack gave a hefty sigh of relief. 'Yes, that's it. Mistaken you for someone else. So glad you weren't that other person.'

Miranda smiled.

Sophie also smiled, with profound relief. 'There,' she said, 'now we can all be comfortable!'

'Mrs Fitzgibbon.' Sir Marcus appeared behind his son and daughter, reaching to take her hand in his firm grip. 'I am glad to see you. Our little party wouldn't be complete without you.'

Miranda would have been hard to please indeed if she had not been flattered by their attention. 'You are very kind, sir.'

'There are only familiar faces here tonight. No one of whom to be nervous. Isn't that so, Jack?'

Jack shuffled his feet. 'Yes, Father.'

'We are all friends here.'

Jack nodded. 'Just so, Father. Never a truer word said.' His gaze shifted uneasily across the room to one of those familiar figures, and Miranda's followed it.

Her heart swelled and her golden-heeled slippers seemed to be floating above the polished floor. Leo was standing by the window, speaking with the Misses McKay. He did not look up, but a smile tugged at his lips and Miranda was sure he was aware of her presence, just as she was aware of his.

They had agreed to keep their secret to themselves, just for a little while. Not because Leo feared Tina would not be overjoyed by their news, but rather because their happiness was so fresh and new. They wanted to enjoy it, just the two of them, for as long as possible.

Tina, in a pale lemon gown which had London modiste sewn all over it, joined her. The other woman seemed a little uncertain of her welcome, but Miranda soon put her mind at ease.

'I do not blame you for telling him the truth. In fact, I am thankful. If it had not been for you, we may still be at cross-purposes.'

'And you are not now?' Tina asked, one arched brow raised. 'My brother's moods have been so violent of late I did not trust my own judgment when he arrived home for luncheon looking as if all his horses had won the Derby.'

Miranda laughed.

Tina's other eyebrow lifted to join the first. 'If I am right, I should congratulate you both, but I expect I am not supposed to know.'

'He hasn't…that is, he hasn't… Yes, it is too early.'

Tina put her out of her misery. 'Don't worry, I won't tell. And Miranda, he *will* ask you.' She breathed a sigh of relief. 'I am so glad it has ended well between you.'

'You have been missing your own family,' Miranda guessed.

'Yes, I have. But I could not have been happy if Leo was not. People think because he is a duke he *should* be happy, but that is not the case. When our father died and Leo took upon himself the mantle of being the head of the Fitzgibbon family, he put aside his own feelings. He changed from the passionate boy he had been into a cold man; I see now that it was the only way he could bear it. But now the time has come for him to look again to his own heart. Oh, Miranda, Leo deserves to be happy. You both do.'

Miranda hardly had time to consider Tina's words, which were near enough to a blessing, when Sophie escaped her duties as hostess to skip to her side. The girl leaned confidingly close, her breath stirring the auburn ringlet that lay against Miranda's cheek.

'Mr Harmon is gone, did you know? Jack says he will not dare to return. The sight of him upset me so but, in a way, seeing him again, reliving the nightmare he put me through, has taken away much of the pain. I have spoken to Father, and he has agreed to another season in London.'

Miranda turned and stared at her. 'Oh, that is good

news, Sophie. You are so pretty and so bright—it would be a shame to rusticate forever.'

Sophie's green eyes shone, and for a time they discussed London and the pleasures to be had there.

'Of course, you must come and stay with me,' Sophie said with a determined air. 'You are far too young to be a widow.'

'Oh, no, Sophie. You are very kind, but—'

Sophie gave an impatient little sigh, glancing towards the window where Leo was still held prisoner by the Misses McKay—literally, if their gloved hands on his arms was any indication. 'I did hope you and Leo might fall in love,' she said wistfully. 'You seemed so ideally suited. Jack said it was a case between you.'

Miranda stared. 'Jack said that?'

'Jack!' Sophie called. Her brother approached, his head held at an unnatural angle because of the height of his starched collar. 'You did tell me you thought it was a case between Leo and Miranda, didn't you?'

Jack twitched his cuffs, embarrassed by his sister's plain speaking. 'Keep your voice down, old girl. Leo will hear you. I only said I *thought* it was. Leo's been as mad as a kite since Mrs Fitzgibbon arrived in town. Up and down and all over the place. Never saw the like. Completely head over heels. Can't help it if she doesn't feel the same. Nothing to do with me, Soph! Anyway, I always hoped you and he would…well, so convenient, what?'

Sophie sniffed. 'You are a fool, Jack. Leo and I would never suit. He's far too bossy for me and I am far too fidgety for him. Find yourself a wife, and then you might stop trying to play matchmaker with me and Leo.'

Jack seemed to be struck forcibly by this piece of advice. 'Why, there's a thought! I believe I know just the girl, too! Nice little thing. Blue eyes. Brown hair. The sweetest smile! Can't remember her name, but it'll come back to me.'

'Just the girl for what, Jack?'

The deep, smooth voice precipitated a short and uncomfortable silence. Jack started and gave Leo a rueful smile, while Sophie hurried off with the excuse that she had other, pressing duties to perform. Miranda met Leo's quizzing glance with her own warm one, and wondered again, with a *frisson* of pleasure, that such a man should be mad with love for her.

As usual Leo was elegance itself, at ease in whatever surroundings he found himself. Beside Jack, his good taste was even more noticeable, and he held himself with supreme confidence. And yet—Miranda felt tenderness well into her heart—with her he had been as unsteady as any youth in the first throes of love.

'Sophie tells me I should marry,' said Jack without the least trace of embarrassment. 'What do you think, Leo?'

Leo pretended to consider. 'Are you prepared to settle down, Jack, and forgo all of your bachelor pleasures?'

'What do you mean?' Jack shuffled uneasily. 'My *club*? Would I have to give up my club? Been a member since I first came to town, Belford. Not something to give up lightly, a man's club.'

Leo looked thoughtful. 'Whether you have to give up your club will depend upon your wife, Jack. What do you think, Mrs Fitzgibbon? Would Jack have to give up the pleasures of his club in order to devote himself entirely to his lady love?'

Miranda took his lead, her expression pensive. 'A certain amount of devotion is important, Duke.'

'Yes, and the club would interfere in that devotion.'

Jack glanced from one to the other with growing dismay. 'What does this "devotion" thing consist of?' he demanded nervously.

'Well, there are compliments to be paid,' Leo returned smartly. 'At least one compliment a day, more if you can manage it. And quiet dinners at home, just the two of you. What else, Miranda?'

'Kissing,' Miranda replied promptly.

Leo's eyebrows rose slowly, and an appreciative gleam deepened the blue of his eyes. 'Yes. Kissing. Much of that, do you think?'

Miranda's cheeks felt a little hot, but she was able to reply calmly, 'Definitely.'

'There you have it then, Jack.' Leo clapped his friend on the back. 'Do you think you'd be able to manage all that?'

Jack was very uncomfortable. 'Good gad! I don't like the sound of it. Quiet dinners at home? No. No, I don't believe I have the time for a wife after all. Just as well I never popped the question to what's her name, eh?' And he moved off at a brisk pace towards the supper table.

Leo hardly waited until his friend was out of earshot, before taking Miranda's arm firmly in his and drawing her into a small, secluded antechamber. It contained a sofa and a huge green plant in an ornate pot, and was divided from the drawing room by a heavy curtain. They were quite private.

Leo settled his love on the sofa, and placed himself beside her, turned slightly, so that he could see her face. She was gazing up at him with brilliant eyes.

'Kissing, Miranda?' he asked darkly.

Miranda laughed softly. Maybe it was the dress, but tonight she felt as beautiful and fascinating as he obviously thought her. And there was that odd sensation again, as if she had known him forever, as if she had been waiting all her life just for him.

'Poor Jack,' Leo murmured. 'He doesn't know what he's missing.' And bending his dark head, he firmly captured her lips with his.

The interlude which followed was very satisfactory to them both. When at last they broke apart, Miranda was flushed and breathless, but perfectly happy. He watched her a moment, smiling in the smug, self-satisfied manner she used to loath but which now, she told herself, she perfectly understood. A man who could kiss as well as Leo kissed had a right to be smug.

'Will you marry me, Miranda?'

Her eyes searched his, while her mind sought and rejected various replies. It was a serious moment, and yet she felt sure enough of Leo to opt for a frivolous answer. Leo saw the teasing smile begin to curve her wide mouth. 'And are you prepared to devote yourself entirely to me?' she murmured, her voice soft and husky.

Leo's arms tightened about her and he felt a strong need to kiss her again. He restrained himself.

'Entirely, my love.'

'You know what Pendle will think of this, Leo. He may very well leave you entirely.'

'If that is the case, then I will bear it as best I can, but I fear he will not leave either of us, my love.'

'Then, yes, I will marry you, Leo.'

There followed another interlude, but this time when Leo lifted his head it was to find that Miranda's eyes had lost their dreamy look. She moved a little away from him, straightening her back slightly, and bracing herself in the way Leo had learned meant his love was about to broach some serious matter.

'Leo, I want to talk to you about Julian.'

Leo forestalled her. 'I know we must talk of Julian. I know you were very…fond of him. Miranda, I do not expect you to feel for me what you felt for him. Not at first. I know you must grieve for him. Julian was my favourite cousin, and I miss him, too. You came to The Grange because it was his gift to you. I saw that from the first. I understand.'

He was smiling at her, a warm, hopeful smile.

'But, Leo, you *don't* understand,' she said, tears shining in her eyes. 'He did leave me The Grange, and I felt it my—my duty to visit it. I didn't expect to love it so. I have always wanted a normal home and a normal life. I thought I could find those things here.'

'Miranda—'

'No, wait.' She gathered herself again. 'By the time I married Julian he was very ill. He…we…' She sighed. 'I know he was devoted to me, but we did not kiss very much, and certainly we did not know a proper married life. I was very fond of him, he was a dear man, and he came to my aid when I most needed him, but I did not love him. Not as I love you.'

Leo was astonished. He remembered his wild jealousy whenever he imagined Julian and Miranda together, and the childish fears that had consumed him whenever she mentioned Julian's name. He had been a fool, he thought in disgust, and nearly laughed aloud. He stopped himself in time. Miranda was watching him with such an anxious expression; laughter was probably not the best option.

'Dearest Miranda,' he said, and first kissed her brow, then the tip of her nose, and then her lips. 'I confess, with some shame, that I have been very envious of my cousin's good fortune, but now I think that I must thank him.'

'Thank him?' she whispered.

'For sending you to me.'

Her gaze slid over his face, searching for the truth in what he was saying, and accepting it.

'Do you think he knew…?'

Leo grinned, he was finding it difficult to keep a

smile off his face. 'Probably. Julian understood more about the human heart than we will ever know. Maybe he realised that what I needed was a saucy, hot-headed girl with whom I could share my vast knowledge of the pleasures of the flesh—'

'And what I needed was a bossy, arrogant man who thought he knew what was best for me,' Miranda retorted, trying not to blush.

He held her slightly away from him. 'Am I bossy?' he asked in surprise.

Miranda didn't reply, but the lift of her brows was answer enough.

He frowned, and spoke defensively. 'If I am a little...autocratic, then it is because I have need to be. I am the head of the Fitzgibbon family, Miranda. It is expected that I run matters. I do not always enjoy what I do, in fact, before I met you, I had begun to find it extremely tiresome, but I am a man who is used to leading. It is natural for me to take charge.'

He stopped, and now it was *his* cheeks which were stained with colour. 'You find this amusing, Miranda?'

'No, of course not. I'm sorry to smile, Leo. I just can't help but be a little amused when you sound so humble and you are so obviously not.'

'Miranda,' he said softly, 'until you came into my life it was very bleak. I did not even realise that was the case, although I knew I was lonely. Not the loneliness of one who is without friends, but an emptiness of the spirit.'

Miranda had lost all desire to laugh. She touched

his arm gently. 'Leo, I have felt that too. Perhaps our meeting was destined after all.'

'A duke has a certain position to uphold, I cannot hide from that. But if I could have you as my duchess, Miranda, I would be the happiest duke in England.'

Tears sparkled in her dark eyes and the words burst out of her. 'Leo, I love you and I want to marry you, but what of my stepmama? She is not exactly good *ton,* and although that distresses me for your sake, I could never abandon her. She has been kind to me, and I love her. Do not ask me to give her up. Do not ask me to choose!'

Miranda's dark eyes gazed into his, her soft mouth trembling with emotion. Very briefly, Leo wondered if his consequence was such that it would allow him to rise above the scandal a relationship-by-marriage to the infamous Decadent Countess would bring down upon his name and that of his family.

Almost at once, he decided he honestly didn't care. He wanted Miranda—he had wanted her even when he thought her the Decadent Countess. How could he allow himself to blight his own happiness by forcing such a choice upon the woman he loved? And he knew enough about Miranda by now to realise she was loyal to a fault. She would never agree to abandon her infamous stepmama, even if her action meant blighting her own happiness.

'If it would make you happy, my love, I would send to Italy for your stepmama right now and throw open my home to her and all her disreputable friends.'

'Leo,' she whispered, teetering on the verge of

hope, 'my stepmama is not in Italy. She is in Somerset. She arrived this afternoon.'

Leo froze for only a second before rising manfully to the occasion. 'All the better, my love!'

Miranda stared at him as if she were not certain she had heard him correctly, and then she gave him a smile that made every word worthwhile. Her heart was in that smile, as well as admiration and relief and sheer love.

'Oh, Leo, I would never ask you to do that, but that you should offer to do so… You must truly love me!'

'Of course I do, Miranda.'

She went into his arms, enjoying every blissful moment. Her journey had come to end. She had found Leo, and now all would be well.

She was hardly aware of Jack's crowing voice, drifting across from the other side of the room. 'See, Sophie! I told you it was a case between 'em!'

*   *   *   *   *

Modern Romance™
...seduction and
passion guaranteed

Tender Romance™
...love affairs that
last a lifetime

Medical Romance™
...medical drama
on the pulse

Historical Romance™
...rich, vivid and
passionate

Sensual Romance™
...sassy, sexy and
seductive

Blaze Romance™
...the temperature's
rising

27 new titles every month.

Live the emotion

MILLS & BOON

dark angel
LYNNE GRAHAM

Knight in shining armour
or avenging angel?

Available from 21st March 2003

Available at most branches of WH Smith,
Tesco, Martins, Borders, Eason, Sainsbury's
and all good paperback bookshops.

0403/135/MB68

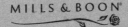

Become a Panel Member

If YOU are a regular United Kingdom buyer of Mills & Boon® Historical Romance™ you might like to tell us your opinion of the books we publish to help us in publishing the books *you* like.

Mills & Boon have a Reader Panel of Historical Romance™ readers. Each person on the panel receives a short questionnaire (taking about five minutes to complete) every third month asking for opinions of the past month's Historical Romances. All people who send in their replies have a chance of winning a FREE year's supply of Historical Romances.

If YOU would like to be considered for inclusion on the panel please fill in and return the following survey. We can't guarantee that everyone will be on the panel but first come will be first considered.

Where did you buy this novel?

❏   WH Smith
❏   Tesco
❏   Borders
❏   Sainsbury's
❏   Direct by mail
❏   Other (please state) _____

What themes do you enjoy most in the Mills and Boon® novels that you read? (Choose all that apply.)

❏   Amnesia
❏   Family drama (including babies/young children)
❏   Hidden/Mistaken identity
❏   Marriage of convenience
❏   Medieval
❏   Regency
❏   Elizabethan England
❏   Forced proximity
❏   Mock engagement or marriage
❏   Revenge

- ❑ Sheikh
- ❑ Shared pasts
- ❑ Western

On average, how many Mills & Boon® novels do you read every month? _____

Please provide us with your name and address:

Name: _____
Address: _____
_____
_____
_____

What is your occupation?
(OPTIONAL)
_____

In which of the following age groups do you belong?
(OPTIONAL)

- ❑ 18 to 24
- ❑ 25 to 34
- ❑ 35 to 49
- ❑ 50 to 64
- ❑ 65 or older

Thank you for your help!
Your feedback is important in helping us offer
quality products you value.

The Reader Service
Reader Panel Questionnaire
FREEPOST CN81
Croydon CR9 3WZ

FREE

2 BOOKS
AND A SURPRISE GIFT!

We would like to take this opportunity to thank you for reading this Mills & Boon® book by offering you the chance to take TWO more specially selected titles from the Historical Romance™ series absolutely FREE! We're also making this offer to introduce you to the benefits of the Reader Service™—

- ★ FREE home delivery
- ★ FREE monthly Newsletter
- ★ FREE gifts and competitions
- ★ Exclusive Reader Service discount
- ★ Books available before they're in the shops

Accepting these FREE books and gift places you under no obligation to buy; you may cancel at any time, even after receiving your free shipment. Simply complete your details below and return the entire page to the address below. *You don't even need a stamp!*

YES! Please send me 2 free Historical Romance books and a surprise gift. I understand that unless you hear from me, I will receive 4 superb new titles every month for just £3.49 each, postage and packing free. I am under no obligation to purchase any books and may cancel my subscription at any time. The free books and gift will be mine to keep in any case.

H3ZEC

Ms/Mrs/Miss/Mr ....Initials ....
BLOCK CAPITALS PLEASE

Surname ....

Address ....

....

....Postcode ....

Send this whole page to:
UK: FREEPOST CN81, Croydon, CR9 3WZ
EIRE: PO Box 4546, Kilcock, County Kildare (stamp required)